THE PAINTED VEIL

William Somerset Maugham was born in 1874 and lived in Paris until he was ten. He was educated at King's School, Canterbury, and at Heidelberg University. He spent some time at St. Thomas's Hospital with the idea of practising medicine, but the success of his first novel, *Liza of Lambeth*, published in 1897, won him over to writing. *Of Human Bondage*, the first of his masterpieces, came out in 1915, and with the publication in 1919 of *The Moon and Sixpence* his reputation as a novelist was established. His position as a successful playwright was being consolidated at the same time. His first play, *A Man of Honour*, was followed by a series of successes just before and after World War I, and his career in the theatre did not end until 1933 with *Sheppey*.

In 1927 Somerset Maugham settled in the South of France and lived there until his death in 1965.

ALSO BY W. SOMERSET MAUGHAM

W. SOMERSET MAUGHAM

The Painted Veil

VINTAGE BOOKS
London

Published by Vintage 2007

8 10 9 7

First published in Great Britain in 1925 by
William Heinemann

Vintage
Random House, 20 Vauxhall Bridge Road,
London SW1V 2SA

www.vintage-books.co.uk

Addresses for companies within The Random House Group Limited
can be found at: www.randomhouse.co.uk/offices.htm

The Random House Group Limited Reg. No. 954009

A CIP catalogue record for this book
is available from the British Library

ISBN 9780099507390

The Random House Group Limited supports The Forest Stewardship
Council (FSC), the leading international forest certification organisation.
All our titles that are printed on Greenpeace approved FSC certified paper
carry the FSC logo. Our paper procurement policy can be found at:
www.rbooks.co.uk/environment

Mixed Sources
Product group from well-managed
forests and other controlled sources
www.fsc.org Cert no. TT-COC-2139
© 1996 Forest Stewardship Council

FSC

Printed and bound in Great Britain by
CPI Cox & Wyman, Reading, RG1 8EX

' . . . the painted veil which those who live call Life.'

Preface

This story was suggested by the lines of Dante that run as follows:

Deh, quando tu sarai tornato al mondo,
E riposato della lunga via,
Seguito il terzo spirito al secondo,
Ricorditi di me, che son la Pia:
Siena mi fè; disfecemi Maremma:
Salsi colui, che, innanellata pria
Disposando m'avea con la sua gemma.

'Pray, when you are returned to the world, and rested from the long journey,' followed the third spirit on the second, 'remember me, who am Pia. Siena made me, Maremma unmade me: this he knows who after betrothal espoused me with his ring.'

I was a student at St. Thomas's Hospital and the Easter vacation gave me six weeks to myself. With my clothes in a gladstone bag and twenty pounds in my pocket I set out. I was twenty. I went to Genoa and Pisa and then to Florence. Here I took a room in the via Laura, from the window of which I could see the lovely dome of the Cathedral, in the apartment of a widow lady, with a daughter, who offered me board and lodging (after a good deal of haggling) for four lire a day. I am afraid that she did not make a very good thing out of it, since my appetite was enormous, and I could devour a mountain of macaroni without inconvenience. She had a vineyard on the Tuscan hills, and my recollection is that the Chianti she got from it was the best I have ever drunk in Italy. Her daughter gave me an Italian lesson every day. She seemed to me then of mature age, but I do not suppose that she was more than twenty-six. She had had trouble. Her betrothed, an officer, had been killed in Abyssinia and she was consecrated to virginity. It was an understood thing that on her mother's death (a buxom, grey-haired, jovial lady who did not mean to die a day before the dear Lord saw fit) Ersilia would enter religion. But she looked forward to this with cheerfulness. She loved a good laugh. We were very gay at luncheon and dinner, but she took her lessons seriously, and when I was stupid or inattentive rapped me over the knuckles with a black ruler. I should have been indignant at being treated like a child if it had not reminded me of the old-fashioned pedagogues I had read of in books and so made me laugh.

I lived laborious days. I started each one by translating a few pages of one of Ibsen's plays so that I might acquire mastery of technique and ease in writing dialogue; then, with Ruskin in my hand, I examined the sights of Florence. I admired according to instructions the tower of Giotto and the bronze doors of Ghiberti. I was properly enthusiastic over the Botticellis in the Uffizi and I turned the scornful shoulder of extreme youth on what the master disapproved of. After luncheon I had my Italian lesson and then going out once more I visited the churches and wandered day-dreaming along the Arno. When dinner was done I went out to look for adventure, but such was my innocence, or at least my shyness, I always came home as virtuous as I had gone out. The Signora, though she had given me a key, sighed with relief when she heard me come in and bolt the door, for she was always afraid I should forget to do this, and I returned to my perusal of the history of the Guelphs and Ghibellines. I was bitterly conscious that not thus behaved the writers of the romantic era, though I doubt whether any of them managed to spend six weeks in Italy on twenty pounds, and I much enjoyed my sober and industrious life.

I had already read the Inferno (with the help of a translation, but conscientiously looking out in a dictionary the words I did not know), so with Ersilia started on the Purgatorio. When we came to the passage I have quoted above she told me that Pia was a gentlewoman of Siena whose husband, suspecting her of adultery and afraid on account of her family to put her to death, took her down to his castle in the Maremma the noxious vapours of which he was confident would do the trick; but she took so long to die that he grew impatient and had her thrown out of the window. I do not know where Ersilia learnt all this, the note in my own Dante was less circumstantial, but the story for some reason caught my imagination. I turned it over in my mind and for many years from time to time would brood over it for two or three days. I used to repeat to myself the line: *Siena mi fè; disfecemi Maremma*. But it was one among many subjects that occupied my fancy and for long periods I forgot it. Of course I saw it as a modern story, and I could not think of a setting in the world of to-day in which such events might plausibly happen. It was not till I made a long journey in China that I found this.

I think this is the only novel I have written in which I started from a story rather than from a character. It is difficult to explain the relation between character and plot. You cannot very well think of a character in the void; the moment you think of him, you think of him in some situation, doing something; so that the character and at least his principle action seem to be the result of a simultaneous act of the imagination. But in this case the characters were chosen to fit the story I gradually evolved; they were constructed from persons I had long known in different circumstances.

I had with this book some of the difficulties that are apt to befall an author. I had originally called my hero and heroine Lane, a common enough name, but it appeared that there were people of that name in Hong-Kong. They brought an action, which the proprietors of the magazine in which my novel was serialised, settled for two hundred and fifty pounds, and I changed the name to Fane. Then the Assistant Colonial Secretary, thinking himself libelled, threatened to institute proceedings. I was surprised, since in England we can put a Prime Minister on the stage or use him as the character of a novel, an Archbishop of Canterbury or a Lord Chancellor, and the tenants of these exalted offices do not turn a hair. It seemed to me strange that the temporary occupant of so insignificant a post should think himself aimed at, but in order to save trouble I changed Hong-Kong to an imaginary colony of Tching-Yen.* The book had already been published when the incident arose and was recalled. A certain number of astute reviewers who had received it did not on one pretext and another return their copies. These have now acquired a bibliographical value, I think there are about sixty of them in existence, and are bought by collectors at a high price.

*Tching-Yen has now been replaced by Hong-Kong.

I

She gave a startled cry.

'What's the matter?' he asked.

Notwithstanding the darkness of the shuttered room he saw her face on a sudden distraught with terror.

'Some one just tried the door.'

'Well, perhaps it was the amah, or one of the boys.'

'They never come at this time. They know I always sleep after tiffin.'

'Who else could it be?'

'Walter,' she whispered, her lips trembling.

She pointed to his shoes. He tried to put them on, but his nervousness, for her alarm was affecting him, made him clumsy, and besides, they were on the tight side. With a faint gasp of impatience she gave him a shoe-horn. She slipped into a kimono and in her bare feet went over to her dressing-table. Her hair was shingled and with a comb she had repaired its disorder before he had laced his second shoe. She handed him his coat.

'How shall I get out?'

'You'd better wait a bit. I'll look out and see that it's all right.'

'It can't possibly be Walter. He doesn't leave the laboratory till five.'

'Who is it then?'

They spoke in whispers now. She was quaking. It occurred to him that in an emergency she would lose her head and on a sudden he felt angry with her. If it wasn't safe why the devil had she said it was? She caught her breath and put her hand on his arm. He followed the direction of her glance. They stood facing the windows that led out on the verandah. They were shuttered and the shutters were bolted. They saw the white china knob of the handle slowly turn. They had heard no one walk along the verandah. It was terrifying to see that silent motion. A minute passed and there was no sound. Then, with the ghastliness of the supernatural, in the same stealthy, noiseless and horrifying manner, they saw the white china knob of the handle at the other window turn also. It was so frightening that Kitty, her nerves failing her, opened her mouth to scream; but, seeing what she was going to do, he swiftly put his hand over it and her cry was smothered in his fingers.

Silence. She leaned against him, her knees shaking, and he was afraid she would faint. Frowning, his jaw set, he carried her to the bed and sat her down upon it. She was as white as the sheet and notwithstanding his tan his cheeks were pale too. He stood by her side looking with fascinated gaze at the china knob. They did not speak. Then he saw that she was crying.

'For God's sake don't do that,' he whispered irritably. 'If we're in for it we're in for it. We shall just have to brazen it out.'

She looked for her handkerchief and knowing what she wanted he gave her her bag.

'Where's your topee?'

'I left it downstairs.'

'Oh, my God!'

'I say, you must pull yourself together. It's a hundred to one it wasn't Walter. Why on earth should he come back at this hour? He never does come home in the middle of the day, does he?'

'Never.'

'I'll bet you anything you like it was the amah.'

She gave him the shadow of a smile. His rich, caressing voice reassured her and she took his hand and affectionately pressed it. He gave her a moment to collect herself.

'Look here, we can't stay here for ever,' he said then. 'Do you feel up to going out on the verandah and having a look?'

'I don't think I can stand.'

'Have you got any brandy in here?'

She shook her head. A frown for an instant darkened his brow, he was growing impatient, he did not quite know what to do. Suddenly she clutched his hand more tightly.

'Suppose he's waiting there?'

He forced his lips to smile and his voice retained the gentle, persuasive tone the effect of which he was so fully conscious of.

'That's not very likely. Have a little pluck, Kitty. How can it possibly be your husband? If he'd come in and seen a strange topee in the hall and come upstairs and found your room locked, surely he would have made some sort of row. It must have been one of the servants. Only a Chinese would turn a handle in that way.'

She did feel more herself now.

'It's not very pleasant even if it was only the amah.'

'She can be squared and if necessary I'll put the fear of God into her. There are not many advantages in being a government official, but you may as well get what you can out of it.'

He must be right. She stood up and turning to him stretched out her arms: he took her in his and kissed her on the lips. It was such rapture that it was pain. She adored him. He released her and she went to the window. She slid back the bolt and opening the shutter a little looked out. There was not a soul. She slipped on to the verandah, looked into her husband's dressing-room and then into her own sitting-room. Both were empty. She went back to the bedroom and beckoned to him.

'Nobody.'

'I believe the whole thing was an optical delusion.'

'Don't laugh. I was terrified. Go into my sitting-room and sit down. I'll put on my stockings and some shoes.'

He did as she bade and in five minutes she joined him. He was smoking a cigarette.

'I say, could I have a brandy and soda?'

'Yes, I'll ring.'

'I don't think it would hurt *you* by the look of things.'

They waited in silence for the boy to answer. She gave the order.

'Ring up the laboratory and ask if Walter is there,' she said then. 'They won't know your voice.'

He took up the receiver and asked for the number. He inquired whether Dr. Fane was in. He put down the receiver.

'He hasn't been in since tiffin,' he told her. 'Ask the boy whether he has been here.'

'I daren't. It'll look so funny if he has and I didn't see him.'

The boy brought the drinks and Townsend helped himself. When he offered her some she shook her head.

'What's to be done if it was Walter?' she asked.

'Perhaps he wouldn't care.'

'Walter?'

Her tone was incredulous.

'It's always struck me he was rather shy. Some men can't bear scenes, you know. He's got sense enough to know that there's nothing to be gained by making a scandal. I don't believe for a minute it was Walter, but even if it was, my impression is that he'll do nothing. I think he'll ignore it.'

She reflected for a moment.

'He's awfully in love with me.'

'Well, that's all to the good. You'll get round him.'

He gave her that charming smile of his which she had

always found so irresistible. It was a slow smile which started in his clear blue eyes and travelled by perceptible degrees to his shapely mouth. He had small white even teeth. It was a very sensual smile and it made her heart melt in her body.

'I don't very much care,' she said, with a flash of gaiety. 'It was worth it.'

'It was my fault.'

'Why did you come? I was amazed to see you.'

'I couldn't resist it.'

'You dear.'

She leaned a little towards him, her dark and shining eyes gazing passionately into his, her mouth a little open with desire, and he put his arms round her. She abandoned herself with a sigh of ecstasy to their shelter.

'You know you can always count on me.' he said.

'I'm so happy with you. I wish I could make you as happy as you make me.'

'You're not frightened any more?'

'I hate Walter,' she answered.

He did not quite know what to say to this, so he kissed her. Her face was very soft against his.

But he took her wrist on which was a little gold watch and looked at the time.

'Do you know what I must do now?'

'Bolt?' she smiled.

He nodded. For one instant she clung to him more closely, but she felt his desire to go, and she released him.

'It's shameful the way you neglect your work. Be off with you.'

He could never resist the temptation to flirt.

'You seem in a devil of a hurry to get rid of me,' he said lightly.

'You know that I hate to let you go.'

Her answer was low and deep and serious. He gave a flattered laugh.

'Don't worry your pretty little head about our mysterious visitor. I'm quite sure it was the amah. And if there's any trouble I guarantee to get you out of it.'

'Have you had a lot of experience?'

His smile was amused and complacent.

'No, but I flatter myself that I've got a head screwed on my shoulders.'

3

She went out on to the verandah and watched him leave the house. He waved his hand to her. It gave her a little thrill as she looked at him; he was forty-one, but he had the lithe figure and the springing step of a boy.

The verandah was in shadow; and lazily, her heart at ease with satisfied love, she lingered. Their house stood in the Happey Valley, on the side of the hill, for they could not afford to live on the more eligible but expensive Peak. But her abstracted gaze scarcely noticed the blue sea and the crowded shipping in the harbour. She could think only of her lover.

Of course it was stupid to behave as they had done that afternoon, but if he wanted her how could she be prudent? He had come two or three times after tiffin, when in the heat of the day no one thought of stirring out, and not even the boys had seen him come and go. It was very difficult at Hong-Kong. She hated the Chinese city and it made her nervous to go into the filthy little house off the Victoria Road in which they were in the habit of meeting. It was a curio dealer's; and the Chinese who were sitting about stared at her unpleasantly; she hated the ingratiating smile of the old man who took her to the back of the shop and then up a dark flight of stairs. The room into which he led her was frowsy and the large wooden bed against the wall made her shudder.

'This is dreadfully sordid, isn't it?' she said to Charlie the first time she met him there.

'It was till you came in,' he answered.

Of course the moment he took her in his arms she forgot everything.

Oh, how hateful it was that she wasn't free, that they both weren't free! She didn't like his wife. Kitty's wandering thoughts dwelt now for a moment on Dorothy Townsend. How unfortunate to be called Dorothy! It dated you. She was thirty-eight at least. But Charlie never spoke of her. Of course he didn't care for her; she bored him to death. But he was a gentleman. Kitty smiled with affectionate irony: it was just like him, silly old thing; he might be unfaithful to her, but he would never allow a word in disparagement of her to cross his lips. She was a tallish woman, taller than Kitty, neither stout nor thin, with a good deal of pale brown hair; she could never have been pretty with anything but the prettiness of youth; her features were good enough without being remarkable and her blue eyes were cold. She had a skin that you would never look at twice and no colour in her cheeks. And she dressed like – well, like what she was, the wife of the Assistant Colonial Secretary at Hong-Kong. Kitty smiled and gave her shoulders a faint shrug.

Of course no one could deny that Dorothy Townsend had a pleasant voice. She was a wonderful mother, Charlie always said that of her, and she was what Kitty's mother called a gentlewoman. But Kitty did not like her. She did not like her casual manner; and the politeness with which she treated you when you went there, to tea or dinner, was exasperating because you could not but feel how little interest she took in you. The fact was, Kitty supposed, that she cared for nothing but her children: there were two boys at school in England, and another boy of six whom she was going to take home next year. Her face was a mask. She smiled and in her pleasant, well-mannered way said the things that were expected of her; but for all her cordiality held you at a distance. She had a few intimate friends in the Colony and they greatly admired her. Kitty wondered whether Mrs. Townsend thought her a little common. She flushed. After all there was no reason for her to put on airs. It was true that her father had been a Colonial Governor and of course it was very grand while it lasted – every one stood up when you entered a room and men took off their hats to you as you passed in your car – but what could be more insignificant than a Colonial Governor when he had retired? Dorothy Townsend's father lived on a pension in a small house at Earl's Court. Kitty's mother would think it a dreadful bore if she asked her to call. Kitty's father, Bernard Garstin, was a K.C. and there was no reason why he should not be made a judge one of these days. Anyhow they lived in South Kensington.

4

Kitty, coming to Hong-Kong on her marriage, had found it hard to reconcile herself to the fact that her social position was determined by her husband's occupation. Of course every one had been very kind and for two or three months they had gone out to parties almost every night; when they dined at Government House the Governor took her in as a bride; but she had understood quickly that as the wife of the Government bacteriologist she was of no particular consequence. It made her angry.

'It's too absurd,' she told her husband. 'Why, there's hardly any one here that one would bother about for five minutes at home. Mother wouldn't dream of asking any of them to dine at our house.'

'You mustn't let it worry you,' he answered. 'It doesn't really matter, you know.'

'Of course it doesn't matter, it only shows how stupid they are, but it is rather funny when you think of all the people who used to come to our house at home that here we should be treated like dirt.'

'From a social standpoint the man of science does not exist,' he smiled.

8

She knew that now, but she had not known it when she married him.

'I don't know that it exactly amuses me to be taken in to dinner by the agent of the P. and O.,' she said, laughing in order that what she said might not seem snobbish.

Perhaps he saw the reproach behind her lightness of manner, for he took her hand and shyly pressed it.

'I'm awfully sorry, Kitty dear, but don't let it vex you.'

'Oh. I'm not going to let it do that.'

5

It couldn't have been Walter that afternoon. It must have been one of the servants and after all they didn't matter. Chinese servants knew everything anyway. But they held their tongues.

Her heart beat a little faster as she remembered the way in which that white china knob slowly turned. They mustn't take risks like that again. It was better to go to the curio shop. No one who saw her go in would think anything of it, and they were absolutely safe there. The owner of the shop knew who Charlie was and he was not such a fool as to put up the back of the Assistant Colonial Secretary. What did anything matter really but that Charlie loved her?

She turned away from the verandah and went back into her sitting-room. She threw herself down on the sofa and stretched out her hand to get a cigarette. Her eye caught sight of a note lying on the top of a book. She opened it. It was written in pencil.

Dear Kitty,
    Here is the book you wanted. I was just going to send it when I met Dr. Fane and he said he'd bring it round himself as he was passing the house.

V.H.

She rang the bell and when the boy came asked him who had brought the book and when.

'Master bring it, missy, after tiffin,' he answered.

Then it had been Walter. She rang up the Colonial Secretary's Office at once and asked for Charlie. She told him what she had just learned. There was a pause before he answered.

'What shall I do?' she asked.

'I'm in the middle of an important consultation. I'm afraid I can't talk to you now. My advice to you is to sit tight.'

She put down the receiver. She understood that he was not alone and she was impatient with his business.

She sat down again, at a desk, and resting her face in her hands sought to think out the situation. Of course Walter might merely have thought she was sleeping: there was no reason why she should not lock herself in. She tried to remember if they had been talking. Certainly they had not been talking loud. And there was the hat. It was maddening of Charlie to have left it downstairs. But it was no use blaming him for that, it was natural enough, and there was nothing to tell that Walter had noticed it. He was probably in a hurry and had just left the book and note on his way to some appointment connected with his work. The strange thing was that he should have tried the door and then the two windows. If he thought she was asleep it was unlike him to disturb her. What a fool she had been!

She shook herself a little and again she felt that sweet pain in her heart which she always felt when she thought of Charlie. It had been worth it. He had said that he would stand by her, and if the worse came to the worse, well . . . Let Walter kick up a row if he chose. She had Charlie; what did she care? Perhaps it would be the best thing for him to know. She had never cared for Walter and since she had loved Charlie Townsend it had irked and bored her to submit to her husband's caresses. She wanted to have nothing more to do with him. She didn't see how he could prove anything. If he accused her she would deny, and if it came to a pass that she could deny no longer, well, she would fling the truth in his teeth, and he could do what he chose.

6

Within three months of her marriage she knew that she had made a mistake; but it had been her mother's fault even more than hers.

There was a photograph of her mother in the room and Kitty's harassed eyes fell on it. She did not know why she kept it there, for she was not very fond of her mother; there was one of her father too, but that was downstairs on the grand piano. It had been done when he took silk and it represented him in a wig and gown. Even they could not make him imposing; he was a little, wizened man, with tired eyes, a long upper lip, and a thin mouth; a facetious photographer had told him to look pleasant, but he had succeeded only in looking severe. It was on this account, for as a rule the down-turned corners of his mouth and the dejection of his eyes gave him an air of mild depression, that Mrs. Garstin, thinking it made him look judicial, had chosen it from among the proofs. But her own photograph showed her in the dress in which she had gone to Court when her husband was made a King's Counsel. She was very grand in the velvet gown, the long train so disposed as to show to advantage, with feathers in her hair and flowers in her hand. She held herself erect. She was a woman of fifty, thin and flat-chested, with prominent cheek-bones and a large, well-shaped nose. She had a great quantity of very smooth black hair and Kitty had always suspected that, if not dyed, it was at least touched up. Her fine black eyes were never still and this was the most noticeable thing about her; for when she was talking to you it was disconcerting to see those restless eyes in that impassive, unlined and yellow face. They moved from one part of you to another, to other persons in the room, and then back to you; you felt that she was criticising you, summing you up, watchful meanwhile of all that went on around her, and that the words she spoke had no connection with her thoughts.

7

Mrs. Garstin was a hard, cruel, managing, ambitious, parsimonious and stupid woman. She was the daughter, one of five, of a solicitor in Liverpool and Bernard Garstin had met her when he was on the Northern Circuit. He had seemed then a young man of promise and her father said he would go far. He hadn't. He was painstaking, industrious and capable, but he had not the will to advance himself. Mrs. Garstin despised him. But she recognised, though with bitterness, that she could only achieve success through him, and she set herself to drive him on the way she desired to go. She nagged him without mercy. She discovered that if she wanted him to do something which his sensitiveness revolted against she had only to give him no peace and eventually, exhausted, he would yield. On her side she set herself to cultivate the people who might be useful. She flattered the solicitors who would send her husband briefs and was familiar with their wives. She was obsequious to the judges and their ladies. She made much of promising politicians.

In twenty-five years Mrs. Garstin never invited any one to dine at her house because she liked him. She gave large dinner parties at regular intervals. But parsimony was as strong in her as ambition. She hated to spend money. She flattered herself that she could make as much show as any one else at half the price. Her dinners were long and elaborate, but thrifty, and she could never persuade herself that people when they were eating and talking knew what they drank. She wrapped sparkling Moselle in a napkin and thought her guests took it for champagne.

Bernard Garstin had a fair, though not a large practice. Men who had been called after him had long outstripped him. Mrs. Garstin made him stand for parliament. The expense of the election was borne by the party, but here again her parsimony balked her ambition, and she could not bring herself to spend enough money to nurse the constituency. The subscriptions Bernard Garstin made to the innumerable funds a candidate is expected to contribute to, were always just a little less than adequate. He was beaten. Though it would have pleased Mrs. Garstin to be a member's wife she bore her disappointment with fortitude. The fact of her husband's standing had brought her in contact with a number of prominent persons and she appreciated the addition to her social consequence. She knew that Bernard would never make his mark in the House. She wanted him to be a member only that he might have a claim on the gratitude of his party and surely to fight two or three losing seats would give him that.

But he was still a junior and many younger men than he had already taken silk. It was necessary that he should too, not only because otherwise he could scarcely hope to be made a judge, but on her account also; it mortified her to go in to dinner after women ten years younger than herself. But here she encountered in her husband an obstinacy which she had not for years been accustomed to. He was afraid that as a K.C. he would get no work. A bird in the hand was worth two in the bush, he told her, to which she retorted that a proverb was the last refuge of the mentally destitute. He suggested to her the possibility that his income would be halved and he knew that there was no argument which could have greater weight with her. She would not listen. She called him pusillanimous. She gave him no peace and at last, as always, he yielded. He applied for silk and it was promptly awarded him.

His misgivings were justified. He made no headway as a leader and his briefs were few. But he concealed any disappointment he may have felt, and if he reproached his wife it was in his heart. He grew perhaps a little more silent, but he had always been silent at home, and no one in his family noticed a change in him. His daughters had never looked upon him as anything but a source of income; it had always seemed perfectly natural that he should lead a dog's life in order to provide them with board and lodging, clothes, holidays and money for odds and ends; and now, understanding that through his fault money was less plentiful, the indifference they had felt for him was tinged with an exasperated contempt. It never occurred to them to ask themselves what were the feelings of the subdued little man who went out early in the morning and came home at night only in time to dress for dinner. He was a stranger to them, but because he was their father they took it for granted that he should love and cherish them.

8

But there was a quality of courage in Mrs. Garstin which in itself was admirable. She let no one in her immediate circle, which to her was the world, see how mortified she was by the frustration of her hopes. She made no change in her style of living. By careful management she was able to give as showy dinners as she had done before, and she met her friends with the same bright gaiety which she had so long cultivated. She had a hard and facile fund of chit-chat which in the society she moved in passed for conversation. She was a useful guest among persons to whom small talk did not come easily, for she was never at a loss with a new topic and could be trusted immediately to break an awkward silence with a suitable observation.

It was unlikely now that Bernard Garstin would ever be made a judge of the High Court, but he might still hope for a County Court judgeship or at the worst an appointment in the Colonies. Meanwhile she had the satisfaction of seeing him appointed Recorder of a Welsh town. But it was on her daughters that she set her hopes. By arranging good marriages for them she expected to make up for all the disappointments of her career. There were two, Kitty and Doris. Doris gave no sign of good looks, her nose was too long and her figure was lumpy; so that Mrs. Garstin could hope no more for her than that she should marry a young man who was well off in a suitable profession.

But Kitty was a beauty. She gave promise of being so when she was still a child, for she had large, dark eyes, liquid and vivacious, brown, curling hair in which there was a reddish tint, exquisite teeth and a lovely skin. Her features would never be very good, for her chin was too square and her nose, though not so long as Doris's, too big. Her beauty depended a good deal on her youth, and Mrs. Garstin realised that she must marry in the first flush of her maidenhood. When she came out she was dazzling: her skin was still her greatest beauty, but her eyes with their long lashes were so starry and yet so melting that it gave you a catch at the heart to look into them. She had a charming gaiety and the desire to please. Mrs. Garstin bestowed upon her all the affection, a harsh, competent, calculating affection, of which she was capable; she dreamed ambitious dreams; it was not a good marriage she aimed at for her daughter, but a brilliant one.

Kitty had been brought up with the knowledge that she was going to be a beautiful woman and she more than suspected her mother's ambition. It accorded with her own desires. She was launched upon the world and Mrs. Garstin performed prodigies in getting herself invited to dances where her daughter might meet eligible men. Kitty was a success. She was amusing as well as beautiful, and very soon she had a dozen men in love with her. But none was suitable, and Kitty, charming and friendly with all, took care to commit herself with none. The drawing-room in South Kensington was filled on Sunday afternoons with amorous youth, but Mrs. Garstin observed, with a grim smile of approval, that it needed no effort on her part to keep them at a distance from Kitty. Kitty was prepared to flirt with them, and it diverted her to play one off against the other, but when they proposed to her, as none failed to do, she refused them with tact but decision.

Her first season passed without the perfect suitor presenting himself, and the second also; but she was young and could afford to wait. Mrs. Garstin told her friends that she thought it a pity for a girl to marry till she was twenty-one. But a third year passed and then a fourth. Two or three of her old admirers proposed again, but they were still penniless, one or two boys younger than herself proposed; a retired Indian Civilian, a K.C.I.E., did the same: he was fifty-three. Kitty still danced a great deal, she went to Wimbledon and Lord's, to Ascot and Henley; she was thoroughly enjoying herself; but still no one whose position and income were satisfactory asked her to marry him. Mrs. Garstin began to grow uneasy. She noticed that Kitty was beginning to attract men of forty and over. She reminded her that she would not be any longer so pretty in a year or two and that young girls were coming out all the time. Mrs. Garstin did not mince her words in the domestic circle and she warned her daughter tartly that she would miss her market.

Kitty shrugged her shoulders. She thought herself as pretty as ever, prettier perhaps, for she had learnt how to dress in the last four years, and she had plenty of time. If she wanted to marry just to be married there were a dozen boys who would jump at the chance. Surely the right man would come along sooner or later. But Mrs. Garstin judged the situation more shrewdly: with anger in her heart for the beautiful daughter who had missed her chances she set her standard a little lower. She turned back to the professional class at which she had sneered in her pride and looked about for a young lawyer or a business man whose future inspired her with confidence.

16

Kitty reached the age of twenty-five and was still unmarried. Mrs. Garstin was exasperated and she did not hesitate often to give Kitty a piece of her very unpleasant mind. She asked her how much longer she expected her father to support her. He had spent sums he could ill afford in order to give her a chance and she had not taken it. It never struck Mrs. Garstin that perhaps her own hard affability had frightened the men, sons of wealthy fathers or heirs to a title, whose visits she had too cordially encouraged. She put down Kitty's failure to stupidity. Then Doris came out. She had a long nose still, and a poor figure, and she danced badly. In her first season she became engaged to Geoffrey Dennison. He was the only son of a prosperous surgeon who had been given a baronetcy during the war. Geoffrey would inherit a title – it is not very grand to be a medical baronet, but a title, thank God, is still a title – and a very comfortable fortune.

Kitty in a panic married Walter Fane.

9

She had known him but a little while and had never taken much notice of him. She had no idea when or where they had first met till after their engagement he told her that it was at a dance to which some friends had brought him. She certainly paid no attention to him then and if she danced with him it was because she was goodnatured and was glad to dance with any one who asked her. She didn't know him from Adam when a day or two later at another dance he came up and spoke to her. Then she remarked that he was at every dance she went to.

'You know, I've danced with you at least a dozen times now and you must tell me your name,' she said to him at last in her laughing way.

He was obviously taken aback.

'Do you mean to say you don't know it? I was introduced to you.'

'Oh, but people always mumble. I shouldn't be at all surprised if you hadn't the ghost of an idea what mine was.'

He smiled at her. His face was grave and a trifle stern, but his smile was very sweet.

'Of course I know it.' He was silent for a moment or two. 'Have you no curiosity?' he asked then.

'As much as most women.'

'It didn't occur to you to ask somebody or other what my name was?'

She was faintly amused; she wondered why he thought it could in the least interest her; but she liked to please, so she looked at him with that dazzling smile of hers and her beautiful eyes, dewy ponds under forest trees, held an enchanting kindness.

'Well, what is it?'

'Walter Fane.'

She did not know why he came to dances, he did not dance very well, and he seemed to know few people. She had a passing thought that he was in love with her; but she dismissed it with a shrug of the shoulders: she had known girls who thought every man they met was in love with them and had always found them absurd. But she gave Walter Fane just a little more of her attention. He certainly did not behave like any of the other youths who had been in love with her. Most of them told her so frankly and wanted to kiss her: a good many did. But Walter Fane never talked of her and very little of himself. He was rather silent; she did not mind that because she had plenty to say and it pleased her to see him laugh when she made a facetious remark; but when he talked it was not stupidly. He was evidently shy. It appeared that he lived in the East and was home on leave.

One Sunday afternoon he appeared at their house in South Kensington. There were a dozen people there, and he sat for some time, somewhat ill at ease, and then went away. Her mother asked her later who he was.

'I haven't a notion. Did you ask him to come here?'

'Yes, I met him at the Baddeleys. He said he'd seen you at various dances. I said I was always at home on Sundays.'

'His name is Fane and he's got some sort of job in the East.'

'Yes, he's a doctor. Is he in love with you?'

'Upon my word, I don't know.'

'I should have thought you knew by now when a young man was in love with you.'

'I wouldn't marry him if he were,' said Kitty lightly.

Mrs. Garstin did not answer. Her silence was heavy with displeasure. Kitty flushed: she knew that her mother did not care now whom she married so long as somehow she got her off her hands.

10

During the next week she met him at three dances and now, his shyness perhaps wearing off a little, he was somewhat more communicative. He was a doctor, certainly, but he did not practise; he was a bacteriologist (Kitty had only a very vague idea what that meant) and he had a job at Hong-Kong. He was going back in the autumn. He talked a good deal about China. She made it a practice to appear interested in whatever people talked to her of, but indeed the life in Hong-Kong sounded quite jolly; there were clubs and tennis and racing and polo and golf.

'Do people dance much there?'

'Oh, yes, I think so.'

She wondered whether he told her these things with a motive. He seemed to like her society, but never by a pressure of the hand, by a glance or by a word, did he give the smallest indication that he looked upon her as anything but a girl whom you met and danced with. On the following Sunday he came again to their house. Her father happened to come in, it was raining and he had not been able to play golf, and he and Walter Fane had a long chat. She asked her father afterwards what they had talked of.

'It appears he's stationed at Hong-Kong. The Chief Justice is an old friend of mine at the Bar. He seems an unusually intelligent young man.'

She knew that her father was as a rule bored to death by the young people whom for her sake and now her sister's he had been forced for years to entertain.

'It's not often you like any of my young men, father,' she said.

His kind, tired eyes rested upon her.

'Are you going to marry him by any chance?'

'Certainly not.'

'Is he in love with you?'

'He shows no sign of it.'

'Do you like him?'

'I don't think I do very much. He irritates me a little.'

He was not her type at all. He was short, but not thick-set, slight rather and thin; dark and clean-shaven, with very regular, clean-cut features. His eyes were almost black, but not large, they were not very mobile and they rested on objects with a singular persistence; they were curious, but not very pleasant eyes. With his straight, delicate nose, his fine brow and well-shaped mouth he ought to have been good-looking. But surprisingly enough he was not. When Kitty began to think of him at all she was surprised that he should have such good features when you took them one by one. His expression was slightly sarcastic and now that Kitty knew him better she realised that she was not quite at ease with him. He had no gaiety.

By the time the season drew to its end they had seen a good deal of one another, but he had remained as aloof and impenetrable as ever. He was not exactly shy with her, but embarrassed; his conversation remained strangely impersonal. Kitty came to the conclusion that he was not in the least in love with her. He liked her and found her easy to talk to, but when he returned to China in November he would not think of her again. She thought it not impossible that he was engaged all the time to some nurse in a hospital at Hong-Kong, the daughter of a clergyman, dull, plain, flat-footed and strenuous; that was the wife that would exactly suit him.

Then came the announcement of Doris's engagement to Geoffrey Dennison. Doris, at eighteen, was making quite a suitable marriage, and she was twenty-five and single. Supposing she did not marry at all? That season the only person who had proposed to her was a boy of twenty who was still at Oxford: she couldn't marry a boy five years younger than herself. She had made a hash of things. Last year she had refused a widowed Knight of the Bath with three children. She almost wished she hadn't. Mother would be horrible now, and Doris, Doris who had always been sacrificed because she, Kitty, was expected to make the brilliant match, would not fail to crow over her. Kitty's heart sank.

II

But one afternoon when she was walking home from Harrod's she chanced to meet Walter Fane in the Brompton Road, He stopped and talked to her. Then, casually, he asked her if she would take a turn with him in the Park. She had no particular wish to go home; it was not just then a very agreeable place. They strolled along, talking as they always talked, of casual things, and he asked her where she was going for the summer.

'Oh, we always bury ourselves in the country. You see, father is exhausted after the term's work and we just go to the quietest place we can find.'

Kitty spoke with her tongue in her cheek, for she knew quite well that her father had not nearly enough work to tire him and even if he had his convenience would never have been consulted in the choice of a holiday. But a quiet place was a cheap place.

'Don't you think those chairs look rather inviting?' said Walter suddenly.

She followed his eyes and saw two green chairs by themselves under a tree on the grass.

'Let us sit in them,' she said.

But when they were seated he seemed to grow strangely abstracted. He was an odd creature. She chattered on, however, gaily enough and wondered why he had asked her to walk with him in the Park. Perhaps he was going to confide in her his passion for the flat-footed nurse in Hong-Kong. Suddenly he turned to her, interrupting her in the middle of a sentence, so that she could not but see that he had not been listening, and his face was chalk white.

'I want to say something to you.'

She looked at him quicky and she saw that his eyes were filled with a painful anxiety. His voice was strained, low and not quite steady. But before she could ask herself what this agitation meant he spoke again.

'I want to ask you if you'll marry me.'

'You could knock me down with a feather,' she answered so surprised that she looked at him blankly.

'Didn't you know I was awfully in love with you?'

'You never showed it.'

'I'm very awkward and clumsy. I always find it more difficult to say the things I mean than the things I don't.'

Her heart began to beat a little more quickly. She had been proposed to often before, but gaily or sentimentally, and she had answered in the same fashion. No one had ever asked her to marry him in a manner which was so abrupt and yet strangely tragic.

'It's very kind of you,' she said, doubtfully.

'I fell in love with you the first time I saw you. I wanted to ask you before, but I could never bring myself to it.'

'I'm not sure if that's very well put,' she chuckled.

She was glad to have an opportunity to laugh a little,

for on that fine, sunny day the air about them seemed on a sudden heavy with foreboding. He frowned darkly.

'Oh, you know what I mean. I didn't want to lose hope. But now you're going away and in the autumn I have to go back to China.'

'I've never thought of you in that way,' she said helplessly.

He said nothing more. He looked down on the grass sullenly. He was a very odd creature. But now that he had told her she felt in some mysterious way that his love was something she had never met before. She was a little frightened, but she was elated also. His impassivity was vaguely impressive.

'You must give me time to think.'

Still he did not say anything. He did not stir. Did he mean to keep her there till she had decided? That was absurd. She must talk it over with her mother. She ought to have got up when she spoke, she had waited thinking he would answer, and now, she did not know why, she found it difficult to make a movement. She did not look at him, but she was conscious of his appearance; she had never seen herself marrying a man so little taller than herself. When you sat close to him you saw how good his features were, and how cold his face. It was strange when you couldn't help being conscious of the devastating passion which was in his heart.

'I don't know you, I don't know you at all,' she said tremulously.

He gave her a look and she felt her eyes drawn to his. They had a tenderness which she had never seen in them before, but there was something beseeching in them, like a dog's that has been whipped, which slightly exasperated her.

'I think I improve on acquaintance,' he said.

'Of course you're shy, aren't you?'

It was certainly the oddest proposal she had ever had. And even now it seemed to her that they were saying to one another the last things you would have expected on such an occasion. She was not in the least in love with him. She did not know why she hesitated to refuse him at once.

'I'm awfully stupid,' he said, 'I want to tell you that I love you more than anything in the world, but I find it so awfully difficult to say.'

Now that was odd too, for inexplicably enough it touched her; he wasn't really cold, of course, it was his manner that was unfortunate: she liked him at that moment better than she had ever liked him before. Doris was to be married in November. He would be on his way to China then and if she married him she would be with him. It wouldn't be very nice to be a bridesmaid at Doris's wedding. She would be glad to escape that. And then Doris as a married woman and herself single! Every one knew how young Doris was and it would make her seem older. It would put her on the shelf. It wouldn't be a very good marriage for her, but it was a marriage, and the fact that she would live in China made it easier. She was afraid of her mother's bitter tongue. Why, all the girls who had come out with her were married long ago and most of them had children; she was tired of going to see them and gushing over their babies. Walter Fane offered her a new life. She turned to him with a smile which she well knew the effect of.

'If I were so rash as to say I'd marry you, when would you want to marry me?'

He gave a sudden gasp of delight, and his white cheeks flushed.

'Now. At once. As soon as possible. We'd go to Italy for our honeymoon. August and September.'

That would save her from spending the summer in a country vicarage, hired at five guineas a week, with her father and mother. In a flash she saw in her mind's eye the announcement in the *Morning Post* that, the bridegroom having to return to the East, the wedding would take place at once. She knew her mother well enough, she could be counted on to make a splash; for the moment at least Doris would be in the background and when Doris's much grander wedding took place she would be far away.

She stretched out her hand.

'I think I like you very much. You must give me time to get used to you.'

'Then it's yes?' he interrupted.

'I suppose so.'

12

She knew him very little then, and now, though they had been married for nearly two years, she knew him but little more. At first she had been touched by his kindness and flattered, though surprised, by his passion. He was extremely considerate; he was very attentive to her comfort; she never expressed the slightest wish without his hastening to gratify it. He was constantly giving her little presents. When she happened to feel ill no one could have been kinder or more thoughtful. She seemed to do him a favour when she gave him the opportunity of doing something tiresome for her. And he was always exceedingly polite. He rose to his feet when she entered a room, he gave her his hand to help her out of a car, if he chanced to meet her in the street he took off his hat, he was solicitous to open the door for her when she left a room, he never came into her bedroom or her boudoir without a knock. He treated her not as Kitty had seen most men treat their wives, but as though she were a fellow-guest in a country house. It was pleasing and yet a trifle comic. She would have felt more at home with him if he had been more casual. Nor did their conjugal relations draw her closer to him. He was passionate then, fierce, oddly hysterical too, and sentimental.

It disconcerted her to realise how emotional he really was. His self-control was due to shyness or to long training, she did not know which; it seemed to her faintly contemptible that when she lay in his arms, his desire appeased, he who was so timid of saying absurd things, who so feared to be ridiculous, should use baby talk. She had offended him bitterly once by laughing and telling him that he was talking the most fearful slush. She had felt his arms grow limp about her, he remained quite silent for a little while, and then without a word released her and went into his own room. She didn't want to hurt his feelings and a day or two later she said to him:

'You silly old thing, I don't mind what nonsense you talk to me.'

He had laughed in a shamefaced way. She had discovered very soon that he had an unhappy disability to lose himself. He was self-conscious. When there was a party and every one started singing Walter could never bring himself to join in. He sat there smiling to show that he was pleased and amused, but his smile was forced; it was more like a sarcastic smirk, and you could not help feeling that he thought all those people enjoying themselves a pack of fools. He could not bring himself to play the round games which Kitty with her high spirits found such a lark. On their journey out to China he had absolutely refused to put on fancy dress when every one else was wearing it. It disturbed her pleasure that he should so obviously think the whole thing a bore.

Kitty was lively; she was willing to chatter all day long and she laughed easily. His silence disconcerted her. He had a way which exasperated her of returning no answer to some casual remark of hers. It was true that it needed no answer, but an answer all the same would have been pleasant. If it was raining and she said: 'It's raining cats and dogs.' she would have liked him to say: 'Yes, isn't it?' He remained silent. Sometimes she would have liked to shake him.

'I said it was raining cats and dogs,' she repeated.

'I heard you,' he answered, with his affectionate smile.

It showed that he had not meant to be offensive. He did not speak because he had nothing to say. But if nobody spoke unless he had something to say, Kitty reflected, with a smile, the human race would very soon lose the use of speech.

13

The fact was, of course, that he had no charm. That was why he was not popular, and she had not been long in Hong-Kong before she discovered that he was not. She remained very vague about his work. It was enough for her to realise, and she did this quite distinctly, that to be the government bacteriologist was no great fry. He seemed to have no desire to discuss that part of his life with her. Because she was willing to be interested in anything at first she had asked him about it. He put her off with a jest.

'It's very dull and technical,' he said on another occasion. 'And it's grossly underpaid.'

He was very reserved. All she knew about his antecedents, his birth, his education, and his life before he met her, she had elicited by direct questioning. It was odd, the only thing that seemed to annoy him was a question; and when, in her natural curiosity, she fired a string of them at him, his answers became at every one more abrupt. She had the wit to see that he did not care to reply because he had anything to hide from her, but merely from a natural secretiveness. It bored him to talk about himself. It made him shy and uncomfortable. He did not know how to be open. He was fond of reading, but he read books which seemed to Kitty very dull. If he was not busy with some scientific treatise he would read books about China or historical works. He never relaxed. She did not think he could. He was fond of games: he played tennis and bridge.

She wondered why he had ever fallen in love with her. She could not imagine any one less suited than herself to this restrained, cold and self-possessed man. And yet it was quite certain that he loved her madly. He would do anything in the world to please her. He was like wax in her hands. When she thought of one side he showed her, a side which only she had seen, she a little despised him. She wondered whether his sarcastic manner, with its contemptuous tolerance for so many persons and things she admired, was merely a façade to conceal a profound weakness. She supposed he was clever, every one seemed to think he was, but except very occasionally when he was with two or three people he liked and was in the mood, she had never found him entertaining. He did not precisely bore her, he left her indifferent.

14

Though Kitty had met his wife at various tea-parties she had been some weeks in Hong-Kong before she saw Charles Townsend. She was introduced to him only when with her husband she went to dine at his house. Kitty was on the defensive. Charles Townsend was Assistant Colonial Secretary and she had no mind to allow him to use her with the condescension which, notwithstanding her good manners she discerned in Mrs. Townsend. The room in which they were received was spacious. It was furnished as was every other drawing-room she had been in at Hong-Kong in a comfortable and homely style. It was a large party. They were the last to come and as they entered Chinese servants in uniform were handing round cocktails and olives. Mrs. Townsend greeted them in her casual fashion and looking at a list told Walter whom he was to take in to dinner.

Kitty saw a tall and very handsome man bear down on them.

'This is my husband.'

'I am to have the privilege of sitting next to you,' he said.

She immediately felt at ease and the sense of hostility

vanished from her bosom. Though his eyes were smiling she had seen in them a quick look of surprise. She understood it perfectly and it made her inclined to laugh.

'I shan't be able to eat any dinner,' he said, 'and if I know Dorothy the dinner's damned good.'

'Why not?'

'I ought to have been told. Some one really ought to have warned me.'

'What about?'

'No one said a word. How was I to know that I was going to meet a raging beauty?'

'Now what am I to say to that?'

'Nothing. Leave me to do the talking. And I'll say it over and over again.'

Kitty, unmoved, wondered what exactly his wife had told him about her. He must have asked. And Townsend looking down on her with his laughing eyes, suddenly remembered.

'What is she like?' he had inquired when his wife told him she had met Dr. Fane's bride.

'Oh, quite a nice little thing. Actressy.'

'Was she on the stage?'

'Oh, no, I don't think so. Her father's a doctor or a lawyer or something. I suppose we shall have to ask them to dinner.'

'There's no hurry, is there?'

When they were sitting side by side at table he told her that he had known Walter Fane ever since he came to the Colony.

'We play bridge together. He's far and away the best bridge player at the Club.'

She told Walter on the way home.

'That's not saying very much, you know.'

'How does he play?'

'Not badly. He plays a winning hand very well, but when he has bad cards he goes all to pieces.'

'Does he play as well as you?'

'I have no illusions about my play. I should describe

myself as a very good player in the second class. Townsend thinks he's in the first. He isn't.'

'Don't you like him?'

'I neither like him nor dislike him. I believe he's not bad at his job and every one says he's a good sportsman. He doesn't very much interest me.'

It was not the first time that Walter's moderation had exasperated her. She asked herself why it was necessary to be so prudent: you either liked people or you didn't. She had liked Charles Townsend very much. And she had not expected to. He was probably the most popular man in the Colony. It was supposed that the Colonial Secretary would retire soon and every one hoped that Townsend would succeed him. He played tennis and polo and golf. He kept racing ponies. He was always ready to do any one a good turn. He never let red tape interfere with him. He put on no airs. Kitty did not know why she had resented hearing him so well spoken of, she could not help thinking he must be very conceited: she had been extremely silly; that was the last thing you could accuse him of.

She had enjoyed her evening. They had talked of the theatres in London, and of Ascot and Cowes, all the things she knew about, so that really she might have met him at some nice house in Lennox Gardens; and later, when the men came into the drawing-room after dinner, he had strolled over and sat beside her again. Though he had not said anything very amusing, he had made her laugh; it must have been the way he said it: there was a caressing sound in his deep, rich voice, a delightful expression in his kind, shining blue eyes, which made you feel very much at home with him. Of course he had charm. That was what made him so pleasant.

He was tall, six foot two at least, she thought, and he had a beautiful figure; he was evidently in very good condition and he had not a spare ounce of fat on him. He was well-dressed, the best-dressed man in the room, and he wore his clothes well. She liked a man to be smart.

Her eyes wandered to Walter: he really should try to be a little better turned out. She noticed Townsend's cuff-links and waistcoat buttons; she had seen similar ones at Cartier's. Of course the Townsends had private means. His face was deeply sunburned, but the sun had not taken the healthy colour from his cheeks. She liked the little trim curly moustache which did not conceal his full red lips. He had black hair, short and brushed very sleek. But of course his eyes, under thick, bushy eyebrows, were his best feature: they were so very blue, and they had a laughing tenderness which persuaded you of the sweetness of his disposition. No man who had those blue eyes could bear to hurt any one.

She could not but know that she had made an impression on him. If he had not said charming things to her his eyes, warm with admiration, would have betrayed him. His ease was delightful. He had no self-consciousness. Kitty was at home in these circumstances and she admired the way in which amid the banter which was the staple of their conversation he insinuated every now and then a pretty, flattering speech. When she shook hands with him on leaving he gave her hand a pressure that she could not mistake.

'I hope we shall see you again soon,' he said casually, but his eyes gave his words a meaning which she could not fail to see.

'Hong-Kong is very small, isn't it?' she said.

15

Who would have thought then that within three months they would be on such terms? He had told her since that he was crazy about her on that first evening. She was the most beautiful thing he had ever seen. He remembered the dress she wore; it was her wedding dress, and he said she looked like a lily of the valley. She knew that he was in love with her before he told her, and a little frightened she kept him at a distance. He was impetuous and it was difficult. She was afraid to let him kiss her, for the thought of his arms about her made her heart beat so fast. She had never been in love before. It was wonderful. And now that she knew what love was she felt a sudden sympathy for the love that Walter bore her. She teased him, playfully, and saw that he enjoyed it. She had been perhaps a little afraid of him, but now she had more confidence. She chaffed him and it amused her to see the slow smile with which at first he received her banter. He was surprised and pleased. One of these days, she thought, he would become quite human. Now that she had learnt something of passion it diverted her to play lightly, like a harpist running his fingers across the strings of his harp, on his affections. She laughed when she saw how she bewildered and confused him.

And when Charlie became her lover the situation between herself and Walter seemed exquisitely absurd. She could hardly look at him, so grave and self-controlled, without laughing. She was too happy to feel unkindly towards him. Except for him, after all, she would never have known Charlie. She had hesitated some time before the final step, not because she did not want to yield to Charlie's passion, her own was equal to his, but because her upbringing and all the conventions of her life intimidated her. She was amazed afterwards (and the final act was due to accident; neither of them had seen the opportunity till it was face to face with them) to discover that she felt in no way different from what she had before. She had expected that it would cause some, she hardly knew what, fantastic change in her so that she would feel like somebody else; and when she had a chance to look at herself in the glass she was bewildered to see the same woman she had seen the day before.

'Are you angry with me?' he asked her.

'I adore you,' she whispered.

'Don't you think you were very silly to waste so much time?'

'A perfect fool.'

16

Her happiness, sometimes almost more than she could bear, renewed her beauty. Just before she married, beginning to lose her first freshness, she had looked tired and drawn. The uncharitable said that she was going off. But there is all the difference between a girl of twenty-five and a married woman of that age. She was like a rosebud that is beginning to turn yellow at the edges of the petals, and then suddenly she was a rose in full bloom. Her starry eyes gained a more significant expression; her skin (that feature which had always been her greatest pride and most anxious care) was dazzling: it could not be compared to the peach or to the flower; it was they that demanded comparison with it. She looked eighteen once more. She was at the height of her glowing loveliness. It was impossible not to remark it and her women friends asked her in little friendly asides if she was going to have a baby. The indifferent who had said she was just a very pretty woman with a long nose admitted that they had misjudged her. She was what Charlie had called her the first time he saw her, a raging beauty.

They managed their intrigue with skill. He had a broad back, he told her ('I will not have you swank about your figure,' she interrupted lightly), and it did not matter about him; but for her sake they mustn't take the smallest risk. They could not meet often alone, not half often enough for him, but he had to think of her first, sometimes in the curio shop, now and then after luncheon in her house when no one was about; but she saw him a good deal here and there. It amused her then to see the formal way he spoke to her, jovial, for he was always that, with the same manner he used with every one. Who could imagine when they heard him chaff her with that charming humour of his that so lately he had held her in his passionate arms?

She worshipped him. He was splendid, in his smart top boots and his white breeches, when he played polo. In tennis clothes he looked a mere boy. Of course he was proud of his figure: it was the best figure she had ever seen. He took pains to keep it. He never ate bread or potatoes or butter. And he took a great deal of exercise. She liked the care he took of his hands; he was manicured once a week. He was a wonderful athlete and the year before he had won the local tennis championship. Certainly he was the best dancer she had ever danced with; it was a dream to dance with him. No one would think he was forty. She told him she did not believe it.

'I believe it's all bluff and you're really twenty-five.'

He laughed. He was well pleased.

'Oh, my dear, I have a boy of fifteen. I'm a middle-aged gent. In another two or three years I shall just be a fat old party.'

'You'll be adorable when you're a hundred.'

She liked his black, bushy eyebrows. She wondered whether it was they that gave his blue eyes their disturbing expression.

He was full of accomplishments. He could play the piano quite well, rag-time, of course, and he could sing a comic song with a rich voice and good humour. She did not believe there was anything he could not do: He was very clever at his work too and she shared his pleasure when he told her that the Governor had particularly congratulated him on the way he had done some difficult job.

'Although it's I as says it,' he laughed, his eyes charming with the love he bore her, 'there's not a fellow in the Service who could have done it better.'

Oh, how she wished that she were his wife rather than Walter's!

Of course it was not certain yet that Walter knew the truth, and if he didn't it was better perhaps to leave well alone; but if he did, well, in the end it would be the best thing for all of them. At first she had been, if not satisfied, at least resigned to seeing Charlie only by stealth; but time had increased her passion and for some while now she had been increasingly impatient of the obstacles which prevented them from being always together. He had told her so often that he cursed his position which forced him to be so discreet, the ties which bound him, and the ties which bound her: how marvellous it would have been, he said, if they were both free! She saw his point of view; no one wanted a scandal, and of course it required a good deal of thinking over before you changed the course of your life; but if freedom were thrust upon them, ah, then, how simple everything would be!

It was not as though any one would suffer very much. She knew exactly what his relations were with his wife. She was a cold woman and there had been no love between them for years. It was habit that held them together, convenience, and of course the children. It was easier for Charlie than for her: Walter loved her; but after all, he was absorbed in his work; and a man always had his club; he might be upset at first, but he would get over it; there was no reason why he should not marry somebody else. Charlie had told her that he could not make out how she came to throw herself away on Walter Fane.

She wondered, half smiling, why a little while before she had been terrified at the thought that Walter had caught them. Of course it was startling to see the handle of the door slowly turn. But after all they knew the worst that Walter could do, and they were ready for it. Charlie would feel as great a relief as she that what they both desired more than anything in the world should be thus forced upon them.

Walter was a gentleman, she would do him the justice to acknowledge that, and he loved her; he would do the right thing and allow her to divorce him. They had made a mistake and the lucky thing was that they had found it out before it was too late. She made up her mind exactly what she was going to say to him and how she would treat him. She would be kind, smiling, and firm. There was no need for them to quarrel. Later on she would always be glad to see him. She hoped honestly that the two years they had spent together would remain with him as a priceless memory.

'I don't suppose Dorothy Townsend will mind divorcing Charlie a bit,' she thought. 'Now the youngest boy is going back to England it will be much nicer for her to be in England too. There's absolutely nothing for her to do in Hong-Kong. She'll be able to spend all the holidays with her boys. And then she's got her father and mother in England.'

It was all very simple and everything could be managed without scandal or ill-feeling. And then she and Charlie could marry. Kitty drew a long sigh. They would be very happy. It was worth going through a certain amount of bother to achieve that. Confusedly, one picture jostling another, she thought of the life they would lead together, of the fun they would have and the little journeys they would take together, the house they would live in, the positions he would rise to and the help she would be to him. He would be very proud of her and she, she adored him.

But through all these day-dreams ran a current of apprehension. It was funny: it was as though the wood and the strings of the orchestra played Arcadian melodies and in the bass the drums, softly but with foreboding, beat a grim tattoo. Sooner or later Walter must come home and her heart beat fast at the thought of meeting him: It was strange that he had gone away that afternoon without saying a word to her. Of course she was not frightened of him; after all what could he do, she repeated to herself; but she could not quite allay her uneasiness. Once more she repeated what she would say to him. What was the good of making a scene? She was very sorry, Heaven knew she didn't want to cause him pain, but she couldn't help it if she didn't love him. It was no good pretending and it was always better to tell the truth. She hoped he wouldn't be unhappy but they had made a mistake and the only sensible thing was to acknowledge it. She would always think kindly of him.

But even as she said this to herself a sudden gust of fear made the sweat start out in the palms of her hands. And because she was frightened she grew angry with him. If he wanted to make a scene, that was his lookout; he must not be surprised if he got more than he bargained for. She would tell him that she had never cared two pins for him and that not a day had passed since their marriage without her regretting it. He was dull. Oh, how he'd bored her, bored her, bored her! He thought himself so much better than any one else, it was laughable; he had no sense of humour; she hated his supercilious air, his coldness, and his self-control. It was easy to be self-controlled when you were interested in nothing and nobody but yourself. He was repulsive to her. She hated to let him kiss her. What had he to be so conceited about? He danced rottenly, he was a wet blanket at a party, he couldn't play or sing, he couldn't play polo and his tennis was no better than anybody else's. Bridge? Who cared about bridge?

Kitty worked herself up into a towering passion. Let him dare to reproach her. All that had happened was his own fault. She was thankful that he knew the truth at last. She hated him and wished never to see him again. Yes, she was thankful that it was all over. Why couldn't he leave her alone? He had pestered her into marrying him and now she was fed up.

'Fed up,' she repeated aloud, trembling with anger. 'Fed up! Fed up!'

She heard the car draw up to the gate of their garden. He was coming up the stairs.

18

He came into the room: Her heart was beating wildly and her hands were shaking; it was lucky that she lay on the sofa. She was holding an open book as though she had been reading. He stood for an instant on the threshold and their eyes met. Her heart sank; she felt on a sudden a cold chill pass through her limbs and she shivered. She had that feeling which you describe by saying that some one was walking over your grave. His face was deathly pale; she had seen it like that once before, when they sat together in the Park and he asked her to marry him. His dark eyes, immobile and inscrutable, seemed preternaturally large. He knew everything.

'You're back early,' she remarked.

Her lips trembled so that she could hardly frame the words. She was terrified. She was afraid she would faint.

'I think it's about the usual time.'

His voice sounded strange to her. It was raised on the last word in order to give his remark a casual air, but it was forced. She wondered if he saw that she was shaking in every limb. It was only by an effort that she did not scream. He dropped his eyes.

'I'm just going to dress.'

He left the room. She was shattered. For two or three minutes she could not stir, but at last, raising herself from the sofa, with difficulty, as though she had had an illness and were still weak, she found her feet. She did not know if her legs would support her. She felt her way by means of chairs and tables to the verandah and then with one hand on the wall went to her room. She put on a tea-gown and when she went back into her boudoir (they only used the drawing-room when there was a party) he was standing at a table looking at the pictures of the *Sketch*. She had to force herself to enter.

'Shall we go down? Dinner is ready.'

'Have I kept you waiting?'

It was dreadful that she could not control the trembling of her lips.

When was he going to speak?

They sat down and for a moment there was silence between them. Then he made a remark and because it was so commonplace it had a sinister air.

'The *Empress* didn't come in to-day,' he said. 'I wonder if she's been delayed by a storm.'

'Was she due to-day?'

'Yes.'

She looked at him now and saw that his eyes were fixed on his plate. He made another observation, equally trivial, about a tennis tournament that was about to be played, and he spoke at length. His voice as a rule was agreeable, with a variety of tone, but now he spoke on one note. It was strangely unnatural. It gave Kitty the impression that he was speaking from a long way off. And all the time his eyes were directed to his plate, or the table, or to a picture on the wall. He would not meet hers. She realised that he could not bear to look at her.

'Shall we go upstairs?' he said when dinner was finished.

'If you like.'

She rose and he held open the door for her. His eyes were cast down as she passed him. When they reached the sitting-room he took up the illustrated paper once more.

'Is this a new *Sketch*? I don't think I've seen it.'

'I don't know. I haven't noticed.'

It had been lying about for a fortnight and she knew that he had looked it through and through. He took it and sat down. She lay again on the sofa and took her book. As a rule in the evening, when they were alone, they played coon-can or patience. He was leaning back in an arm-chair, in a comfortable attitude, and his attention seemed absorbed by the illustration he was looking at. He did not turn the page. She tried to read, but she could not see the print before her eyes. The words were blurred. Her head began to ache violently.

When would he speak?

They sat in silence for an hour. She gave up the pretence of reading, and letting her novel fall on her lap, gazed into space. She was afraid to make the smallest gesture or the smallest sound. He sat quite still, in that same easy attitude, and stared with those wide, immobile eyes of his at the picture. His stillness was strangely menacing. It gave Kitty the feeling of a wild beast prepared to spring.

When suddenly he stood up she started. She clenched her hands and she felt herself grow pale. Now!

'I have some work to do,' he said in that quiet, toneless voice, his eyes averted. 'If you don't mind I'll go into my study. I daresay you'll have gone to bed by the time I've finished.'

'I *am* rather tired to-night.'

'Well, good-night.'

'Good-night.'

He left the room.

19

As soon as she could next morning she rang Townsend up at his office:

'Yes, what is it?'

'I want to see you.'

'My dear, I'm awfully busy. I'm a working man.'

'It's very important. Can I come down to the office?'

'Oh, no, I wouldn't do that if I were you.'

'Well, come here then.'

'I can't possibly get away. What about this afternoon?

And don't you think it would be better if I didn't come to your house?'

'I must see you at once.'

There was a pause and she was afraid that she had been cut off.

'Are you there?' she asked anxiously.

'Yes, I was thinking. Has anything happened?'

'I can't tell you over the telephone.'

There was another silence before he spoke again.

'Well, look here, I can manager to see you for ten minutes at one if that'll do. You'd better go to Ku-Chou's and I'll come along as soon as I can.'

'The curio shop?' she asked in dismay.

'Well, we can't meet in the lounge at the Hong-Kong Hotel very well,' he answered.

She noticed a trace of irritation in his voice.

'Very well. I'll go to Ku-Chou's.'

20

She got out of her rickshaw in the Victoria Road and walked up the steep, narrow lane till she came to the shop. She lingered outside a moment as though her attention were attracted by the bric-a-brac which was displayed. But a boy who was standing there on the watch for customers, recognising her at once, gave her a broad smile of connivance. He said something in Chinese to some one within and the master, a little, fat-faced man in a black gown, came out and greeted her. She walked in quickly.

'Mr. Townsend no come yet. You go top-side, yes?'

She went to the back of the shop and walked up the rickety, dark stairs. The Chinese followed her and unlocked the door that led into the bedroom. It was stuffy and there was an acrid smell of opium. She sat down on a sandalwood chest.

In a moment she heard a heavy step on the creaking

stairs. Townsend came in and shut the door behind him. His face bore a sullen look, as he saw her it vanished, and he smiled in that charming way of his. He took her quickly in his arms and kissed her lips.

'Now what's the trouble?'

'It makes me feel better just to see you,' she smiled.

He sat down on the bed and lit a cigarette.

'You look rather washed out this morning.'

'I don't wonder,' she answered. 'I don't think I closed my eyes all night.'

He gave her a look. He was smiling still, but his smile was a little set and unnatural. She thought there was a shade of anxiety in his eyes.

'He knows,' she said.

There was an instant's pause before he answered.

'What did he say?'

'He hasn't said anything.'

'What!' He looked at her sharply. 'What makes you think he knows?'

'Everything. His look. The way he talked at dinner.'

'Was he disagreeable?'

'No, on the contrary, he was scrupulously polite. For the first time since we married he didn't kiss me good-night.'

She dropped her eyes. She was not sure if Charlie understood. As a rule Walter took her in his arms and pressed his lips to hers and would not let them go. His whole body grew tender and passionate with his kiss.

'Why do you imagine he didn't say anything?'

'I don't know.'

There was a pause. Kitty sat very still on the sandal-wood box and looked with anxious attention at Town-send. His face once more was sullen and there was a frown between his brows. His mouth dropped a little at the corners. But all at once he looked up and a gleam of malicious amusement came into his eyes.

'I wonder if he *is* going to say anything.'

She did not answer. She did not know what he meant.

'After all, he wouldn't be the first man who's shut his eyes in a case of this sort. What has he to gain by making a row? If he'd wanted to make a row he would have insisted on coming into your room.' His eyes twinkled and his lips broke into a broad smile. 'We should have looked a pair of damned fools.'

'I wish you could have seen his face last night.'

'I expect he was upset. It was naturally a shock. It's a damned humiliating position for any man. He always looks a fool. Walter doesn't give me the impression of a fellow who'd care to wash a lot of dirty linen in public.'

'I don't think he would,' she answered reflectively. 'He's very sensitive, I've discovered that.'

'That's all to the good as far as we're concerned. You know, it's a very good plan to put yourself in somebody else's shoes and ask yourself how you would act in his place. There's only one way in which a man can save his face when he's in that sort of position and that is to pretend he knows nothing. I bet you anything you like that that is exactly what he's going to do.'

The more Townsend talked the more buoyant he became. His blue eyes sparkled and he was once more his gay and jovial self. He irradiated an encouraging confidence.

'Heavens knows, I don't want to say anything disagreeable about him, but when you come down to brass tacks a bacteriologist is no great shakes. The chances are that I shall be Colonial Secretary when Simmons goes home, and it's to Walter's interest to keep on the right side of me. He's got his bread and butter to think of, like the rest of us: do you think the Colonial Office are going to do much for a fellow who makes a scandal? Believe me, he's got everything to gain by holding his tongue and everything to lose by kicking up a row.'

Kitty moved uneasily. She knew how shy Walter was and she could believe that the fear of a scene, and the dread of public attention, might have influence upon him; but she could not believe that he would be affected by

43

the thought of a material advantage. Perhaps she didn't know him very well, but Charlie didn't know him at all.

'Has it occurred to you that he's madly in love with me?'

He did not answer, but he smiled at her with roguish eyes. She knew and loved that charming look of his.

'Well, what is it? I know you're going to say something awful.'

'Well, you know, women are often under the impression that men are much more madly in love with them than they really are.'

For the first time she laughed. His confidence was catching.

'What a monstrous thing to say.'

'I put it to you that you haven't been bothering much about your husband lately. Perhaps he isn't quite so much in love with you as he was.'

'At all events I shall never delude myself that *you* are madly in love with me,' she retorted.

'That's where you're wong.'

Ah, how good it was to hear him say that! She knew it and her belief in his passion warmed her heart. As he spoke he rose from the bed and came and sat down beside her on the sandalwood box. He put his arm round her waist.

'Don't worry your silly little head a moment longer,' he said. 'I promise you there's nothing to fear. I'm as certain as I am of anything that he's going to pretend he knows nothing. You know, this sort of thing is awfully difficult to prove. You say he's in love with you; perhaps he doesn't want to lose you altogether. I swear I'd accept anything rather than that if you were my wife.'

She leaned towards him. Her body became limp and yielding against his arm. The love she felt for him was almost torture. His last words had struck her: perhaps Walter loved her so passionately that he was prepared to accept any humiliation if sometimes she would let him love her. She could understand that; for that was how she felt towards Charlie. A thrill of pride passed through her, and at the same time a faint sensation of contempt for a man who could love so slavishly.

She put her arm lovingly round Charlie's neck.

'You're simply wonderful. I was shaking like a leaf when I came here and you've made everything all right.'

He took her face in his hand and kissed her lips.

'Darling.'

'You're such a comfort to me,' she sighed.

'I'm sure you need not be nervous. And you know I'll stand by you. I won't let you down.'

She put away her fears, but for an instant unreasonably she regretted that her plans for the future were shattered. Now that all danger was past she almost wished that Walter were going to insist on a divorce.

'I knew I could count on you,' she said.

'So I should hope.'

'Oughtn't you to go and have your tiffin?'

'Oh, damn my tiffin.'

He drew her more closely to him and now she was held tight in his arms. His mouth sought hers.

'Oh, Charlie, you must let me go.'

'Never.'

She gave a little laugh, a laugh of happy love and of triumph; his eyes were heavy with desire. He lifted her to her feet and not leting her go but holding her close to his breast he locked the door.

21

All through the afternoon she thought of what Charlie had said about Walter. They were dining out that evening and when he came back from the Club she was dressing. He knocked at her door.

'Come in.'

He did not open.

'I'm going straight along to dress. How long will you be?'

'Ten minutes.'

He said nothing more, but went to his own room. His voice had that constrained note which she had heard in it the night before. She felt fairly sure of herself now. She was ready before he was and when he came downstairs she was already seated in the car.

'I'm afraid I've kept you waiting,' he said.

'I shall survive it,' she replied, and she was able to smile as she spoke.

She made an observation or two as they drove down the hill, but he answered curtly. She shrugged her shoulders; she was growing a trifle impatient: if he wanted to sulk, let him, she didn't care. They drove in silence till they reached their destination. It was a large dinner party. There were too many people and too many courses. While Kitty chatted gaily with her neighbours she watched Walter. He was deathly pale and his face was pinched.

'Your husband is looking rather washed out. I thought he didn't mind the heat. Has he been working very hard?'

'He always works hard.'

'I suppose you're going away soon?'

'Oh, yes, I think I shall go to Japan as I did last year,' she said. 'The doctor says I must get out of the heat if I don't want to go all to pieces.'

Walter did not as usual when they were dining out give her a little smiling glance now and then. He never looked at her. She had noticed that when he came down to the car he kept his eyes averted, and he did the same when, with his usual politeness, he gave her his hand to alight. Now, talking with the women on either side of him, he did not smile, but looked at them with steady and unblinking eyes; and really his eyes looked enormous and in that pale face coal black. His face was set and stern.

'He must be an agreeable companion,' thought Kitty ironically.

The idea of those unfortunate ladies trying to indulge in small talk with that grim mask not a little diverted her.

Of course he knew; there was no doubt about that, and he was furious with her. Why hadn't he said anything? Was it really because, though angry and hurt, he loved her so much that he was afraid she would leave him. The thought made her ever so slightly despise him, but good-naturedly: after all, he was her husband and he provided her with board and lodging; so long as he didn't interfere with her and let her do as she liked she would be quite nice to him. On the other hand perhaps his silence was due merely to a morbid timidity. Charlie was right when he said that no one would hate a scandal more than Walter. He never made a speech if he could help it. He had told her once that when he was subpoenaed as a witness on a case where he was to give expert evidence he had hardly slept for a week before. His shyness was a disease.

And there was another thing: men were very vain, and so long as no one knew what had happened it might be that Walter would be content to ignore it. Then she wondered whether by any possibility Charlie was right when he suggested that Walter knew which side his bread was buttered. Charlie was the most popular man in the Colony and soon would be Colonial Secretary. He could be very useful to Walter: on the other hand he could make himself very unpleasant if Walter put his back up. Her heart exulted as she thought of her lover's strength and determination; she felt so defenceless in his virile arms. Men were strange: it would never have occurred to her that Walter was capable of such baseness, and yet you never knew; perhaps his seriousness was merely a mask for a mean and pettifogging nature. The more she considered it the more likely it seemed that Charlie was right; and she turned her glance once more on her husband. There was no indulgence in it.

It happened that just then the women on either side of

him were talking with their neighbours and he was left alone. He was staring straight in front of him, forgetful of the party, and his eyes were filled with a mortal sadness. It gave Kitty a shock.

22

Next day when she was lying down after luncheon, dozing, she was aroused by a knock at her door.

'Who is it?' she cried irritably.

At that hour she was unaccustomed to be disturbed.

'I.'

She recognised her husband's voice and she sat up quickly.

'Come in.'

'Did I wake you?' he asked as he entered.

'In point of fact you did,' she answered in the natural tone she had adopted with him for the last two days.

'Will you come into the next room. I want to have a little talk with you.'

Her heart gave a sudden beat against her ribs.

'I'll put on a dressing-gown.'

He left her. She slipped her bare feet into mules and wrapped herself in a kimono. She looked in the glass; she was very pale and she put on some rouge. She stood at the door for a moment, nerving herself for the interview, and then with a bold face joined him.

'How did you manage to get away from the Laboratory at this hour?' she said. 'I don't often see you at this sort of time.'

'Won't you sit down?'

He did not look at her. He spoke gravely. She was glad to do as he asked: her knees were a little shaky, and unable to continue in that jocular tone she kept silent. He sat also and lit a cigarette. His eyes wandered restlessly about the room. He seemed to have some difficulty in starting.

Suddenly he looked full at her; and because he had held his eyes so long averted, his direct gaze gave her such a fright that she smothered a cry.

'Have you ever heard of Mei-tan-fu?' he asked. 'There's been a good deal about it in the papers lately.'

She stared at him in astonishment. She hesitated.

'Is that the place where there's cholera? Mr. Arbuthnot was talking about it last night.'

'There's an epidemic. I believe it's the worst they've had for years. There was a medical missionary there. He died of cholera three days ago. There's a French convent there and of course there's the Customs man. Every one else has got out.'

His eyes were still fixed on her and she could not lower hers. She tried to read his expression, but she was nervous, and she could only discern a strange watchfulness. How could he look so steadily? He did not even blink.

'The French nuns are doing what they can. They've turned the orphanage into a hospital. But the people are dying like flies. I've offered to go and take charge.'

'You?'

She started violently. Her first thought was that if he went she would be free and without let or hindrance could see Charlie. But the thought shocked her. She felt herself go scarlet. Why did he watch her like that? She looked away in embarrassment.

'Is that necessary?' she faltered.

'There's not a foreign doctor in the place.'

'But you're not a doctor, you're a bacteriologist.'

'I am an M.D., you know, and before I specialised I did a good deal of general work in a hospital. The fact that I'm first and foremost a bacteriologist is all to the good. It will be an admirable chance for research work.'

He spoke almost flippantly and when she glanced at him she was surprised to see in his eyes a gleam of mockery. She could not understand.

'But won't it be awfully dangerous?'

'Awfully.'

He smiled. It was a derisive grimace. She leaned her forehead on her hand. Suicide. It was nothing short of that. Dreadful! She had not thought he would take it like that. She couldn't let him do that. It was cruel. It was not her fault if she did not love him. She couldn't bear the thought that he should kill himself for her sake. Tears flowed softly down her cheeks.

'What are you crying for?'

His voice was cold.

'You're not obliged to go, are you?'

'No, I go of my own free will.'

'Please don't, Walter. It would be too awful if something happened. Supposing you died?'

Though his face remained impassive the shadow of a smile once more crossed his eyes. He did not answer.

'Where is this place?' she asked after a pause.

'Mei-tan-fu? It's on a tributary of the Western River. We should go up the Western River and then by chair.'

'Who is we?'

'You and I.'

She looked at him quickly. She thought she had heard amiss. But now the smile in his eyes had travelled to his lips. His dark eyes were fixed on her.

'Are you expecting me to come too?'

'I thought you'd like to.'

Her breath began to come very fast. A shudder passed through her.

'But surely it's no place for a woman. The missionary sent his wife and children down weeks ago and the A.P.C. man and his wife came down. I met her at a tea-party. I've just remembered that she said they left some place on account of cholera.'

'There are five French nuns there.'

Panic seized her.

'I don't know what you mean. It would be madness for me to go. You know how delicate I am. Dr. Hayward said I must get out of Hong-Kong on account of the heat. I could never stand the heat up there. And cholera: I should be frightened out of my wits. It's just asking for trouble. There's no reason for me to go. I should die.'

He did not answer. She looked at him in her desperation and she could hardly restrain a cry. His face had a sort of black pallor which suddenly terrified her. She saw in it a look of hatred. Was it possible that he wanted her to die? She answered her own outrageous thought.

'It's absurd. If you think you ought to go it's your own lookout. But really you can't expect me to. I hate illness. A cholera epidemic. I don't pretend to be very brave and I don't mind telling you that I haven't pluck for that. I shall stay here until it's time for me to go to Japan.'

'I should have thought that you would want to accompany me when I am about to set out on a dangerous expedition.'

He was openly mocking her now. She was confused. She did not quite know whether he meant what he said or was merely trying to frighten her.

'I don't think any one could reasonably blame me for refusing to go to a dangerous place where I had no business or where I could be of no use.'

'You could be of the greatest use; you could cheer and comfort me.'

She grew even a little paler.

'I don't understand what you're talking about.'

'I shouldn't have thought it needed more than average intelligence.'

'I'm not going, Walter. It's monstrous to ask me.'

'Then I shall not go either. I shall immediately file my petition.'

23

She looked at him blankly. What he said was so unexpected that at the first moment she could hardly gather its sense.

'What on earth are you talking about?' she faltered.

Even to herself her reply rang false, and she saw the look of disdain which it called forth on Walter's stern face.

'I'm afraid you've thought me a bigger fool than I am.'

She did not quite know what to say. She was undecided whether indignantly to assert her innocence or to break out into angry reproaches. He seemed to read her thoughts.

'I've got all the proof necessary.'

She began to cry. The tears flowed from her eyes without any particular anguish and she did not dry them: to weep gave her a little time to collect herself. But her mind was blank. He watched her without concern, and his calmness frightened her. He grew impatient.

'You're not going to do much good by crying, you know.'

His voice, so cold and hard, had the effect of exciting in her a certain indignation. She was recovering her nerve.

'I don't care. I suppose you have no objection to my divorcing you. It means nothing to a man.'

'Will you allow me to ask why I should put myself to the smallest inconvenience on your account?'

'It can't make any difference to you. It's not much to ask you to behave like a gentleman.'

'I have much too great a regard for your welfare.'

She sat up now and dried her eyes.

'What *do* you mean?' she asked him.

'Townsend will marry you only if he is co-respondent and the case is so shameless that his wife is forced to divorce him.'

'You don't know what you're talking about,' she cried. 'You stupid fool.'

His tone was so contemptuous that she flushed with anger. And perhaps her anger was greater because she had never before heard him say to her any but sweet, flattering and delightful things. She had been accustomed to find him subservient to all her whims.

'If you want the truth you can have it. He's only too

anxious to marry me. Dorothy Townsend is perfectly willing to divorce him and we shall be married the moment we're free.'

'Did he tell you that in so many words or is that the impression you have gained from his manner?'

Walter's eyes shone with bitter mockery. They made Kitty a trifle uneasy. She was not quite sure that Charlie had ever said exactly that in so many words.

'He said it over and over again.'

'That's a lie and you know it's a lie.'

'He loves me with all his heart and soul. He loves me as passionately as I love him. You've found out. I'm not going to deny anything. Why should I? We've been lovers for a year and I'm proud of it. He means everything in the world to me and I'm glad that you know at last. We're sick to death of secrecy and compromise and all the rest of it. It was a mistake that I ever married you, I never should have done it, I was a fool. I never cared for you. We never had anything in common. I don't like the people you like and I'm bored by the things that interest you. I'm thankful it's finished.'

He watched her without a gesture and without a movement of his face. He listened attentively and no change in his expression showed that what she said affected him.

'Do you know why I married you?'

'Because you wanted to be married before your sister Doris.'

It was true, but it gave her a funny little turn to realise that he knew it. Oddly enough, even in that moment of fear and anger, it excited her compassion. He faintly smiled.

'I had no illusions about you,' he said. 'I knew you were silly and frivolous and empty-headed. But I loved you. I knew that your aims and ideals were vulgar and commonplace. But I loved you. I knew that you were second-rate. But I loved you. It's comic when I think how hard I tried to be amused by the things that amused you and how anxious I was to hide from you that I wasn't ignorant and vulgar and scandal-mongering and stupid. I knew how frightened you were of intelligence and I did everything I could to make you think me as big a fool as the rest of the men you knew. I knew that you'd only married me for convenience. I loved you so much, I didn't care. Most people, as far as I can see, when they're in love with some one and the love isn't returned feel that they have a grievance. They grow angry and bitter. I wasn't like that. I never expected you to love me, I didn't see any reason that you should, I never thought myself very lovable. I was thankful to be allowed to love you and I was enraptured when now and then I thought you were pleased with me or when I noticed in your eyes a gleam of good-humoured affection. I tried not to bore you with my love; I knew I couldn't afford to do that and I was always on the lookout for the first sign that you were impatient with my affection. What most husbands expect as a right I was prepared to receive as a favour.'

Kitty, accustomed to flattery all her life, had never heard such things said to her before. Blind wrath, driving out fear, arose in her heart: it seemed to choke her, and she felt the blood-vessels in her temples swell and throb. Wounded vanity can make a woman more vindictive than a lioness robbed of her cubs. Kitty's jaw, always a little too square, protruded with an apish hideousness and her beautiful eyes were black with malice. But she kept her temper in check.

'If a man hasn't what's necessary to make a woman love him, it's his fault, not hers.'

'Evidently.'

His derisive tone increased her irritation. She felt that she could wound him more by maintaining her calm.

'I'm not very well-educated and I'm not very clever. I'm just a perfectly ordinary young woman. I like the things that the people like among whom I've lived all my life. I like dancing and tennis and theatres and I like the men who play games. It's quite true that I've always been bored by you and by the things you like. They mean nothing to me and I don't want them to. You dragged me round those interminable galleries in Venice: I should have enjoyed myself much more playing golf at Sandwich.'

'I know.'

'I'm sorry if I haven't been all that you expected me to be. Unfortunately I always found you physically repulsive. You can hardly blame me for that.'

'I don't.'

Kitty could more easily have coped with the situation if he had raved and stormed. She could have met violence with violence. His self-control was inhuman and she hated him now as she had never hated him before.

'I don't think you're a man at all. Why didn't you break into the room when you knew I was there with Charlie? You might at least have tried to thrash him. Were you afraid?'

But the moment she had said this she flushed, for she was ashamed. He did not answer, but in his eyes she read an icy disdain. The shadow of a smile flickered on his lips.

'It may be that, like a historical character, I am too proud to fight.'

Kitty, unable to think of anything to answer, shrugged her shoulders. For a moment longer he held her in his immobile gaze.

'I think I've said all I had to say: if you refuse to come to Mei-tan-fu I shall file my petition.'

'Why won't you consent to let me divorce you?'

He took his eyes off her at last. He leaned back in his chair and lit a cigarette. He smoked it to the end without saying a word. Then, throwing away the butt, he gave a little smile. He looked at her once more.

'If Mrs. Townsend will give me her assurance that she will divorce her husband and if he will give me his written promise to marry you within a week of the two decrees being made absolute, I will do that.'

There was something in the way he spoke which disconcerted her. But her self-respect obliged her to accept his offer in the grand manner.

'That is very generous of you, Walter.'

To her astonishment he burst suddenly into a shout of laughter. She flushed angrily.

'What are you laughing at? I see nothing to laugh at.'

'I beg your pardon. I daresay my sense of humour is peculiar.'

She looked at him frowning. She would have liked to say something bitter and wounding, but no rejoinder occurred to her. He looked at his watch.

'You had better look sharp if you want to catch Townsend at his office. If you decide to come with me to Mei-tan-fu it would be necessary to start the day after tomorrow.'

'Do you want me to tell him to-day?'

'They say there is no time like the present.'

Her heart began to beat a little faster. It was not uneasiness that she felt, it was, she didn't quite know what it was. She wished she could have had a little longer; she would have liked to prepare Charlie. But she had the fullest confidence in him, he loved her as much as she loved him, and it was treacherous even to let the thought cross her mind that he would not welcome the necessity that was forced upon them. She turned to Walter gravely.

'I don't think you know what love is. You have no conception how desperately in love Charlie and I are with one another. It really is the only thing that matters and every sacrifice that our love calls for will be as easy as falling off a log.'

He gave a little bow, but said nothing, and his eyes followed her as she walked with measured step from the room.

24

She sent in a little note to Charlie on which she had written: *'Please see me. It is urgent.'* A Chinese boy asked her to wait and brought the answer that Mr. Townsend would see her in five minutes. She was unaccountably nervous. When at last she was ushered into his room Charlie came forward to shake hands with her, but the moment the boy, having closed the door, left them alone he dropped the affable formality of his manner.

'I say, my dear, you really mustn't come her in working hours. I've got an awful lot to do and we don't want to give people a chance to gossip.'

She gave him a long look with those beautiful eyes of her and tried to smile, but her lips were stiff and she could not.

'I wouldn't have come unless it was necessary.'

He smiled and took her arm.

'Well, since you're here come and sit down.'

It was a bare room, narrow, with a high ceiling; its walls were painted in two shades of terra cotta. The only furniture consisted of a large desk, a revolving chair for Townsend to sit in and a leather arm-chair for visitors. It intimidated Kitty to sit in this. He sat at the desk. She had never seen him in spectacles before; she did not know that he used them. When he noticed that her eyes were on them he took them off.

'I only use them for reading,' he said.

Her tears came easily and now, she hardly knew why, she began to cry. She had no deliberate intention of deceiving, but rather an instinctive desire to excite his sympathy. He looked at her blankly.

'Is anything the matter? Oh, my dear, don't cry.'

She took out her handkerchief and tried to check her

sobs. He rang the bell and when the boy came to the door went to it.

'If any one asks for me say I'm out.'

'Very good, sir.'

The boy closed the door. Charlie sat on the arm of the chair and put his arm round Kitty's shoulders.

'Now, Kitty dear, tell me all about it.'

'Walter wants a divorce,' she said.

She felt the pressure of his arm on her shoulder cease. His body stiffened. There was a moment's silence, then Townsend rose from her chair and sat down once more in his.

'What exactly do you mean?' he said.

She looked at him quickly, for his voice was hoarse, and she saw that his face was dully red.

'I've had a talk with him. I've come straight from the house now. He says he has all the proof he wants.'

'You didn't commit yourself, did you? You didn't acknowledge anything?'

Her heart sank.

'No,' she answered.

'Are you quite sure?' he asked, looking at her sharply.

'Quite sure,' she lied again.

He leaned back in his chair and stared vacantly at the map of China which was hanging on the wall in front of him. She watched him anxiously. She was somewhat disconcerted at the manner in which he had received the news. She had expected him to take her in his arms and tell her he was thankful, for now they could be together always; but of course men were funny. She was crying softly, not now to arouse sympathy, but because it seemed the natural thing to do.

'This is a bloody mess we've got into,' he said at length. 'But it's no good losing our heads. Crying isn't going to do us any good, you know.'

She noticed the irritation in his voice and dried her eyes.

'It's not my fault, Charlie. I couldn't help it.'

'Of course you couldn't. It was just damned bad luck. I was just as much to blame as you were. The thing to do now is to see how we're going to get out of it. I don't suppose you want to be divorced any more than I do.'

She smothered a gasp. She gave him a searching look. He was not thinking of her at all.

'I wonder what his proofs really are. I don't know how he can actually prove that we were together in that room. On the whole we've been about as careful as any one could be. I'm sure that old fellow at the curio shop wouldn't have given us away. Even if he'd seen us go in there's not reason why we shouldn't hunt curios together.'

He was talking to himself rather than to her.

'It's easy enough to bring charges, but it's damned difficult to prove them; any lawyer will tell you that. Our line is to deny everything, and if he threatens to bring an action we'll tell him to go to hell and we'll fight it.'

'I couldn't go into court, Charlie.'

'Why on earth not? I'm afraid you'll have to. God knows, I don't want a row, but we can't take it lying down.'

'Why need we defend it?'

'What a question to ask. After all, it's not only you that are concerned, I'm concerned too. But as a matter of fact I don't think you need be afraid of that. We shall be able to square your husband somehow. The only thing that worries me is the best way to set about it.'

It looked as though an idea occurred to him, for he turned towards her with his charming smile and his tone, a moment before abrupt and business-like, became ingratiating.

'I'm afraid you've been awfully upset, poor little woman. It's too bad.' He stretched out his hand and took hers. 'It's a scrape we've got into, but we shall get out of it. It's not . . . ' He stopped and Kitty had a suspicion that he had been about to say that it was not the first he had got out of. 'The greatest thing is to keep our heads. You know I shall never let you down.'

'I'm not frightened. I don't care what he does.'

He smiled still, but perhaps his smile was a trifle forced.

'If the worst comes to the worst I shall have to tell the Governor. He'll curse me like hell, but he's a good fellow and a man of the world. He'll fix it up somehow. It wouldn't do him any good if there was a scandal.'

'What can he do?' asked Kitty.

'He can bring pressure to bear on Walter. If he can't get at him through his ambition he'll get at him through his sense of duty.'

Kitty was a little chilled. She did not seem able to make Charlie see how desperately grave the situation was. His airiness made her impatient. She was sorry that she had come to see him in his office. The surroundings intimidated her. It would have been much easier to say what she wanted if she could have been in his arms with hers round his neck.

'You don't know Walter,' she said.

'I know that every man has his price.'

She loved Charlie with all her heart, but his reply disconcerted her; for such a clever man it was a stupid thing to say.

'I don't think you realise how angry Walter is. You haven't seen his face and the look of his eyes.'

He did not reply for a moment, but looked at her with a slight smile. She knew what he was thinking. Walter was the bacteriologist and occupied a subordinate position; he would hardly have the impudence to make himself a nuisance to the upper officials of the Colony.

'It's no good deceiving yourself, Charlie,' she said earnestly. 'If Walter has made up his mind to bring an action nothing that you or anybody else can say will have the slightest influence.'

His face once more grew heavy and sulky.

'Is it his idea to make me co-respondent?'

'At first it was. At last I managed to get him to consent to let me divorce him.'

'Oh, well, that's not so terrible.' His manner relaxed again and she saw the relief in his eyes. 'That seems to me a very good way out. After all, it's the least a man can do, it's the only decent thing.'

'But he makes a condition.'

He gave her an inquiring glance and he seemed to reflect.

'Of course I'm not a very rich man, but I'll do anything in my power.'

Kitty was silent. Charlie was saying things which she would never have expected him to say. And they made it difficult for her to speak. She had expected to blurt it out in one breath, held in his loving arms, with her burning face hid on his breast.

'He agrees to my divorcing him if your wife will give him the assurance that she will divorce you.'

'Anything else?'

Kitty could hardly find her voice.

'And – it's awfully hard to say, Charlie, it sounds dreadful – if you'll promise to marry me within a week of the decrees being made absolute.'

25

For a moment he was silent. Then he took her hand again and pressed it gently.

'You know, darling,' he said, 'whatever happens we must keep Dorothy out of this.'

She looked at him blankly.

'But I don't understand. How can we?'

'Well, we can't only think of ourselves in this world. You know, other things being equal, there's nothing in this world I'd love more than to marry you. But it's quite out of the question. I know Dorothy: nothing would induce her to divorce me.'

Kitty was becoming horribly frightened. She began to cry again. He got up and sat down beside her with his arm round her waist.

'Try not to upset yourself, darling. We *must* keep our heads.'

'I thought you loved me . . . '

'Of course I love you,' he said tenderly. 'You surely can't have any doubt of that now.'

'If she won't divorce you Walter will make you corespondent.'

He took an appreciable time to answer. His tone was dry.

'Of course that would ruin my career, but I'm afraid it wouldn't do you much good. If the worst came to the worst I should make a clean breast of it to Dorothy; she'd be dreadfully hurt and wretched, but she'd forgive me.' He had an idea. 'I'm not sure if the best plan wouldn't be to make a clean break of it anyhow. If she went to your husband I daresay she could persuade him to hold his tongue.'

'Does that mean you don't want her to divorce you?'

'Well, I have got my boys to think of, haven't I? And naturally I don't want to make her unhappy. We've always got on very well together. She's been an awfully good wife to me, you know.'

'Why did you tell me that she meant nothing to you?'

'I never did. I said I wasn't in love with her. We haven't slept together for years except now and then, on Christmas Day for instance, or the day before she was going home or the day she came back. She isn't a woman who cares for that sort of thing. But we've always been excellent friends. I don't mind telling you that I depend on her more than any one has any idea of.'

'Don't you think it would have been better to leave me alone then?'

She found it strange that with terror catching her breath she could speak so calmly.

'You were the loveliest little thing I'd seen for years. I

just fell madly in love with you. You can't blame me for that.'

'After all, you said you'd never let me down.'

'But, good God, I'm not going to let you down. We've got in an awful scrape and I'm going to do everything that's humanly possible to get you out of it.'

'Except the one obvious and natural thing.'

He stood up and returned to his own chair.

'My dear, you must be reasonable. We'd much better face the situation frankly. I don't want to hurt your feelings, but really I must tell you the truth. I'm very keen on my career. There's no reason why I shouldn't be a Governor one of these days, and it's a damned soft job to be a Colonial Governor. Unless we can hush this up I don't stand a dog's chance. I may not have to leave the service, but there'll always be a black mark against me. If I do have to leave the service then I must go into business in China where I know people. In either case my only chance is for Dorothy to stick to me.'

'Was it necessary to tell me that you wanted nothing in the world but me?'

The corners of his mouth drooped peevishly.

'Oh, my dear, it's rather hard to take quite literally the things a man says when he's in love with you.'

'Didn't you mean them?'

'At the moment.'

'And what's to happen to me if Walter divorces me?'

'If we really haven't a leg to stand on of course we won't defend. There shouldn't be any publicity and people are pretty broad-minded nowadays.'

For the first time Kitty thought of her mother. She shivered. She looked again at Townsend. Her pain now was tinged with resentment.

'I'm sure you'd have no difficulty in bearing any inconvenience that I had to suffer,' she said.

'We're not going to get much further by saying disagreeable things to one another,' he answered.

She gave a cry of despair. It was dreadful that she should

love him so devotedly and yet feel such bitterness towards him. It was not possible that he understood how much he meant to her.

'Oh, Charlie, don't you know how I love you?'

'But, my dear, I love you. Only we're not living in a desert island and we've got to make the best we can out of the circumstances that are forced upon us. You really must be reasonable.'

'How can I be reasonable? To me our love was everything and you were my whole life. It is not very pleasant to realise that to you it was only an episode.'

'Of course it wasn't an episode. But you know, when you ask me to get my wife, to whom I'm very much attached, to divorce me, and ruin my career by marrying you, you're asking a good deal.'

'No more than I'm willing to do for you.'

'The circumstances are rather different.'

'The only difference is that you don't love me.'

'One can be very much in love with a woman without wishing to spend the rest of one's life with her.'

She gave him a quick look and despair seized her. Heavy tears rolled down her cheeks.

'Oh, how cruel! How can you be so heartless?'

She began to sob hysterically. He gave an anxious glance at the door.

'My dear, do try and control yourself.'

'You don't know how I love you,' she gasped. 'I can't live without you. Have you no pity for me?'

She could not speak any more. She wept without restraint.

'I don't want to be unkind and, Heaven knows I don't want to hurt your feelings, but I must tell you the truth.'

'It's the ruin of my whole life. Why couldn't you leave me alone? What harm had I ever done you?'

'Of course if it does you any good to put all the blame on me you may.'

Kitty blazed with sudden anger.

'I suppose I threw myself at your head. I suppose I gave you no peace till you yielded to my entreaties.'

'I don't say that. But I certainly should never have thought of making love to you if you hadn't made it perfectly clear that you were ready to be made love to.'

Oh, the shame of it! She knew that what he said was true. His face now was sullen and worried and his hands moved uneasily. Every now and then he gave her a little glance of exasperation.

'Won't your husband forgive you?' he said after a while.

'I never asked him.'

Instinctively he clenched his hands. She saw him suppress the exclamation of annoyance which came to his lips.

'Why don't you go to him and throw yourself on his mercy? If he's as much in love with you as you say he's bound to forgive you.'

'How little you know him!'

26

She wiped her eyes. She tried to pull herself together.

'Charlie, if you desert me I shall die.'

She was driven now to appeal to his compassion. She ought to have told him at once. When he knew the horrible alternative that was placed before her his generosity, his sense of justice, his manliness, would be so vehemently aroused that he would think of nothing but her danger. Oh, how passionately she desired to feel his dear, protecting arms around her!

'Walter wants me to go to Mei-tan-fu.'

'Oh, but that's the place where the cholera is. They've got the worst epidemic that they've had for fifty years. It's no place for a woman. You can't possibly go there.'

'If you let me down I shall have to.'

'What do you mean? I don't understand.'

'Walter is taking the place of the missionary doctor who died. He wants me to go with him.'

'When?'

'Now. At once.'

Townsend pushed back his chair and looked at her with puzzled eyes.

'I may be very stupid, but I can't make head or tail out of what you're saying. If he wants you to go to this place with him what about a divorce?'

'He's given me my choice. I must either go to Mei-tan-fu or else he'll bring an action.'

'Oh, I see.' Townsend's tone changed ever so slightly. 'I think that's rather decent of him, don't you?'

'Decent?'

'Well, it's a damned sporting thing of him to go there. It's not a thing I'd fancy. Of course he'll get a C.M.G. for it when he comes back.'

'But me, Charlie?' she cried, with anguish in her voice.

'Well, I think if he wants you to go, under the circumstances I don't see how you can very well refuse.'

'It means death. Absolutely certain death.'

'Oh, damn it all, that's rather an exaggeration. He would hardly take you if he thought that. It's no more risk for you than for him. In point of fact there's no great risk if you're careful. I've been here when there's been cholera and I haven't turned a hair. The great thing is not to eat anything uncooked, no raw fruit or salads, or anything like that, and see that your drinking water is boiled.' He was gaining confidence as he proceeded, and his speech was fluent; he was even becoming less sullen and more alert; he was almost breezy. 'After all, it's his job, isn't it? He's interested in bugs. It's rather a chance for him if you come to think of it.'

'But me, Charlie?' she repeated, not with anguish now, but with consternation.

'Well, the best way to understand a man is to put yourself in his shoes. From his point of view you've been rather a naughty little thing and he wants to get you out of harm's way. I always thought he never wanted to divorce you, he doesn't strike me as that sort of chap; but he made what he thought was a very generous offer and you put his back up by turning it down. I don't want to blame you, but really for all our sakes I think you ought to have given it a little consideration.'

'But don't you see it'll kill me? Don't you know that he's taking me there because he *knows* it'll kill me.'

'Oh, my dear, don't talk like that. We're in a damned awkward position and really it's no time to be melodramatic.'

'You've made up your mind not to understand.' Oh, the pain in her heart, and the fear! She could have screamed. 'You can't send me to certain death. If you have no love or pity for me you must have just ordinary human feeling.'

'I think it's rather hard on me to put it like that. As far as I can make out your husband is behaving very generously. He's willing to forgive you if you'll let him. He wants to get you away and this opportunity has presented itself to take you to some place where for a few months you'll be out of harm's way. I don't pretend that Mei-tanfu is a health resort, I never knew a Chinese city that was, but there's no reason to get the wind up about it. In fact that's the worst thing you can do. I believe as many people die from sheer fright in an epidemic as because they get infected.'

'But I'm frightened now. When Walter spoke of it I almost fainted.'

'At the first moment I can quite believe it was a shock, but when you come to look at it calmly you'll be all right. It'll be the sort of experience that not every one has had.'

'I thought, I thought . . . '

She rocked to and fro in an agony. He did not speak, and once more his face wore that sullen look which till lately she had never known. Kitty was not crying now. She was dry-eyed, calm, and though her voice was low it was steady.

'Do you want me to go?'

'It's Hobson's choice, isn't it?'

'Is it?'

'It's only fair to you to tell you that if your husband brought an action for divorce and won it I should not be in a position to marry you.'

It must have seemed an age to him before she answered. She rose slowly to her feet.

'I don't think that my husband ever thought of bringing an action.'

'Then why in God's name have you been frightening me out of my wits?' he asked.

She looked at him coolly.

'He knew that you'd let me down.'

She was silent. Vaguely, as when you are studying a foreign language and read a page which at first you can make nothing of, till a word or a sentence gives you a clue; and on a sudden a suspicion, as it were, of the sense flashes across your troubled wits, vaguely she gained an inkling into the workings of Walter's mind. It was like a dark and ominous landscape seen by a flash of lightning and in a moment hidden again by the night. She shuddered at what she saw.

'He made that threat only because he knew that you'd crumple up at it, Charlie. It's strange that he should have judged you so accurately. It was just like him to expose me to such a cruel disillusion.'

Charlie looked down at the sheet of blotting paper in front of him. He was frowning a little and his mouth was sulky. But he did not reply.

'He knew that you were vain, cowardly and self-seeking. He wanted me to see it with my own eyes. He knew that you'd run like a hare at the approach of danger. He knew how grossly deceived I was in thinking that you were in love with me, because he knew that you were incapable of loving any one but yourself. He knew you'd sacrifice me without a pang to save your own skin.'

'If it really gives you any satisfaction to say beastly things to me I suppose I've got no right to complain.

Women always are unfair and they generally manage to put a man in the wrong. But there is something to be said on the other side.'

She took no notice of his interruption.

'And now I know all that he knew. I know that you're callous and heartless, I know that you're selfish, selfish beyond words, and I know that you haven't the nerve of a rabbit, I know you're a liar and a humbug, I know that you're utterly contemptible. And the tragic part is' – her face was on a sudden distraught with pain – 'the tragic part is that notwithstanding I love you with all my heart.'

'Kitty.'

She gave a bitter laugh. He had spoken her name in that melting, rich tone of his which came to him so naturally and meant so little.

'You fool,' she said.

He drew back quickly, flushing and offended; he could not make her out. She gave a look in which there was a glint of amusement.

'You're beginning to dislike me, aren't you? Well, dislike me. It doesn't make any difference to me now.'

She began to put on her gloves.

'What are you going to do?' he asked.

'Oh, don't be afraid, you'll come to no harm. You'll be quite safe.'

'For God's sake, don't talk like that, Kitty,' he answered and his deep voice rang with anxiety. 'You must know that everything that concerns you concerns me. I shall be frightfully anxious to know what happens. What are you going to say to your husband?'

'I'm going to tell him that I'm prepared to go to Mei-tan-fu with him.'

'Perhaps when you consent he won't insist.'

He could not have known why, when he said this, she looked at him so strangely.

'You're not really frightened?' he asked her.

'No,' she said. 'You've inspired me with courage. To go

into the midst of a cholera epidemic will be a unique experience and if I die it – well, I die.'

'I was trying to be as kind to you as I could.'

She looked at him again. Tears sprang into her eyes once more and her heart was very full. The impulse was almost irresistible to fling herself on his breast and crush her lips against his. It was no use.

'If you want to know,' she said, trying to keep her voice steady, 'I go with death in my heart and fear. I do not know what Walter has in that dark, twisted mind of his, but I'm shaking with terror. I think it may be that death will be really a release.'

She felt that she could not hold on to her self-control for another moment. She walked swiftly to the door and let herself out before he had time to move from his chair. Townsend gave a long sigh of relief. He badly wanted a brandy and soda.

27

Walter was in when she got home. She would have liked to go straight to her room, but he was downstairs, in the hall, giving instructions to one of the boys. She was so wretched that she welcomed the humiliation to which she must expose herself. She stopped and faced him.

'I'm coming with you to that place,' she said.

'Oh, good.'

'When do you want me to be ready?'

'To-morrow night.'

She did not know what spirit of bravado entered into her. His indifference was like the prick of a spear. She said a thing that surprised herself.

'I suppose I needn't take more than a few summer things and a shroud, need I?'

She was watching his face and knew that her flippancy angered him.

'I've already told your amah what you'll want.'

She nodded and went up to her room. She was very pale.

28

They were reaching their destination at last. They were borne in chairs, day after day, along a narrow causeway between interminable rice-fields. They set out at dawn and travelled till the heat of the day forced them to take shelter in a wayside inn and then went on again till they reached the town where they had arranged to spend the night. Kitty's chair headed the procession and Walter followed her; then in a struggling line came the coolies that bore their bedding, stores and equipment. Kitty passed through the country with unseeing eyes. All through the long hours, the silence broken only by an occasional remark from one of the bearers or a snatch of uncouth song, she turned over in her tortured mind the details of that heart-rending scene in Charlie's office. Recalling what he had said to her and what she had said to him, she was dismayed to see what an arid and businesslike turn their conversation had taken. She had not said what she wanted to say and she had not spoken in the tone she intended. Had she been able to make him see her boundless love, the passion in her heart, and her helplessness, he could never have been so inhuman as to leave her to her fate. She had been taken unawares. She could hardly believe her ears when he told her, more clearly than with words, that he cared nothing for her. That was why she had not even cried very much, she had been so dazed. She had wept since, wept miserably.

At night in the inns, sharing the principal guest chamber with her husband and conscious that Walter, lying on his camp bed, a few feet away from her, lay awake, she dug her teeth in the pillow so that no sound might escape her. But in the day-time, protected by the curtains of her chair, she allowed herself to give way. Her pain was so great that she could have screamed at the top of her voice; she had never known that one could suffer so much; and she asked herself desperately what she had done to deserve it. She could not make out why Charlie did not love her: it was her fault, she supposed, but she had done everything she knew to make him fond of her. They had always got on so well, they laughed all the time they were together, they were not only lovers but good friends. She could not understand; she was broken. She told herself that she hated and despised him; but she had no idea how she was going to live if she was never to see him again. If Walter was taking her to Mei-tan-fu as a punishment he was making a fool of himself, for what did she care now what became of her? She had nothing to live for any more. It was rather hard to be finished with life at twenty-seven.

29

On the steamer that took them up the Western River Walter read incessantly, but at meal-times he endeavoured to make some kind of conversation. He talked to her as though she were a stranger with whom he happened to be making the journey, of indifferent things, from politeness, Kitty imagined, or because so he could render more marked the gulf that separated them.

In a flash of insight she had told Charlie that Walter had sent her to him with the threat of divorce as the alternative to her accompanying him to the stricken city in order that she might see for herself how indifferent, cowardly and selfish he was. It was true. It was a trick which accorded very well with his sardonic humour. He knew exactly what would happen and he had given her amah necessary instructions before her return. She had caught in his eyes a disdain which seemed to include her lover as well as herself. He said to himself, perhaps, that if he had been in Townsend's place nothing in the world would have hindered him from making any sacrifice to gratify her smallest whim. She knew that was true also. But then, when her eyes were opened, how could he make her do something which was so dangerous, and which he must know frightened her so terribly? At first she thought he was only playing with her and till they actually started, no, later, till they left the river and took to the chairs for the journey across country, she thought he would give that little laugh of his and tell her that she need not come. She had no inkling what was in his mind. He could not really desire her death. He had loved her so desperately. She knew what love was now and she remembered a thousand signs of his adoration. For him really, in the French phrase, she did make fine weather and foul. It was impossible that he did not love her still. Did you cease to love a person because you had been treated cruelly? She had not made him suffer as Charlie had made her suffer and yet, if Charlie made a sign, notwithstanding everything, even though she knew him now, she would abandon all the world had to offer and fly to his arms. Even though he had sacrificed her and cared nothing for her, even though he was callous and unkind, she loved him.

At first she thought that she had only to bide her time, and sooner or later Walter would forgive her. She had been too confident of her power over him to believe that it was gone for ever. Many waters could not quench love. He was weak if he loved her, and felt that love her he must. But now she was not quite sure. When in the evening he sat reading in the straight-backed blackwood chair of the inn with the light of a hurricane lamp on his face she was able to watch him at her ease. She lay on the pallet on which her bed presently would be set and she was in shadow. Those straight, regular features of his made his face look very severe. You could hardly believe that it was possible for them on occasion to be changed by so sweet a smile. He was able to read as calmly as though she were a thousand miles away; she saw him turn the pages and she saw his eyes move regularly as they travelled from line to line. He was not thinking of her. And when, the table being set and dinner brought in, he put aside his book and gave her a glance (not knowing how the light on his face threw into distinctness his expression), she was startled to see in his eyes a look of physical distaste. Yes, it startled her. Was it possible that his love had left him entirely? Was it possible that he really designed her death? It was absurd. That would be the act of a madman. It was odd, the little shiver that ran through her as the thought occurred to her that perhaps Walter was not quite sane.

30

Suddenly her bearers, long silent, began to speak and one of them, turning round, with words she could not understand and with a gesture, sought to attract her attention. She looked in the direction he pointed and there, on the top of a hill, saw an archway; she knew by now that it was a memorial in compliment of a fortunate scholar or a virtuous widow, she had passed many of them since they left the river; but this one, silhouetted against the westering sun, was more fantastic and beautiful than any she had seen. Yet, she knew not why, it made her uneasy; it had a significance which she felt but could not put into words: Was it a menace that she vaguely discerned or was it derision? She was passing a grove of bamboos and they leaned over the causeway strangely as if they would detain her; though the summer evening was windless their narrow green leaves shivered a little. It gave her the sensation that some one hidden among them was watching her as she passed. Now they came to the foot of the hill and the rice-fields ceased. The bearers took it with a swinging stride. The hill was covered close with little green mounds, close, close to one another, so that the ground was ribbed like the sea-sand when the tide has gone out; and this she knew too for she had passed just such a spot as they approached each populous city and left it. It was the graveyard. Now she knew why the bearers had called her attention to the archway that stood on the crest of the hill: they had reached the end of their journey.

They passed through the archway and the chair-bearers paused to change the pole from shoulder to shoulder. One of them wiped his sweating face with a dirty rag. The causeway wound down. There were bedraggled houses on each side. Now the night was falling. But the bearers on a sudden broke into excited talk and with a jump that shook her ranged themselves as near as they could to the wall. In a moment she knew what had startled them, for as they stood there, chattering to one another, four peasants passed, quick and silent, bearing a new coffin, unpainted, and its fresh wood gleamed white in the approaching darkness. Kitty felt her heart beat in terror against her ribs. The coffin passed, but the bearers stood still; it seemed as though they could not summon up the will to go on. But there was a shout from behind and they started. They did not speak now.

They walked for a few minutes longer and then turned sharply into an open gateway. The chair was set down. She had arrived.

31

It was a bungalow and she entered the sitting-room. She sat down while the coolies, straggling in one by one, brought in their loads. Walter in the courtyard gave directions where this or that was to be placed. She was very tired. She was startled to hear an unknown voice.

'May I come in?'

She flushed and grew pale. She was overwrought and it made her nervous to meet a stranger. A man came out of the darkness, for the long low room was lit only by a shaded lamp, and held out his hand.

'My name is Waddington. I am the Deputy Commissioner.'

'Oh, the Customs. I know. I heard that you were here.'

In that dim light she could see only that he was a little thin man, no taller than she, with a bald head and a small, bare face.

'I live just at the bottom of the hill, but coming in this way you wouldn't have seen my house. I thought you'd be too fagged to come and dine with me, so I've ordered your dinner here and I've invited myself.'

'I'm delighted to hear it.'

'You'll find the cook's not bad. I kept on Watson's boys for you.'

'Watson was the missionary who was here?'

'Yes. Very nice fellow. I'll show you his grave tomorrow if you like.'

'How kind you are,' said Kitty, with a smile.

At that moment Walter came in. Waddington had introduced himself to him before coming in to see Kitty and now he said:

'I've just been breaking it to your missus that I'm dining with you. Since Watson died I haven't had anybody much to talk to but the nuns, and I can never do myself justice in French. Besides, there is only a limited number of subjects you can talk to them about.'

'I've just told the boy to bring in some drinks,' said Walter.

The servant brought whisky and soda and Kitty noticed that Waddington helped himself generously. His manner of speaking and his easy chuckle had suggested to her when he came in that he was not quite sober.

'Here's luck,' he said. Then, turning to Walter: 'You've got your work cut out for you here. They're dying like flies. The magistrate's lost his head and Colonel Yü, the officer commanding the troops, is having a devil of a job to prevent them from looting. If something doesn't happen soon we shall all be murdered in our beds. I tried to get the nuns to go, but of course they wouldn't. They all want to be martyrs, damn them.'

He spoke lightly and there was in his voice a sort of ghostly laughter so that you could not listen to him without smiling.

'Why haven't you gone?' asked Walter.

'Well, I've lost half my staff and the others are ready to lie down and die at any minute. Somebody's got to stay and keep things together.'

'Have you been inoculated?'

'Yes. Watson did me. But he did himself too, and it didn't do him much good, poor blighter.' He turned to Kitty and his funny little face was gaily puckered. 'I don't think there's any great risk if you take proper precautions. Have your milk and water boiled and don't eat fresh fruit or uncooked vegetables. Have you brought any gramophone records with you?'

'No, I don't think so,' said Kitty.

'I'm sorry for that. I was hoping you would. I haven't had any for a long time and I'm sick of my old ones.'

The boy came in to ask if they would have dinner.

'You won't dress to-night, will you?' asked Waddington. 'My boy died last week and the boy I have now is a fool, so I haven't been dressing in the evening.'

'I'll go and take off my hat,' said Kitty.

Her room was next door to that in which they sat. It was barely furnished. An amah was kneeling on the floor, the lamp beside her, unpacking Kitty's things.

32

The dining-room was small and the greater part of it was filled by an immense table. On the walls were engravings of scenes from the Bible and illuminated texts.

'Missionaries always have large dining-tables,' Waddington explained. 'They get so much a year more for every child they have and they buy their tables when they marry so that there shall be plenty of room for little strangers.'

From the ceiling hung a large paraffin lamp, so that Kitty was able to see better what sort of a man Waddington was. His baldness had deceived her into thinking him no longer young, but she saw now that he must be well under forty. His face, small under a high, rounded forehead, was unlined and fresh-coloured; it was ugly like a monkey's, but with an ugliness that was not without charm; it was an amusing face. His features, his nose and his mouth, were hardly larger than a child's, and he had small, very bright blue eyes. His eyebrows were fair and scanty. He looked like a funny little old boy. He helped himself constantly to liquor and as dinner proceeded it became evident that he was far from sober. But if he was drunk it was without offensiveness, gaily, as a satyr might be who had stolen a wine-skin from a sleeping shepherd.

He talked of Hong-Kong; he had many friends there and he wanted to know about them. He had been down for the races a year before and he talked of ponies and their owners.

'By the way, what about Townsend?' he asked suddenly. 'Is he going to become Colonial Secretary?'

Kitty felt herself flush, but her husband did not look at her.

'I shouldn't wonder,' he answered.

'He's the sort that gets on.'

'Do you know him?' asked Walter.

'Yes, I know him pretty well. We travelled out from home together once.'

From the other side of the river they heard the beating of gongs and the clatter of fire-crackers. There, so short a way from them, the great city lay in terror; and death, sudden and ruthless, hurried through its tortuous streets. But Waddington began to speak of London. He talked of the theatres. He knew everything that was being played at the moment and he told them what pieces he had seen when he was last home on leave. He laughed as he recollected the humour of this low comedian and sighed as he reflected on the beauty of that star of musical comedy. He was pleased to be able to boast that a cousin of his had married one of the most celebrated. He had lunched with her and she had given him her photograph. He would show it to them when they came and dined with him at the Customs.

Walter looked at his guest with a cold and ironic gaze, but he was evidently not a little amused by him, and he made an effort to show a civil interest in topics of which Kitty was well aware he knew nothing. A faint smile lingered on his lips. But Kitty, she knew not why, was filled with awe. In the house of that dead missionary, over against the stricken city, they seemed immeasurably apart from all the world. Three solitary creatures and strangers to each other.

Dinner was finished and she rose from the table.

'Do you mind if I say good-night to you? I'm going to bed.'

'I'll take myself off, I expect the doctor wants to go to bed too,' answered Waddington. 'We must be out early to-morrow.'

He shook hands with Kitty. He was quite steady on his feet, but his eyes were shining more than ever.

'I'll come and fetch you,' he told Walter, 'and take you to see the Magistrate and Colonel Yü, and then we'll go along to the Convent. You've got your work cut out, I can tell you.'

33

Her night was tortured with strange dreams. She seemed to be carried in her chair and she felt the swaying motion as the bearers marched with their long, uneven stride. She entered cities, vast and dim, where the multitude thronged about her with curious eyes. The streets were narrow and tortuous and in the open shops, with their strange wares, all traffic stopped as she went by and those who bought and those who sold, paused. Then she came to the memorial arch and its fantastic outline seemed on a sudden to gain a monstrous life; its capricious contours were like the waving arms of a Hindu god, and, as she passed under it, she heard the echo of mocking laughter. But then Charlie Townsend came towards her and took her in his arms, lifting her out of the chair, and said it was all a mistake, he had never meant to treat her as he had, for he loved her and he couldn't live without her. She felt his kisses on her mouth and she wept with joy, asking him why he had been so cruel, but though she asked she knew it did not matter. And then there was a hoarse, abrupt cry and they were separated, and between, hurrying silently, coolies passed in their ragged blue and they bore a coffin.

She awoke with a start.

The bungalow stood half way down a steep hill and from her window she saw the narrow river below her and opposite, the city. The dawn had just broken and from the river rose a white mist shrouding the junks that lay moored close to one another like peas in a pod. There were hundreds of them, and they were silent, mysterious in that ghostly light, and you had a feeling that their crews lay under an enchantment, for it seemed that it was not sleep, but something strange and terrible, that held them so still and mute.

The morning drew on and the sun touched the mist so that it shone whitely like the ghost of snow on a dying star. Though on the river it was light so that you could discern palely the lines of the crowded junks and the thick forest of their masts, in front it was a shining wall the eye could not pierce. But suddenly from that white cloud a tall, grim and massive bastion emerged. It seemed not merely to be made visible by the all-discovering sun but rather to rise out of nothing at the touch of a magic wand. It towered, the stronghold of a cruel and barbaric race, over the river. But the magician who built worked swiftly and now a fragment of coloured wall crowned the bastion; in a moment, out of the mist, looming vastly and touched here and there by a yellow ray of sun, there was seen a cluster of green and yellow roofs. Huge they seemed and you could make out no pattern; the order, if order there was, escaped you; wayward and extravagant, but of an unimaginable richness. This was no fortress, nor a temple, but the magic palace of some emperor of the gods where no man might enter. It was too airy, fantastic and unsubstantial to be the work of human hands; it was the fabric of a dream.

The tears ran down Kitty's face and she gazed, her hands clasped to her breast and her mouth, for she was breathless, open a little. She had never felt so light of heart and it seemed to her as though her body were a shell that lay at her feet and she pure spirit. Here was Beauty. She took it as the believer takes in his mouth the wafer which is God.

34

Since Walter went out early in the morning, came back at tiffin only for half an hour, and did not then return till dinner was just ready, Kitty found herself much alone. For some days she did not stir from the bungalow. It was very hot and for the most part she lay in a long chair by the open window, trying to read. The hard light of mid-day had robbed the magic palace of its mystery and now it was no more than a temple on the city wall, garish and shabby, but because she had seen it once in such an ecstasy it was never again quite common-place; and often at dawn or at dusk, and again at night, she found herself able to recapture something of that beauty. What had seemed to her a mighty bastion was but the city wall and on this, massive and dark, her eyes rested continually.

Behind its crenellations lay the city in the dread grip of the pestilence.

Vaguely she knew that terrible things were happening there, not from Walter who when she questioned him (for otherwise he rarely spoke to her) answered with a humorous nonchalance which sent a shiver down her spine; but from Waddington and from the amah. The people were dying at the rate of a hundred a day, and hardly any of those who were attacked by the disease recovered from it; the gods had been brought out from the abandoned temples and placed in the streets; offerings were laid before them and sacrifices made, but they did not stay the plague. The people died so fast that it was hardly possible to bury them. In some houses the whole family had been swept away and there was none to perform the funeral rights. The officer commanding the troops was a masterful man and if the city was not given over to riot and arson it was due to his determination. He forced his soldiers to bury such as there was no one else to bury and he had shot with his own hand an officer who demurred at entering a stricken house.

Kitty sometimes was so frightened that her heart sank within her and she would tremble in every limb. It was all very well to say that the risk was small if you took reasonable precautions: she was panic-stricken. She turned over in her mind crazy plans of escape. To get away, just to get away, she was prepared to set out as she was and make her way alone, without anything but what she stood up in, to some place of safety. She thought of throwing herself on the mercy of Waddington, telling him everything and beseeching him to help her to get back to Hong-Kong. If she flung herself on her knees before her husband, and admitted that she was frightened, frightened, even though he hated her now he must have enough human feeling in him to pity her.

It was out of the question. If she went, where could she go? Not to her mother; her mother would make her see very plainly that, having married her off, she counted on being rid of her; and besides she did not want to go to her mother. She wanted to go to Charlie, and he did not want her. She knew what he would say if she suddenly appeared before him. She saw the sullen look of his face and the shrewd hardness behind his charming eyes. It would be difficult for him to find words that sounded well. She clenched her hands. She would have given anything to humiliate him as he had humiliated her. Sometimes she was seized with such a frenzy that she wished she had let Walter divorce her, ruining herself if only she could have ruined him too. Certain things he had said to her made her blush with shame when she recalled them.

35

The first time she was alone with Waddington she brought the conversation round to Charlie. Waddington had spoken of him on the evening of their arrival. She pretended that he was no more than an acquaintance of her husband.

'I never much cared for him,' said Waddington. 'I've always thought him a bore.'

'You must be very hard to please,' returned Kitty, in the bright, chaffing way she could assume so easily. 'I suppose he's far and away the most popular man in Hong-Kong.'

'I know. That is his stock in trade. He's made a science of popularity. He has the gift of making every one he meets feel that he is the one person in the world he wants to see. He's always ready to do a service that isn't any trouble to himself, and even if he doesn't do what you want he manages to give you the impression that it's only because it's not humanly possible.'

'That is surely an attractive trait.'

'Charm and nothing but charm at last grows a little tiresome, I think. It's a relief then to deal with a man who isn't quite so delightful but a little more sincere. I've known Charlie Townsend for a good many years and once or twice I've caught him with the mask off – you see, I never mattered, just a subordinate official in the Customs – and I know that he doesn't in his heart give a damn for any one in the world but himself.'

Kitty, lounging easily in her chair, looked at him with smiling eyes. She turned her wedding-ring round and round her finger.

'Of course he'll get on. He knows all the official ropes. Before I die I have every belief that I shall address him as Your Excellency and stand up when he enters the room.'

'Most people think he deserves to get on. He's generally supposed to have a great deal of ability.'

'Ability? What nonsense! He's a very stupid man. He gives you the impression that he dashes off his work and gets it through from sheer brilliancy. Nothing of the kind. He's as industrious as a Eurasian clerk.'

'How has he got the reputation of being so clever?'

'There are many foolish people in the world and when a man in a rather high position puts on no frills, slaps them on the back, and tells them he'll do anything in the world for them, they are very likely to think him clever. And then of course, there's his wife. There's an able woman if you like. She has a good sound head and her advice is always worth taking. As long as Charlie Townsend's got her to depend on he's pretty safe never to do a foolish thing, and that's the first thing necessary for a man to get on in Government service. They don't want clever men; clever men have ideas, and ideas cause trouble; they want men who have charm and tact and who can be counted on never to make a blunder. Oh, yes, Charlie Townsend will get to the top of the tree all right.'

'I wonder why you dislike him?'

'I don't dislike him.'

'But you like his wife better?' smiled Kitty.

'I'm an old-fashioned little man and I like a well-bred woman.'

'I wish she were well-dressed as well as well-bred.'

'Doesn't she dress well? I never noticed.'

'I've always heard that they were a devoted couple,' said Kitty, watching him through her eye-lashes.

'He's very fond of her: I will give him that credit. I think that is the most decent thing about him.'

'Cold praise.'

'He has his little flirtations, but they're not serious. He's much too cunning to let them go to such lengths as might cause him inconvenience. And of course he isn't a passionate man; he's only a vain one. He likes admiration. He's fat and forty now, he does himself too well, but he was very good-looking when he first came to the Colony. I've often heard his wife chaff him about his conquests.'

'She doesn't take his flirtations very seriously?'

'Oh, no, she knows they don't go very far. She says she'd like to be able to make friends of the poor little things who fall to Charlie; but they're always so common. She says it's really not very flattering to her that the women who fall in love with her husband are so uncommonly second-rate.'

36

When Waddington left her Kitty thought over what he had so carelessly said. It hadn't been very pleasant to hear and she had had to make something of an effort not to show how much it touched her. It was bitter to think that all he said was true. She knew that Charlie was stupid and vain, hungry for flattery, and she remembered the complacency with which he had told her little stories to prove his cleverness. He was proud of a low cunning. How worthless must she be if she had given her heart so passionately to such a man because – because he had nice eyes and a good figure! She wished to despise him, because so long as she only hated him she knew that she was very near loving him. The way he had treated her should have opened her eyes. Walter had always held him in contempt. Oh, if she could only get him out of her mind altogether! And had his wife chaffed him about her obvious infatuation for him? Dorothy would have liked to make a friend of her, but that she found her second-rate. Kitty smiled a little: how indignant her mother would be to know that her daughter was considered that!

But at night she dreamt of him again. She felt his arms pressing her close and the hot passion of his kisses on her lips. What did it matter if he was fat and forty? She laughed with soft affection because he minded so much; she loved him all the more for his childlike vanity and she could be sorry for him and comfort him. When she awoke tears were streaming from her eyes.

She did not know why it seemed to her so tragic to cry in her sleep.

37

She saw Waddington every day, for he strolled up the hill to the Fanes' bungalow when his day's work was done; and so after a week they had arrived at an intimacy which under other circumstances they could scarcely have achieved in a year. Once when Kitty told him she didn't know what she would do there without him he answered, laughing:

'You see, you and I are the only people here who walk quite quietly and peaceably on solid ground. The nuns walk in heaven and your husband – in darkness.'

Though she gave a careless laugh she wondered what he meant. She felt that his merry little blue eyes were scanning her face with an amiable, but disconcerting attention. She had discovered already that he was shrewd and she had a feeling that the relations between herself and Walter excited his cynical curiosity. She found a certain amusement in baffling him. She liked him and she knew that he was kindly disposed towards her. He was not witty nor brilliant, but he had a dry and incisive way of putting things which was diverting, and his funny, boyish face under that bald skull, all screwed up with laughter, made his remarks sometimes extremely droll. He had lived for many years in outports, often with no man of his own colour to talk to, and his personality had developed in eccentric freedom. He was full of fads and oddities. His frankness was refreshing. He seemed to look upon life in a spirit of banter, and his ridicule of the Colony at Hong-Kong was acid; but he laughed also at the Chinese officials in Mei-tan-fu and at the cholera which decimated the city. He could not tell a tragic story or one of heroism without making it faintly absurd. He had many anecdotes of his adventures during twenty years in China, and you concluded from them that the earth was a very grotesque, bizarre and ludicrous place.

Though he denied that he was a Chinese scholar (he swore that the Sinologues were as mad as march hares) he spoke the language with ease. He read little and what he knew he had learned from conversation. But he often told Kitty stories from the Chinese novels and from Chinese history and though he told them with that airy badinage which was natural to him it was good-humoured and even tender. It seemed to her that, perhaps unconsciously, he had adopted the Chinese view that the Europeans were barbarians and their life a folly: in China alone was it so led that a sensible man might discern in it a sort of reality. Here was food for reflection: Kitty had never heard the Chinese spoken of as anything but decadent, dirty and unspeakable. It was as though the corner of a curtain were lifted for a moment, and she caught a glimpse of a world rich with a colour and significance she had not dreamt of.

He sat there, talking, laughing and drinking.

'Don't you think you drink too much?' said Kitty to him boldly.

'It's my great pleasure in life,' he answered. 'Besides, it keeps the cholera out.'

When he left her he was generally drunk, but he carried

his liquor well. It made him hilarious, but not disagreeable.

One evening Walter, coming back earlier than usual, asked him to stay to dinner. A curious incident happened. They had their soup and their fish and then with the chicken a fresh green salad was handed to Kitty by the boy.

'Good God, you're not going to eat that,' cried Waddington, as he saw Kitty take some.

'Yes, we have it every night.'

'My wife likes it,' said Walter.

The dish was handed to Waddington, but he shook his head.

'Thank you very much, but I'm not thinking of committing suicide just yet.'

Walter smiled grimly and helped himself. Waddington said nothing more, in fact he became strangely taciturn, and soon after dinner he left them.

It was true that they ate salad every night. Two days after their arrival the cook, with the unconcern of the Chinese, had sent it in and Kitty, without thinking, took some. Walter leaned forward quickly.

'You oughtn't to eat that. The boy's crazy to serve it.'

'Why not?' asked Kitty, looking at him full in the face.

'It's always dangerous, it's madness now. You'll kill yourself.'

'I thought that was the idea,' said Kitty.

She began to eat it coolly. She was seized with she knew not what spirit of bravado. She watched Walter with mocking eyes. She thought that he grew a trifle pale, but when the salad was handed to him he helped himself. The cook, finding they did not refuse it, sent them some in every day and every day, courting death, they ate it. It was grotesque to take such a risk. Kitty, in terror of the disease, took it with the feeling not only that she was thus maliciously avenging herself on Walter, but that she was flouting her own desperate fears.

38

It was the day after this that Waddington, coming to the bungalow in the afternoon, when he had sat a little asked Kitty if she would not go for a stroll with him. She had not been out of the compound since their arrival. She was glad enough.

'There are not many walks, I'm afraid,' he said. 'But we'll go to the top of the hill.'

'Oh, yes, where the archway is. I've seen it often from the terrace.'

One of the boys opened the heavy doorway for them and they stepped out into the dusty lane. They walked a few yards and then Kitty, seizing Waddington's arm in fright, gave a startled cry.

'Look!'

'What's the matter?'

At the foot of the wall that surrounded the compound a man lay on his back with his legs stretched out and his arms thrown over his head. He wore the patched blue rags and the wild mop of hair of the Chinese beggar.

'He looks as if he were dead,' Kitty gasped.

'He is dead. Come along; you'd better look the other way. I'll have him moved when we come back.'

But Kitty was trembling so violently that she could not stir.

'I've never seen any one dead before.'

'You'd better hurry up and get used to it then, because you'll see a good many before you've done with this cheerful spot.'

He took her hand and drew it in his arm. They walked for a little in silence.

'Did he die of cholera?' she said at last.

'I suppose so.'

They walked up the hill till they came to the archway. It was richly carved. Fantastic and ironical it stood like a landmark in the surrounding country. They sat down on the pedestal and faced the wide plain. The hill was sown close with the little green mounds of the dead, not in lines but disorderly, so that you felt that beneath the surface they must strangely jostle one another. The narrow causeway meandered sinuously among the green rice-fields. A small boy seated on the neck of a water-buffalo drove it slowly home, and three peasants in wide straw hats lolloped with sidelong gait under their heavy loads. After the heat of the day it was pleasant in that spot to catch the faint breeze of the evening and the wide expanse of country brought a sense of restful melancholy to the tortured heart. But Kitty could not rid her mind of the dead beggar.

'How can you talk and laugh and drink whisky when people are dying all around you?' she asked suddenly.

Waddington did not answer. He turned round and looked at her, then he put his hand on her arm.

'You know, this is no place for a woman,' he said gravely. 'Why don't you go?'

She gave him a sidelong glance from beneath her long lashes and there was the shadow of a smile on her lips.

'I should have thought under the circumstances a wife's place was by her husband's side.'

'When they telegraphed to me that you were coming with Fane I was astonished. But then it occurred to me that perhaps you'd been a nurse and all this sort of thing was in the day's work. I expected you to be one of those grim-visaged females who lead you a dog's life when you're ill in hospital. You could have knocked me down with a feather when I came into the bungalow and saw you sitting down and resting. You looked very frail and white and tired.'

'You couldn't expect me to look my best after nine days on the road.'

'You look frail and white and tired now, and if you'll allow me to say so, desperately unhappy.'

Kitty flushed because she could not help it, but she was able to give a laugh that sounded merry enough.

'I'm sorry you don't like my expression. The only reason I have for looking unhappy is that since I was twelve I've known that my nose was a little too long. But to cherish a secret sorrow is a most effective pose: you can't think how many sweet young men have wanted to console me.'

Waddington's blue and shining eyes rested on her and she knew that he did not believe a word she said. She did not care so long as he pretended to.

'I knew that you hadn't been married very long and I came to the conclusion that you and your husband were madly in love with each other. I couldn't believe that he had wished you to come, but perhaps you had absolutely refused to stay behind.'

'That's a very reasonable explanation,' she said lightly.

'Yes, but it isn't the right one.'

She waited for him to go on, fearful of what he was about to say, for she had a pretty good idea of his shrewdness and was aware that he never hesitated to speak his mind, but unable to resist the desire to hear him talk about herself.

'I don't think for a moment that you're in love with your husband. I think you dislike him, I shouldn't be surprised if you hated him. But I'm quite sure you're afraid of him.'

For a moment she looked away. She did not mean to let Waddington see that anything he said affected her.

'I have a suspicion that you don't very much like my husband,' she said with cool irony.

'I respect him. He has brains and character; and that, I may tell you, is a very unusual combination. I don't suppose you know what he is doing here, because I don't think he's very expansive with you. If any man single-handed can put a stop to this frightful epidemic he's going to do it. He's doctoring the sick, cleaning the city up, trying to get the drinking water pure. He doesn't mind where he goes nor what he does. He's risking his life twenty times a day. He's got Colonel Yü in his pocket and he's induced him to put the troops at his disposal. He's even put a little pluck into the magistrate and the old man is really trying to do something. And the nuns at the convent swear by him. They think he's a hero.'

'Don't you?'

'After all this isn't his job, is it? He's a bacteriologist. There was no call for him to come here. He doesn't give me the impression that he's moved by compassion for all these dying Chinamen. Watson was different. He loved the human race. Though he was a missionary it didn't make any difference to him if they were Christian, Buddhist or Confucian; they were just human beings. Your husband isn't here because he cares a damn if a hundred thousand Chinese die of cholera; he isn't here either in the interests of science. Why is he here?'

'You'd better ask him.'

'It interests me to see you together. I sometimes wonder how you behave when you're alone. When I'm there you're acting, both of you, and acting damned badly, by George. You'd neither of you get thirty bob a week in a touring company if that's the best you can do.'

'I don't know what you mean,' smiled Kitty, keeping up a pretence of frivolity which she knew did not deceive.

'You're a very pretty woman. It's funny that your husband should never look at you. When he speaks to you it sounds as though it were not his voice but somebody else's.'

'Do you think he doesn't love me?' asked Kitty in a low voice, hoarsely, putting aside suddenly her lightness.

'I don't know. I don't know if you fill him with such a repulsion that it gives him goose-flesh to be near you or if he's burning with a love that for some reason he will not allow himself to show. I've asked myself if you're both here to commit suicide.'

Kitty had seen the startled glance and then the scrutinising look Waddington gave them when the incident of the salad took place.

'I think you're attaching too much importance to a few lettuce leaves,' she said flippantly. She rose. 'Shall we go home? I'm sure you want a whisky and soda.'

'You're not a heroine at all events. You're frightened to death. Are you sure you don't want to go away?'

'What has it got to do with you?'

'I'll help you.'

'Are *you* going to fall to my look of secret sorrow? Look at my profile and tell me if my nose isn't a trifle too long.'

He gazed at her reflectively, that malicious, ironical look in his bright eyes, but mingled with it, a shadow, like a tree standing at a river's edge and its reflection in the water, was an expression of singular kindliness. It brought sudden tears to Kitty's eyes.

'Must you stay?'

'Yes.'

They passed under the flamboyant archway and walked down the hill. When they came to the compound they saw the body of the dead beggar. He took her arm, but she released herself. She stood still.

'It's dreadful, isn't it?'

'What? Death.'

'Yes. It makes everything else seem so horribly trivial. He doesn't look human. When you look at him you can hardly persuade yourself that he's ever been alive. It's hard to think that not so very many years ago he was just a little boy tearing down the hill and flying a kite.'

She could not hold back the sob that choked her.

39

A few days later Waddington, sitting with Kitty, a long glass of whisky and soda in his hand, began to speak to her of the convent.

'The Mother Superior is a very remarkable woman,' he said. 'The Sisters tell me that she belongs to one of the greatest families in France, but they won't tell me which; the Mother Superior, they say, doesn't wish it to be talked of.'

'Why don't you ask her if it interests you?' smiled Kitty.

'If you knew her you'd know it was impossible to ask her an indiscreet question.'

'She must certainly be very remarkable if she can impress you with awe.'

'I am the bearer of a message from her to you. She has asked me to say that, though of course you may not wish to adventure into the very centre of the epidemic, if you do not mind that it will give her great pleasure to show you the convent.'

'It's very kind of her. I shouldn't have thought she was aware of my existence.'

'I've spoken about you; I go there two or three times a week just now to see if there's anything I can do; and I daresay your husband has told them about you. You must be prepared to find that they have an unbounded admiration for him.'

'Are you a Catholic?'

His malicious eyes twinkled and his funny little face was puckered with laughter.

'Why are you grinning at me?' asked Kitty.

'Can any good come out of Galilee? No, I'm not a Catholic. I describe myself as a member of the Church of England, which I suppose is an inoffensive way of saying that you don't believe in anything very much. . . . When the Mother Superior came here ten years ago she brought seven nuns with her and of those all but three are dead. You see, at the best of times, Mei-tan-fu is not a health resort. They live in the very middle of the city, in the poorest district, they work very hard and they never have a holiday.'

'But are there only three and Mother Superior now?'

'Oh, no, more have taken their places. There are six of

them now. When one of them died of cholera at the beginning of the epidemic two others came up from Canton.'

Kitty shivered a little.

'Are you cold?'

'No, it was only some one walking over my grave.'

'When they leave France they leave it forever. They're not like the Protestant missionaries who have a year's leave every now and then. I always think that must be the hardest thing of all. We English have no very strong attachment to the soil, we can make ourselves at home in any part of the world, but the French, I think, have an attachment to their country which is almost a physical bond. They're never really at ease when they're out of it. It always seems to me very moving that these women should make just that sacrifice. I suppose if I *were* a Catholic it would seem very natural to me.'

Kitty looked at him coolly. She could not quite understand the emotion with which the little man spoke and she asked herself whether it was a pose. He had drunk a good deal of whisky and perhaps he was not quite sober.

'Come and see for yourself,' he said, with his bantering smile, quickly reading her thought. 'It's not nearly so risky as eating a tomato.'

'If you're not frightened there's no reason why I should be.'

'I think it'll amuse you. It's like a little bit of France.'

40

They crossed the river in a sampan. A chair was waiting for Kitty at the landing-stage and she was carried up the hill to the water-gate. It was through this that the coolies came to fetch water from the river and they hurried to and fro with huge buckets hanging from the yoke on their shoulder, splashing the causeway so that it was as wet as though it had heavily rained. Kitty's bearers gave short, sharp cries to urge them to make way.

'Of course all business is at a standstill,' said Waddington, walking by her side. 'Under normal circumstances you have to fight you way through the coolies carrying loads up and down to the junks.'

The street was narrow and winding so that Kitty lost all sense of the direction in which she was going. Many of the shops were closed. She had grown used on the journey up to the untidiness of a Chinese street, but here was the litter of weeks, garbage and refuse; and the stench was so horrible that she had to put her handkerchief to her face. Passing through Chinese cities she had been incommoded by the staring of the crowd, but now she noticed that no more than an indifferent glance was thrown at her. The passers-by, scattered rather than as usual thronging, seemed intent on their own affairs. They were cowed and listless. Now and then as they went by a house they heard the beating of gongs and the shrill, sustained lament of unknown instruments. Behind those closed doors one was lying dead.

'Here we are,' said Waddington at last.

The chair was set down at a small doorway, surmounted by a cross, in a long white wall, and Kitty stepped out. He rang the bell.

'You musn't expect anything very grand, you know. They're miserably poor.'

The door was opened by a Chinese girl, and after a word or two from Waddington she led them into a little room on the side of the corridor. It contained a large table covered with a chequered oilcloth and round the walls was a set of stiff chairs. At one end of the room was a statue, in plaster, of the Blessed Virgin. In a moment a nun came in, short and plump, with a homely face, red cheeks and merry eyes. Waddington, introducing Kitty to her, called her Soeur St. Joseph.

'C'est la dame du docteur?' she asked, beaming, and

then added that the Mother Superior would join them directly.

Sister St. Joseph could speak no English and Kitty's French was halting; but Waddington, fluent, voluble and inaccurate, maintained a stream of facetious comment which convulsed the good-humoured nun. Her cheerful, easy laughter not a little astonished Kitty. She had an idea that the religious were always grave and this sweet and childlike merriment touched her.

41

The door opened, to Kitty's fancy not quite naturally but as though it swung back of itself on its hinges, and the Mother Superior entered the little room. She stood for an instant on the threshold and a grave smile hovered upon her lips as she looked at the laughing Sister and Waddington's puckered, clownish face. Then she came forward and held out her hand to Kitty.

'Mrs. Fane?' She spoke in English with a good deal of accent, but with a correct pronunciation, and she gave the shadow of a bow. 'It is a great pleasure to me to make the acquaintance of the wife of our good and brave doctor.'

Kitty felt that the Superior's eyes held her in a long and unembarrassed look of appraisal. It was so frank that it was not uncivil; you felt that here was a woman whose business it was to form an opinion of others and to whom it never occurred that subterfuge was necessary. With a dignified affability she motioned to her visitors to take chairs and herself sat down. Sister St. Joseph, smiling still but silent, stood at the side but a little behind the Superior.

'I know you English like tea,' said the Mother Superior, 'and I have ordered some. But I must make my excuses if it is served in the Chinese fashion. I know that Mr. Waddington prefers whisky, but that I am afraid I cannot offer him.'

She smiled and there was a hint of malice in her grave eyes.

'Oh, come, *ma mère*, you speak as if I were a confirmed drunkard.'

'I wish you could say that you never drink, Mr. Waddington.'

'I can at all events say that I never drink except to excess.'

The Mother Superior laughed and translated into French for Sister St. Joseph the flippant remark. She looked at him with lingering, friendly eyes.

'We must make allowances for Mr. Waddington because two or three times when we had no money at all and did not know how we were to feed our orphans Mr. Waddington came to our rescue.'

The convert who had opened the door for them now came in with a tray on which were Chinese cups, a teapot, and a little plate of the French cakes called *Madeleines*.

'You must eat the *Madeleines*,' said the Mother Superior, 'because Sister St. Joseph made them for you herself this morning.'

They talked of commonplace things. The Mother Superior asked Kitty how long she had been in China and if the journey from Hong-Kong had greatly tired her. She asked her if she had been in France and if she did not find the climate of Hong-Kong trying. It was a conversation trivial but friendly, which gained a peculiar saviour from the circumstances. The parlour was very quiet, so that you could hardly believe that you were in the midst of the populous city. Peace dwelt there. And yet all round about the epidemic was raging and the people, terrified and restless, were kept in check but by the strong will of a soldier who was more than half a brigand. Within the convent walls the infirmary was crowded with sick and dying soldiers, and of the orphans in the nuns' charge a quarter were dead.

Kitty, impressed she hardly knew why, observed the

grave lady who asked her these amiable questions. She was dressed in white and the only colour on her habit was the red heart that burned on her breast. She was a woman of middle age, she might have been forty or fifty, it was impossible to say, for there were few wrinkles on her smooth, pale face, and you received the impression that she was far from young chiefly from the dignity of her bearing, her assurance, and the emaciation of her strong and beautiful hands. The face was long, with a large mouth and large, even teeth; the nose, though not small, was delicate and sensitive; but it was the eyes, under their thin black brows, which gave her face its intense and tragic character. They were very large, black, and though not exactly cold, by their calm steadiness strangely compelling. Your first thought when you looked at Mother Superior was that as a girl she must have been beautiful, but in a moment you realised that this was a woman whose beauty, depending on character, had grown with advancing years. Her voice was deep, low and controlled, and whether she spoke in English or in French she spoke slowly. But the most striking thing about her was the air she had of authority tempered by Christian charity; you felt in her the habit of command. To be obeyed was natural to her, but she accepted obedience with humility. You could not fail to see that she was deeply conscious of the authority of the church which upheld her. But Kitty had a surmise that notwithstanding her austere demeanour she had for human frailty a human tolerance; and it was impossible to look at her grave smile when she listened to Waddington, unabashed, talking nonsense, without being sure that she had a lively sense of the ridiculous.

But there was some other quality in her which Kitty vaguely felt, but could not put a name to. It was something that notwithstanding the Mother Superior's cordiality and the exquisite manners which made Kitty feel like an awkward school-girl, held her at a distance.

42

'*Monsieur ne mange rien,*' said Sister St. Joseph.

'Monsieur's palate is ruined by Manchu cooking,' replied the Mother Superior.

The smile left Sister St. Joseph's face and she assumed an expression of some primness. Waddington, a roguish glance in his eyes, took another cake. Kitty did not understand the incident.

'To prove to you how unjust you are, *ma mère*, I will ruin the excellent dinner that awaits me.'

'If Mrs. Fane would like to see over the convent I shall be glad to show her.' The Mother Superior turned to Kitty with a deprecating smile. 'I am sorry you should see it just now when everything is in disorder. We have so much work and not enough Sisters to do it. Colonel Yü has insisted on our putting our infirmary at the disposal of sick soldiers and we have had to make the *réfectoire* into an infirmary for our orphans.'

She stood at the door to allow Kitty to pass and together, followed by Sister St. Joseph and Waddington, they walked along cool white corridors. They went first into a large, bare room where a number of Chinese girls were working at elaborate embroideries. They stood up when the visitors entered and the Mother Superior showed Kitty specimens of the work.

'We go on with it notwithstanding the epidemic because it takes their minds off the danger.'

They went to a second room in which younger girls were doing plain sewing, hemming and stitching, and then into a third where there were only tiny children under the charge of a Chinese covert. They were playing noisily and when the Mother Superior came in they crowded round her, mites of two and three, with their black Chinese eyes and their black hair; and they seized her hands and hid themselves in her great skirts. An enchanting smile lit up her grave face, and she fondled them; she spoke little chaffing words which Kitty, ignorant though she was of Chinese, could tell were like caresses. She shuddered a little, for in their uniform dress, sallow-skinned, stunted, with their flat noses, they looked to her hardly human. They were repulsive. But the Mother Superior stood among them like Charity itself. When she wished to leave the room they would not let her go, but clung to her, so that, with smiling expostulations, she had to use a gentle force to free herself. They at all events found nothing terrifying in this great lady.

'You know of course,' she said, as they walked along another corridor, 'that they are only orphans in the sense that their parents have wished to be rid of them. We give them a few cash for every child that is brought in, otherwise they will not take the trouble, but do away with them.' She turned to the Sister. 'Have any come to day?' she asked.

'Four.'

'Now, with the cholera, they are more than ever anxious not to be burdened with useless girls.'

She showed Kitty the dormitories and then they passed a door on which was painted the word *infirmerie*. Kitty heard groans and loud cries and sounds as though beings not human were in pain.

'I will not show you the infirmary,' said the Mother Superior in her placid tones. 'It is not a sight that one would wish to see.' A thought struck her. 'I wonder if Dr. Fane is there?'

She looked interrogatively at the Sister and she, with her merry smile, opened the door and slipped in. Kitty shrank back as the open door allowed her to hear more horribly the turmoil within. Sister St. Joseph came back.

'No, he has been and will not be back again till later.'

'What about number six?'

'*Pauvre garçon,* he's dead.'

The Mother Superior crossed herself and her lips moved in a short and silent prayer.

They passed by a courtyard and Kitty's eyes fell upon two long shapes that lay side by side on the ground covered with a piece of blue cotton. The Superior turned to Waddington.

'We are so short of beds that we have to put two patients in one and the moment a sick man dies he must be bundled out in order to make room for another.' But she gave Kitty a smile. 'Now we will show you our chapel. We are very proud of it. One of our friends in France sent us a little while ago a life-size statue of the Blessed Virgin.'

43

The chapel was no more than a long low room with whitewashed walls and rows of deal benches; at the end was the altar on which stood the image; it was in plaster of Paris painted in crude colours; it was very bright and new and garish. Behind it was a picture in oils of the Crucifixion with the two Marys at the foot of the Cross in extravagant attitudes of grief. The drawing was bad and the dark pigments were put on with an eye that knew nothing of the beauty of colour. Around the walls were the Stations of the Cross painted by the same unfortunate hand. The chapel was hideous and vulgar.

The nuns on entering knelt down to say a prayer and then, rising, the Mother Superior began once more to chat with Kitty.

'Everything that can be broken is broken when it comes here, but the statue presented to us by our benefactor came from Paris without so much as the smallest chip. There is no doubt that it was a miracle.'

Waddington's malicious eyes gleamed, but he held his tongue.

'The altarpiece and the Stations of the Cross were painted by one of our Sisters, Soeur St. Anselme.' The Mother Superior crossed herself. 'She was a real artist. Unfortunately, she fell a victim to the epidemic. Do you not think that they are very beautiful?'

Kitty faltered an affirmative. On the altar were bunches of paper flowers and the candlesticks were distractingly ornate.

'We have the privilege of keeping here the Blessed Sacrament.'

'Yes?' said Kitty, not understanding.

'It has been a great comfort to us during this time of so terrible trouble.'

They left the chapel and retraced their steps to the parlour in which they had first sat.

'Would you like to see the babies that came in this morning before you go?'

'Very much,' said Kitty.

The Mother Superior led them into a tiny room on the other side of the passage. On a table, under a cloth, there was a singular wriggling. The Sister drew back the cloth and displayed four tiny, naked infants. They were very red and they made funny restless movements with their arms and legs; their quaint little Chinese faces were screwed up into strange grimaces. They looked hardly human; queer animals of an unknown species, and yet there was something singularly moving in the sight. The Mother Superior looked at them with an amused smile.

'They seem very lively. Sometimes they are brought in only to die. Of course we baptise them the moment they come.'

'The lady's husband will be pleased with them,' said Sister St. Joseph. 'I think he could play by the hour with the babies. When they cry he has only to take them up, and he makes them comfortable in the crook of his arm, so that they laugh with delight.'

Then Kitty and Waddington found themselves at the door. Kitty gravely thanked the Mother Superior for the trouble she had taken. The nun bowed with a condescension that was at once dignified and affable.

'It has been a great pleasure. You do not know how kind and helpful your husband has been to us. He has been sent to us by Heaven. I am glad that you came with him. When he goes home it must be a great comfort to him to have you there with your love and your – your sweet face. You must take care of him and not let him work too hard. You must look after him for all our sakes.'

Kitty flushed. She did not know what to say. The Mother Superior held out her hand and while she held it Kitty was conscious of those cool, thoughtful eyes which rested on her with detachment and yet with something that looked like a profound understanding.

Sister St. Joseph closed the door behind them and Kitty got into her chair. They went back through the narrow, winding streets. Waddington made a casual remark: Kitty did not answer. He looked round, but the side curtains of the chair were drawn and he could not see her. He walked on in silence. But when they reached the river and she stepped out to his surprise he saw that her eyes were streaming with tears.

'What is the matter?' he asked, his face puckered into an expression of dismay.

'Nothing.' She tried to smile. 'Only foolishness.'

44

Alone once more in the sordid parlour of the dead missionary, lying on the long chair that faced the window, her abstracted eyes on the temple across the river (now again at the approach of evening aerial and lovely), Kitty tried to set in order the feelings in her heart. She would never have believed that this visit to the convent could so have moved her. She had gone from curiosity. She had nothing else to do and after looking for so many days at the walled city across the water she was not unwilling to have at least a glimpse of its mysterious streets.

But once within the convent it had seemed to her that she was transported into another world situated strangely neither in space nor time. Those bare rooms and the white corridors, austere and simple, seemed to possess the spirit of something remote and mystical. The little chapel, so ugly and vulgar, in its very crudeness was pathetic; it had something which was wanting in the greatness of a cathedral, with its stained glass and its pictures: it was very humble; and the faith which had adorned it, the affection which cherished it, had endued it with a delicate beauty of the soul. The methodical way in which the convent's work was carried on in the midst of the pestilence showed a coolness in the face of danger and a practical sense, almost ironical it was so matter of fact, which were deeply impressive. In Kitty's ears rang still the ghastly sounds she heard when for a moment Sister St. Joseph opened the infirmary door.

It was unexpected the way they had spoken of Walter. First the Sister and then the Mother Superior herself, and the tone of her voice had been very gentle when she praised him. Oddly enough it gave her a little thrill of pride to know that they thought so well of him. Waddington also had told something of what Walter was doing; but it was not only his competence that the nuns praised (in Hong-Kong she had known that he was thought clever), they spoke of his thoughtfulness and his tenderness. Of course he could be very tender. He was at his best when you were ill; he was too intelligent to exasperate, and his touch was pleasant, cool and soothing. By some magic he seemed able by his mere presence to relieve your suffering. She knew that she would never see again in his eyes the look of affection which she had once been· so used to that she found it merely exasperating. She knew now how immense was his capacity for loving; in some odd way he was pouring it out on these wretched sick who had only him to look to. She did not feel jealousy, but a sense of emptiness; it was as though a support that she had grown so accustomed to as not to realise its presence were suddenly withdrawn from her so that she swayed this way and that like a thing that was top-heavy.

She had only contempt for herself because once she had felt contempt for Walter. He must have known how she regarded him and he had accepted her estimate without bitterness. She was a fool and he knew it and because he loved her it had made no difference to him. She did not hate him now, nor feel resentment of him, but fear rather and perplexity. She could not admit but that he had remarkable qualities, sometimes she thought that there was even in him a strange and unattractive greatness; it was curious then that she could not love him, but loved still a man whose worthlessness was now so clear to her. After thinking, thinking, all through those long days she rated accurately Charles Townsend's value; he was a common fellow and his qualities were second-rate. If she could only tear from her heart the love that still lingered there! She tried not to think of him.

Waddington too thought highly of Walter. She alone had been blind to his merit. Why? Because he loved her and she did not love him. What was it in the human heart that made you despise a man because he loved you? But Waddington had confessed that he did not like Walter. Men didn't. It was easy to see that those two nuns had for him a feeling which was very like affection. He was different with women; notwithstanding his shyness you felt in him an exquisite kindliness.

45

But after all it was the nuns that had most deeply touched her. Sister St. Joseph, with her merry face and apple red cheeks; she had been one of the little band that came out to China with the Mother Superior ten years before and she had seen one after another of her companions die of disease, privation and homesickness; and yet she remained cheerful and happy. What was it that gave her that naïve and charming humour? And the Mother Superior. Kitty in fancy stood again in her presence and once more she felt humble and ashamed. Though she was so simple and unaffected she had a native dignity which inspired awe, and you could not imagine that any one could treat her without respect. Sister St. Joseph by the way she stood, by every small gesture and the intonation of her answers, had shown the deep submission in which she held herself; and Waddington, frivolous and impertinent, had shown by his tone that he was not quite at his ease. Kitty thought it unnecessary to have told her that the Mother Superior belonged to one of the great families of France; there was that in her bearing which suggested ancient race, and she had the authority of one who has never known that it is possible to be disobeyed. She had the condescension of a great lady and the humility of a saint. There was in her strong, handsome and ravaged face an austerity that was passionate; and at the same time she had a solicitude and a gentleness which permitted those little children to cluster, noisy and unafraid, in the assurance of her deep affection. When she had looked at the four new-born babies she had worn a smile that was sweet and yet profound: it was like a ray of sunshine on a wild and desolate heath. What Sister St. Joseph had said so carelessly of Walter moved Kitty strangely; she knew that he had desperately wanted her to bear a child, but she had never suspected from his reticence that he was capable with a baby of showing without embarrassment a charming and playful tenderness. Most men were silly and awkward with babies. How strange he was!

But to all that moving experience there had been a shadow (a dark lining to the silver cloud), insistent and plain, which disconcerted her. In the sober gaiety of Sister St. Joseph, and much more in the beautiful courtesy of the Mother Superior, she had felt an aloofness which oppressed her. They were friendly and even cordial, but at the same time they held something back, she knew not what, so that she was conscious that she was nothing but a casual stranger. There was a barrier between her and them. They spoke a different language not only of the tongue but of the heart. And when the door was closed upon her she felt that they had put her out of their minds so completely, going about their neglected work again without delay, that for them she might never have existed. She felt shut out not only from that poor little convent, but from some mysterious garden of the spirit after which with all her soul she hankered. She felt on a sudden alone as she had never felt alone before. That was why she had wept.

And now, throwing back her head wearily, she sighed: 'Oh, I'm so worthless.'

46

That evening Walter came back to the bungalow a little earlier than usual. Kitty was lying on the long chair by the open window. It was nearly dark.

'Don't you want a lamp?' he asked.

'They'll bring it when dinner is ready.'

He talked to her always quite casually, of trifling things, as though they were friendly acquaintances, and there was never anything in his manner to suggest that he harboured malice in his heart. He never met her eyes and he never smiled. He was scrupulously polite.

'Walter, what do you propose we should do if we get through the epidemic?' she asked.

He waited for a moment before answering. She could not see his face.

'I haven't thought.'

In the old days she said carelessly whatever came into her head; it never occurred to her to think before she spoke; but now she was afraid of him; she felt her lips tremble and her heart beat painfully.

'I went to the convent this afternoon.'

'So I heard.'

She forced herself to speak though she could hardly frame the words.

'Did you really want me to die when you brought me here?'

'If I were you I'd leave well alone, Kitty. I don't think any good will come of talking about what we should do much better to forget.'

'But you don't forget; neither do I. I've been thinking a great deal since I came here. Won't you listen to what I have to say?'

'Certainly.'

'I treated you very badly. I was unfaithful to you.'

He stood stock still. His immobility was strangely terrifying.

'I don't know whether you'll understand what I mean. That sort of thing doesn't mean very much to a woman when it's over. I think women have never quite understood the attitude that men take up.' She spoke abruptly, in a voice she would hardly have recognised as her own. 'You know what Charlie was and you knew what he'd do. Well, you were quite right. He's a worthless creature. I suppose I shouldn't have been taken in by him if I hadn't been as worthless as he. I don't ask you to forgive me. I don't ask you to love me as you used to love me. But couldn't we be friends? With all these people dying in thousands round us, and with those nuns in their convent . . . '

'What have they got to do with it?' he interrupted.

'I can't quite explain. I had such a singular feeling when I went there to-day. It all seems to mean so much. It's all so terrible and their self-sacrifice is so wonderful; I can't help feeling it's absurd and disproportionate, if you understand what I mean, to distress yourself because a foolish woman has been unfaithful to you. I'm much too worthless and insignificant for you to give me a thought.'

He did not answer, but he did not move away; he seemed to be waiting for her to continue.

'Mr. Waddington and the nuns have told me such wonderful things about you. I'm very proud of you, Walter.'

'You used not to be; you used to feel contempt for me. Don't you still?'

'Don't you know that I'm afraid of you?'

Again he was silent.

'I don't understand you,' he said at last. 'I don't know what it is you want.'

'Nothing for myself. I only want you to be a little less unhappy.'

She felt him stiffen and his voice was very cold when he answered.

'You're mistaken in thinking I'm unhappy. I have a great deal too much to do to think of you very often.'

'I have wondered if the nuns would allow me to go and work at the convent. They are very shorthanded and if I could be of any help I should be grateful to them.'

'It is not easy work or pleasant work. I doubt if it would amuse you long.'

'Do you absolutely despise me, Walter?'

'No.' He hesitated and his voice was strange. 'I despise myself.'

47

It was after dinner. As usual Walter sat by the lamp and read. He read every evening till Kitty went to bed and then went into a laboratory which he had fitted up in one of the bungalow's empty rooms. Here he worked late into the night. He slept little. He was occupied with she knew not what experiments. He told her nothing of his work; but even in the old days he had been reticent on this: he was not by nature expansive. She thought deeply of what he had just said to her: the conversation had led to nothing. She knew him so little that she could not be sure if he was speaking the truth or not. Was it possible that, whereas he now existed so ominously for her, she had entirely ceased to exist for him? Her conversation which had entertained him once because he loved her, now that he loved her no longer might be merely tedious to him. It mortified her.

She looked at him. The light of the lamp displayed his profile as though it were a cameo. With his regular and finely-cut features it was very distinguished, but it was more than severe, it was grim: that immobility of his, only his eyes moving as he perused each page, was vaguely terrifying. Who would have thought that this hard face could be melted by passion to such a tenderness of expression? She knew and it excited in her a little shiver of distaste. It was strange that though he was good-looking as well as honest, reliable and talented, it had been so impossible for her to love him. It was a relief that she need never again submit to his caresses.

He would not answer when she had asked him whether in forcing her to come here he had really wished to kill her. The mystery of this fascinated and horrified her. He was so extraordinarily kind; it was incredible that he could have had such a devilish intention. He must have suggested it only to frighten her and to get back on Charlie (that would be like his sardonic humour) and then from obstinacy or from fear of looking foolish insisted on her going through with it.

Yes, he said he despised himself. What did he mean by that? Once again Kitty looked at his calm cool face. She might not even be in the room, he was so unconscious of her.

'Why do you despise yourself?' she asked, hardly knowing that she spoke, as though she were continuing without a break the earlier conversation.

He put down his book and observed her reflectively. He seemed to gather his thoughts from a remote distance.

'Because I loved you.'

She flushed and looked away. She could not bear his

cold, steady and appraising gaze. She understood what he meant. It was a little while before she answered.

'I think you do me an injustice,' she said. 'It's not fair to blame me because I was silly and frivolous and vulgar. I was brought up like that. All the girls I know are like that . . . It's like reproaching some one who has no ear for music because he's bored at a symphony concert. Is it fair to blame me because you ascribed to me qualities I hadn't got? I never tried to deceive you by pretending I was anything I wasn't. I was just pretty and gay. You don't ask for a pearl necklace or a sable coat at a booth in a fair; you ask for a tin trumpet and a toy balloon.'

'I don't blame you.'

His voice was weary. She was beginning to feel a trifle impatient with him. Why could he not realise, what suddenly had become so clear to her, that beside all the terror of death under whose shadow they lay and beside the awe of the beauty which she had caught a glimpse of that day, their own affairs were trivial? What did it really matter if a silly woman had committed adultery and why should her husband, face to face with the sublime, give it a thought? It was strange that Walter with all his cleverness should have so little sense of proportion. Because he had dressed a doll in gorgeous robes and set her in a sanctuary to worship her, and then discovered that the doll was filled with sawdust he could neither forgive himself nor her. His soul was lacerated. It was all make-believe that he had lived on, and when the truth shattered it he thought reality itself was shattered. It was true enough, he would not forgive her because he could not forgive himself.

She thought that she heard him give a faint sigh and she shot a rapid glance at him. A sudden thought struck her and it took her breath away. She only just refrained from giving a cry.

Was it what they called – a broken heart – that he suffered from?

48

All the next day Kitty thought of the convent; and the morning after, early, soon after Walter had gone, taking the amah with her to get chairs, she crossed the river. It was barely day and the Chinese crowding the ferry boat, some in the blue cotton of the peasant, others in the black robes of respectability, had a strange look of the dead being borne over the water to the land of shadow. And when they stepped ashore they stood for a little at the landing-place uncertainly as though they did not quite know where to go, before desultorily, in twos and threes, they wandered up the hill.

At that hour the streets of the city were very empty so that more than ever it seemed a city of the dead. The passers-by had an abstracted air so that you might almost have thought them ghosts. The sky was unclouded and the early sun shed a heavenly mildness on the scene; it was difficult to imagine, on that blithe, fresh and smiling morn, that the city lay gasping, like a man whose life is being throttled out of him by a maniac's hands, in the dark clutch of the pestilence. It was incredible that nature (the blue of the sky was clear like a child's heart) should be so indifferent when men were writhing in agony and going to their death in fear. When the chairs were set down at the convent door a beggar arose from the ground and asked Kitty for alms. He was clad in faded and shape-less rags that looked as though he had raked them out of a muck-heap, and through their rents you saw his skin hard and rough and tanned like the hide of a goat; his bare legs were emaciated, and his head, with its shock of coarse grey hair (the cheeks hollow, the eyes wild), was the head of a madman. Kitty turned from him in fright-ened horror, and the chair-bearers in gruff tones bade him begone, but he was importunate, and to be rid of him, shuddering, Kitty gave him a few cash.

The door was opened and the amah explained that Kitty wished to see the Mother Superior. She was taken once more into the stiff parlour in which it seemed a window had never been opened, and here she sat so long that she began to think her message had not been delivered. At last the Mother Superior came in.

'I must ask you to excuse me for keeping you waiting,' she said. 'I did not expect you and I was occupied.'

'Forgive me for troubling you. I am afraid I have come at an inconvenient moment.'

The Mother Superior gave her a smile, austere but sweet, and begged her to sit down. But Kitty saw that her eyes were swollen. She had been weeping. Kitty was startled, for she had received from the Mother Superior the impression that she was a woman whom earthly troubles could not greatly move.

'I am afraid something has happened,' she faltered. 'Would you like me to go away? I can come another time.'

'No, no. Tell me what I can do for you. It is only – only that one of our Sisters died last night.' Her voice lost its even tone and her eyes filled with tears. 'It is wicked of me to grieve, for I know that her good and simple soul has flown straight to heaven; she was a saint; but it is difficult always to control one's weakness. I am afraid I am not always very reasonable.'

'I'm so sorry, I'm so dreadfully sorry,' said Kitty.

Her ready sympathy brought a sob into her voice.

'She was one of the Sisters who came out from France with me ten years ago. There are only three of us left now. I remember, we stood in a little group at the end of the boat (what do you call it, the bow?) and as we steamed out of the harbour at Marseilles and we saw the golden figure of Saint-Marie la Grace, we said a prayer together. It had been my greatest wish since I entered religion to be allowed to come to China, but when I saw the land grow distant I could not prevent myself from weeping. I was their Superior; it was not a very good example I was giving my daughters. And then Sister St. Francis Xavier – that is the name of the Sister who died last night – took my hand and told me not to grieve; for wherever we were, she said, there was France and there was God.'

That severe and handsome face was distorted by the grief which human nature wrung from her and by the effort to restrain the tears which her reason and her faith refused. Kitty looked away. She felt that it was indecent to peer into that struggle.

'I have been writing to her father. She, like me, was her mother's only daughter. They were fisher folk in Brittany, and it will be hard for them. Oh, when will this terrible epidemic cease? Two of our girls have been attacked this morning and nothing but a miracle can save them. These Chinese have no resistance. The loss of Sister St. Francis is very severe. There is so much to do and now fewer than ever to do it. We have Sisters at our other houses in China who are eager to come, all our Order, I think, would give anything in the world (only they have nothing) to come here; but it is almost certain death; and so long as we can manage with the Sisters we have I am unwilling that others should be sacrificed.'

'That encourages me, *ma mère*,' said Kitty. 'I have been feeling that I had come at a very unfortunate moment. You said the other day that there was more work than the Sisters could do, and I was wondering if you would allow me to come and help them. I do not mind what I do if I can only be useful. I should be thankful if you just set me to scrub the floors.'

The Mother Superior gave an amused smile and Kitty was astonished at the mobile temperament which could so easily pass from mood to mood.

'There is no need to scrub the floors. That is done after a fashion by the orphans.' She paused and looked kindly at Kitty. 'My dear child, do you not think that you have done enough in coming with your husband here? That is more than many wives would have had the courage to do, and for the rest how can you be better occupied than in giving him peace and comfort when he comes home to you after the day's work? Believe me, he needs then all your love and all your consideration.'

Kitty could not easily meet the eyes which rested on her with a detached scrutiny and with an ironical kindliness.

'I have nothing whatever to do from morning till night,' said Kitty. 'I feel that there is so much to be done that I cannot bear to think that I am idle. I don't want to make a nuisance of myself, and I know that I have no claim either on your kindness or on your time, but I mean what I say and it would be a charity that you were doing me if you would let me be of some help to you.'

'You do not look very strong. When you did us the pleasure of coming to see us the day before yesterday it seemed to me that you were very pale. Sister St. Joseph thought that perhaps you were going to have a baby.'

'No, no,' cried Kitty, flushing to the roots of her hair.

The Mother Superior gave a little, silvery laugh.

'It is nothing to be ashamed of, my dear child, nor is there anything improbable in the supposition. How long have you been married?'

'I am very pale because I am naturally pale, but I am very strong, and I promise you I am not afraid of work.'

Now the Superior was complete mistress of herself. She assumed unconsciously the air of authority which was habitual to her and she held Kitty in an appraising scrutiny. Kitty felt unaccountably nervous.

'Can you speak Chinese?'

'I'm afraid not,' answered Kitty.

'Ah, that is a pity. I could have put you in charge of the elder girls. It is very difficult just now, and I am afraid they will get – what do you call? Out of hand?' she concluded with a tentative sound.

'Could I not be of help to the Sisters in nursing? I am

not at all afraid of the cholera. I could nurse the girls or the soldiers.'

The Mother Superior, unsmiling now, a reflective look on her face, shook her head.

'You do not know what the cholera is. It is a dreadful thing to see. The work in the infirmary is done by soldiers and we need a Sister only to supervise. And so far as the girls are concerned . . . no, no, I am sure your husband would not wish it; it is a terrible and frightening sight.'

'I should grow used to it.'

'No, it is out of the question. It is our business and our privilege to do such things, but there is no call for you to do so.'

'You make me feel very useless and very helpless. It seems incredible that there should be nothing that I can do.'

'Have you spoken to your husband of your wish?'

'Yes.'

The Mother Superior looked at her as though she were delving into the secrets of her heart, but when she saw Kitty's anxious and appealing look she gave a smile.

'Of course you are a Protestant?' she asked.

'Yes.'

'It doesn't matter. Dr. Watson, the missionary who died, was a Protestant, and it made no difference. He was all that was most charming to us. We owe him a deep debt of gratitude.'

Now the flicker of a smile passed over Kitty's face, but she did not say anything. The Mother Superior seemed to reflect. She rose to her feet.

'It is very good of you. I think I can find something for you to do. It is true that now Sister St. Francis has been taken from us, it is impossible for us to cope with the work. When will you be ready to start?'

'Now.'

'*A la bonne heure.* I am content to hear you say that.'

'I promise you I will do my best. I am very grateful to you for the opportunity that you are giving me.'

117

The Mother Superior opened the parlour door, but as she was going out she hesitated. Once more she gave Kitty a long, searching and sagacious look. Then she laid her hand gently on her arm.

'You know, my dear child, that one cannot find peace in work or in pleasure, in the world or in a convent, but only in one's soul.'

Kitty gave a little start, but the Mother Superior passed swiftly out.

49

Kitty found the work a refreshment to her spirit. She went to the convent every morning soon after sunrise and did not return to the bungalow till the westering sun flooded the narrow river and its crowded junks with gold. The Mother Superior gave into her care the smaller children. Kitty's mother had brought to London from her native Liverpool a practical sense of housewifery and Kitty, notwithstanding her air of frivolity, had always had certain gifts to which she referred only in bantering tones. Thus she could cook quite well and she sewed beautifully. When she disclosed this talent she was set to supervise the stitching and hemming of the younger girls. They knew a little French and every day she picked up a few words of Chinese so that it was not difficult for her to manage. At other times she had to see that the smaller children did not get into mischief; she had to dress and undress them and take care that they rested when rest was needed. There were a good many babies and these were in charge of amahs, but she was bidden to keep an eye on them. None of the work was very important and she would have liked to do something which was more arduous; but the Mother Superior paid no attention to her entreaties and Kitty stood sufficiently in awe of her not to be importunate.

For the first few days she had to make something of an

effort to overcome the faint distaste she felt for these little girls, in their ugly uniforms, with their stiff black hair, their round yellow faces, and their staring, sloe-black eyes. But she remembered the soft look which had transfigured so beautifully the countenance of the Mother Superior when on Kitty's first visit to the convent she had stood surrounded by those ugly little things, and she would not allow herself to surrender to her instinct. And presently, taking in her arms one or other of the tiny creatures, crying because of a fall or a cutting tooth, when Kitty found that a few soft words, though in a language the child could not understand, the pressure of her arms and the softness of her cheek against the weeping yellow face, could comfort and console, she began to lose all her feeling of strangeness. The small children, without any fear of her, came to her in their childish troubles and it gave her a peculiar happiness to discern their confidence. It was the same with the older girls, those to whom she taught sewing; their bright, clever smiles and the pleasure she could give them by a word of praise, touched her. She felt that they liked her and, flattered and proud, she liked them in return.

But there was one child that she could not grow used to. It was a little girl of six, an idiot with a huge hydro-cephalic head that swayed top-heavily on a small, squat body, large vacant eyes and a drooling mouth; the creature spoke hoarsely a few mumbled words; it was revolting and horrible; and for some reason it conceived an idiot attachment for Kitty so that it followed her about as she changed her place from one part of the large room to another. It clung to her skirt and rubbed its face against her knees. It sought to fondle her hands. She shivered with disgust. She knew it yearned for caresses and she could not bring herself to touch it.

Once, speaking of it to Sister St. Joseph, she said that it was a pity it lived. Sister St. Joseph smiled and stretched out her hand to the misformed thing. It came and rubbed its bulging forehead against it.

'Poor little mite,' said the nun. 'She was brought here positively dying. By the mercy of Providence I was at the door just as she came. I thought there was not a moment to lose so I baptised her at once. You would not believe what trouble we have had to keep her with us. Three or four times we thought that her little soul would escape to heaven.'

Kitty was silent. Sister St. Joseph in her loquacious way began to gossip of other things. And next day when the idiot child came to her and touched her hand Kitty nerved herself to place it in a caress on the great bare skull. She forced her lips into a smile. But suddenly the child, with an idiot perversity, left her; it seemed to lose interest in her, and that day and the following days paid her no attention. Kitty did not know what she had done and tried to lure it to her with smiles and gestures, but it turned away and pretended not to see her.

50

Since the nuns were busy from morning till night with a hundred duties Kitty saw little of them but at the services in the bare, humble chapel. On her first day the Mother Superior, catching sight of her seated at the back behind the girls on the benches according to their ages, stopped and spoke to her.

'You must not think it necessary for you to come to the chapel when we do,' she said. 'You are a Protestant and you have your own convictions.'

'But I like to come, Mother. I find that it rests me.'

The Mother Superior gave her a moment's glance and slightly inclined her grave head.

'Of course you will do exactly as you choose. I merely wanted you to understand that you are under no obligation.'

But with Sister St. Joseph Kitty soon became on terms not of intimacy perhaps but of familiarity. The economy of the convent was in her charge and to look after the material well-being of that big family kept the Sister on her feet all day. She said that the only time she had to rest was that which she devoted to prayer. But it pleased her towards evening when Kitty was with the girls at their work to come in and, vowing that she was tired out and had not a moment to spare, sit down for a few minutes and gossip. When she was not in the presence of the Mother Superior she was a talkative, merry creature, fond of a joke, and she did not dislike a bit of scandal. Kitty stood in no fear of her, her habit did not prevent Sister St. Joseph from being a good-natured, homely woman, and she chattered with her gaily. She did not mind with her showing how badly she talked French and they laughed with one another over Kitty's mistakes. The Sister taught her every day a few useful words of Chinese. She was a farmer's daughter and at heart she was still a peasant.

'I used to keep the cows when I was little,' she said, 'like St. Joan of Arc. But I was too wicked to have visions. It was fortunate, I think, for my father would certainly have whipped me if I had. He used often to whip me, the good old man, for I was a very naughty little girl. I am ashamed sometimes when I think now of the pranks I used to play.'

Kitty laughed at the thought that this corpulent, middle-aged nun could ever have been a wayward child. And yet there was something childlike in her still so that your heart went out to her: she seemed to have about her an aroma of the countryside in autumn when the apple trees are laden with fruit and the crops are in and safely housed. She had not the tragic and austere saintliness of the Mother Superior, but a gaiety that was simple and happy.

'Do you never wish to go home again, *ma soeur*?' asked Kitty.

'Oh, no. It would be too hard to come back. I love to be here and I am never so happy as when I am among the orphans. They're so good, they're so grateful. But it is all very well to be a nun (*on a beau être religieuse*) still one has a mother and one cannot forget that one drank the milk of her breasts. She is old, my mother, and it is hard never to see her again; but then she is fond of her daughter-in-law, and my brother is good to her. His son is growing up now, I should think they will be glad of an extra pair of strong arms on the farm; he was only a child when I left France, but he promised to have a fist that you could fell an ox with.'

It was almost impossible in that quiet room, listening to the nun, to realise that on the other side of these four walls cholera was raging. Sister St. Joseph had an unconcern which conveyed itself to Kitty.

She had a naïve curiosity about the world and its inhabitants. She asked Kitty all kinds of questions about London and England, a country, she thought, where so thick was the fog that you could not see your hand at mid-day, and she wanted to know if Kitty went to balls and whether she lived in a grand house and how many brothers and sisters she had. She spoke often of Walter. The Mother Superior said he was wonderful and every day they prayed for him. How lucky Kitty was to have a husband who was so good and so brave and so clever.

51

But sooner or later Sister St. Joseph returned to the subject of the Mother Superior. Kitty had been conscious from the beginning that the personality of this woman dominated the convent. She was regarded by all that dwelt there with love certainly and with admiration, but also with awe and not a little dread. Notwithstanding her kindliness Kitty herself felt like a schoolgirl in her presence. She was never quite at her ease with her, for she was filled with a sentiment which was so strange that it embarrassed her: reverence. Sister St. Joseph with an ingenuous desire to impress, told Kitty how great the family was to which the Mother Superior belonged; she had among her ancestors persons of historic importance and she was *un peu cousine* with half the kings of Europe: Alphonso of Spain had hunted at her father's, and they had *châteaux* all over France. It must have been hard to leave so much grandeur. Kitty listened smilingly, but not a little impressed.

'*Du reste*, you have only to look at her,' said the Sister, 'to see that, *comme famille, c'est le dessus du panier*.'

'She has the most beautiful hands that I have ever seen,' said Kitty.

'Ah, but if you only knew how she had used them. She is not afraid of work, *notre bonne mère*.'

When they had come to this city there had been nothing. They had built the convent. The Mother Superior had made the plans and supervised the work. The moment they arrived they began to save the poor little unwanted girls from the baby-tower and the cruel hands of the midwife. At first they had had no beds to sleep in and no glass to keep out the night air ('and there is nothing,' said Sister St. Joseph, 'which is more unwholesome'); and often they had no money left, not only to pay the builders, but even to buy their simple fare; they lived like peasants, what was she saying? the peasants in France, *tenez*, the men who worked for her father, would have thrown to the pigs the food they ate. And then the Mother Superior would collect her daughters round her and they would kneel and pray; and the Blessed Virgin would send money. A thousand francs would arrive by post next day, or a stranger, an Englishman (a Protestant, if you please) or even a Chinaman would knock at the door while they were actually on their knees and bring them a present. Once they were in such straits that they all made a vow to the Blessed Virgin that they would recite a *neuvaine* in her honour if she succoured them, and, would you believe it? that funny Mr. Waddington came to see us next day and saying that we looked as though we all wanted a good plate of roast beef gave us a hundred dollars.

What a comic little man he was, with his bald head and his little shrewd eyes (*ses petits yeux malins*) and his jokes. *Mon Dieu*, how he murdered the French language, and yet you could not help laughing at him. He was always in a good humour. All through this terrible epidemic he carried himself as if he were enjoying a holiday. He had a heart quite French and a wit so that you could hardly believe he was English. Except for his accent. But sometimes Sister St. Joseph thought he spoke badly on purpose to make you laugh. Of course his morals were not all one could wish; but still that was his business (with a sigh, a shrug and a shake of the head) and he was a bachelor and a young man.

'What is wrong with his morals, *ma soeur*?' asked Kitty smiling.

'Is it possible that you do not know? It is a sin for me to tell you. I have no business to say such things. He lives with a Chinese woman, that is to say, not a Chinese woman, but a Manchu. A princess, it appears, and she loves him to distraction.'

'That sounds quite impossible,' cried Kitty.

'No, no, I promise you, it is everything that is most true. It is very wicked of him. Those things are not done. Did you not hear, when you first came to the convent and he would not eat the *madeleines* that I had made expressly, that *notre bonne mère* said his stomach was deranged by Manchu cooking? That was what she meant and you should have seen the head that he made. It is a story altogether curious. It appears that he was stationed at Hankow during the revolution when they were massacring the Manchus and this good little Waddington saved the lives of one of their great families. They are related to the Imperial Family. The girl fell violently in love with him and – well, the rest you can imagine. And then when he left Hankow she ran away and followed him and now she follows him everywhere, and he has had to resign himself to keep her, poor fellow, and I daresay he is very fond of her; they are quite charming sometimes, these Manchu women. But what am I thinking of? I have a thousand things to do and I sit here. I am a bad religious. I am ashamed of myself.'

52

Kitty had a queer feeling that she was growing. The constant occupation distracted her mind and the glimpses she had of other lives and other outlooks awakened her imagination. She began to regain her spirits; she felt better and stronger. It had seemed to her that she could do nothing now but weep; but to her surprise, and not a little to her confusion, she caught herself laughing at this and that. It began to seem quite natural to live in the midst of a terrible epidemic. She knew that people were dying to the right and left of her, but she ceased very much to think of it. The Mother Superior had forbidden her to go into the infirmaries and the closed doors excited her curiosity. She would have liked to peep in, but could not do so without being seen, and she did not know what punishment the Mother Superior would inflict upon her. It would be dreadful to be sent away. She was devoted to the children now and they would miss her if she went; in fact she did not know what they would do without her.

And one day it occurred to her that she had neither thought of Charles Townsend nor dreamt of him for a week. Her heart gave a sudden thud against her ribs: she was cured. She could think of him now with indifference. She loved him no longer. Oh, the relief and the sense of liberation! It was strange to look back and remember how passionately she had yearned for him; she thought she would die when he failed her; she thought life thenceforward had nothing to offer but misery. And now already she was laughing. A worthless creature. What a fool she had made of herself! And now, considering him calmly, she wondered what on earth she had seen in him. It was lucky that Waddington knew nothing, she could never have endured his malicious eyeing and his ironical innuendoes. She was free, free at last, free! She could hardly prevent herself from laughing aloud.

The children were playing some romping game and it was her habit to look on with an indulgent smile, restraining them when they made too much noise and taking care that in their boisterousness none was hurt; but now in her high spirits, feeling as young as any of them, she joined in the game. The little girls received her with delight. They chased up and down the room, shouting at the top of their shrill voices, with fantastic and almost barbarous glee. They grew so excited that they leaped into the air with joy. The noise was terrific.

Suddenly the door opened and the Mother Superior stood on the threshold. Kitty, abashed, extricated herself from the clutches of a dozen little girls who with wild shrieks had seized her.

'Is this how you keep these children good and quiet?' asked the Mother Superior, a smile on her lips.

'We were having a game, Mother. They got excited. It is my fault, I led them on.'

The Mother Superior came forward and as usual the children clustered about her. She put her hands round their narrow shoulders and playfully pulled their little yellow ears. She looked at Kitty with a long, soft look. Kitty was flushed and she was breathing quickly. Her liquid eyes were shining and her lovely hair, disarranged in all the struggling and the laughter, was in adorable confusion.

'*Que vous êtes belle, ma chère enfant,*' said the Mother Superior. 'It does the heart good to look at you. No wonder these children adore you.'

Kitty blushed deeply and, she knew not why, tears suddenly filled her eyes. She covered her face with her hands.

'Oh, Mother, you make me ashamed.'

'Come, do not be silly. Beauty is also a gift of God, one of the most rare and precious, and we should be thankful if we are happy enough to possess it and thankful, if we are not, that others possess it for our pleasure.'

She smiled again and as though Kitty were a child too gently patted her soft cheek.

53

Since she had been working at the convent Kitty had seen less of Waddington. Two or three times he had come down to the river bank to meet her and they had walked up the hill together. He came in to drink a whisky and soda, but he would seldom stay to dinner. One Sunday, however, he suggested that they should take their luncheon with them and go in chairs to a Buddhist monastery. It was situated ten miles from the city and had some reputation as a place of pilgrimage. The Mother Superior, insisting that Kitty must have a day's rest, would not let her work on Sundays and Walter of course was as busy then as usual.

They started early in order to arrive before the heat of the day and were carried along a narrow causeway between rice-fields. Now and then they passed comfortable farm-houses nestling with friendly intimacy in a grove of bamboos. Kitty enjoyed the idleness; it was pleasant after being cooped up in the city to see about her the wide country. They came to the monastery, straggling low buildings by the side of the river, agreeably shaded by trees, and were led by smiling monks throughout courtyards, empty with a solemn emptiness, and shown temples with grimacing gods. In the sanctuary sat the Buddha, remote and sad, wistful, abstracted and faintly smiling. There was about everything a sense of dejection; the magnificence was shoddy and ruined; the gods were dusty and the faith that had made them was dying. The monks seemed to stay on sufferance, as though they awaited a notice to quit; and in the smile of the abbot, with his beautiful politeness, was the irony of resignation. One of these days the monks would wander away from the shady, pleasant wood, and the buildings, crumbling and neglected, would be battered by fierce storms and besieged by the surrounding nature. Wild creepers would twine themselves about the dead images and the trees would grow in the courtyards. Then the gods would dwell there no longer, but evil spirits of darkness.

54

They sat on the steps of a little building (four lacquered columns and a high, tiled roof under which stood a great bronze bell) and watched the river flow sluggish and with many a bend towards the stricken city. They could see its crenellated walls. The heat hung over it like a pall. But the river, though it flowed so slowly, had still a sense of movement and it gave one a melancholy feeling of the transitoriness of things. Everything passed, and what trace of its passage remained? It seemed to Kitty that they were all, the human race, like the drops of water in that river and they flowed on, each so close to the other and yet so far apart, a nameless flood, to the sea. When all things lasted so short a time and nothing mattered very much, it seemed pitiful that men, attaching an absurd importance to trivial objects, should make themselves and one another so unhappy.

'Do you know Harrington Gardens?' she asked Waddington, with a smile in her beautiful eyes.

'No. Why?'

'Nothing; only it's a long way from here. It's where my people live.'

'Are you thinking of going home?'

'No.'

'I suppose you'll be leaving here in a couple of months.

The epidemic seems to be abating and the cool weather should see the end of it.'

'I almost think I shall be sorry to go.'

For a moment she thought of the future. She did not know what plans Walter had in mind. He told her nothing. He was cool, polite, silent and inscrutable. Two little drops in that river that flowed silently towards the unknown; two little drops that to themselves had so much individuality and to the onlooker were but an undistinguishable part of the water.

'Take care the nuns don't start converting you,' said Waddington, with his malicious little smile.

'They're much too busy. Nor do they care. They're wonderful and so kind; and yet – I hardly know how to explain it – there is a wall between them and me. I don't know what it is. It is as though they possessed a secret which made all the difference in their lives and which I was unworthy to share. It is not faith; it is something deeper and more – more significant: they walk in a different world from ours and we shall always be strangers to them. Each day when the convent door closes behind me I feel that for them I have ceased to exist.'

'I can understand that it is something of a blow to your vanity,' he returned mockingly.

'My vanity.'

Kitty shrugged her shoulders. Then, smiling once more, she turned to him lazily.

'Why did you never tell me that you lived with a Manchu princess?'

'What have those gossiping old women been telling you? I am sure that it is a sin for nuns to discuss the private affairs of the Customs officials.'

'Why should you be so sensitive?'

Waddington glanced down, sideways, so that it gave him an air of slyness. He faintly shrugged his shoulders.

'It's not a thing to advertise. I do not know that it would greatly add to my chances of promotion in the service.'

'Are you very fond of her?'

He looked up now and his ugly little face had the look of a naughty schoolboy's.

'She's abandoned everything for my sake, home, family, security and self-respect. It's a good many years now since she threw everything to the winds to be with me. I've sent her away two or three times, but she's always come back; I've run away from her myself, but she's always followed me. And now I've given it up as a bad job; I think I've got to put up with her for the rest of my life.'

'She must really love you to distraction.'

'It's a rather funny sensation, you know,' he answered, wrinkling a perplexed forehead. 'I haven't the smallest doubt that if I really left her, definitely, she would commit suicide. Not with any ill-feeling towards me, but quite naturally, because she was unwilling to live without me. It is a curious feeling it gives one to know that. It can't help meaning something to you.'

'But it's loving that's the important thing, not being loved. One's not even grateful to the people who love one; if one doesn't love them, they only bore one.'

'I have no experience of the plural,' he replied. 'Mine is only in the singular.'

'Is she really an Imperial Princess?'

'No, that is a romantic exaggeration of the nuns. She belongs to one of the great families of the Manchus, but they have, of course, been ruined by the revolution. She is all the same a very great lady.'

He said it in a tone of pride, so that a smile flickered in Kitty's eyes.

'Are you going to stay here for the rest of your life then?'

'In China? Yes. What would she do elsewhere? When I retire I shall take a little Chinese house in Peking and spend the rest of my days there.'

'Have you any children?'

'No.'

She looked at him curiously. It was strange that this

little bald-headed man with his monkey face should have aroused in the alien woman so devastating a passion. She could not tell why the way he spoke of her, notwithstanding his casual manner and his flippant phrases, gave her the impression so strongly of the woman's intense and unique devotion. It troubled her a little.

'It does seem a long way to Harrington Gardens,' she smiled.

'Why do you say that?'

'I don't understand anything. Life is so strange. I feel like some one who's lived all his life by a duck-pond and suddenly is shown the sea. It makes me a little breathless, and yet it fills me with elation. I don't want to die, I want to live. I'm beginning to feel a new courage. I feel like one of those old sailors who set sail for undiscovered seas and I think my soul hankers for the unknown.'

Waddington looked at her reflectively. Her abstracted gaze rested on the smoothness of the river. Two little drops that flowed silently, silently towards the dark, eternal sea.

'May I come and see the Manchu lady?' asked Kitty, suddenly raising her head.

'She can't speak a word of English.'

'You've been very kind to me, you've done a great deal for me, perhaps I could show her by my manner that I had a friendly feeling towards her.'

Waddington gave a thin, mocking little smile, but he answered with good-humour.

'I will come and fetch you one day and she shall give you a cup of jasmine tea.'

She would not tell him that this story of an alien love had from the first moment strangely intrigued her fancy, and the Manchu Princess stood now as the symbol of something that vaguely, but insistently, beckoned to her. She pointed enigmatically to a mystic land of the spirit.

55

But a day or two later Kitty made an unforeseen discovery.

She went to the convent as usual and set about her first work of seeing that the children were washed and dressed. Since the nuns held firmly that the night air was harmful, the atmosphere in the dormitory was close and fetid. After the freshness of the morning it always made Kitty a little uncomfortable and she hastened to open such windows as would. But to-day she felt all of a sudden desperately sick and with her head swimming she stood at the window trying to compose herself. It had never been as bad as this before. Then nausea overwhelmed her and she vomited. She gave a cry so that the children were frightened, and the older girl who was helping her ran up and, seeing Kitty white and trembling, stopped short with an exclamation. Cholera! The thought flashed through Kitty's mind and then a deathlike feeling came over her; she was seized with terror, she struggled for a moment against the night that seemed agonisingly to run through her veins; she felt horribly ill; and then darkness.

When she opened her eyes she did not at first know where she was. She seemed to be lying on the floor and, moving her head slightly, she thought that there was a pillow under it. She could not remember. The Mother Superior was kneeling by her side, holding smelling salts to her nose, and Sister St. Joseph stood looking at her. Then it came back. Cholera! She saw the consternation on the nuns' faces. Sister St. Joseph looked huge and her outline was blurred. Once more terror overwhelmed her.

'Oh, Mother, Mother,' she sobbed. 'Am I going to die? I don't want to die.'

'Of course you're not going to die,' said the Mother Superior.

She was quite composed and there was even amusement in her eyes.

'But it's cholera. Where's Walter? Has he been sent for? Oh, Mother, Mother.'

She burst into a flood of tears. The Mother Superior gave her hand and Kitty seized it as though it were a hold upon the life she feared to lose.

'Come, come, my dear child, you mustn't be so silly. It's not cholera or anything of the kind.'

'Where's Walter?'

'Your husband is much too busy to be troubled. In five minutes you'll be perfectly well.'

Kitty looked at her with staring, harassed eyes. Why did she take it so calmly? It was cruel.

'Keep perfectly quiet for a minute,' said the Mother Superior. 'There is nothing to alarm yourself about.'

Kitty felt her heart beat madly. She had grown so used to the thought of cholera that it had ceased to seem possible that she could catch it. Oh, the fool she had been! She knew she was going to die. She was frightened. The girls brought in a long rattan chair and placed it by the window.

'Come, let us lift you,' said the Mother Superior. 'You will be more comfortable on the *chaise longue*. Do you think you can stand?'

She put her hands under Kitty's arms and Sister St. Joseph helped her to her feet. She sank exhausted into the chair.

'I had better shut the window,' said Sister St. Joseph. 'The early morning air cannot be good for her.'

'No, no,' said Kitty. 'Please leave it open.'

It gave her confidence to see the blue sky. She was shaken, but certainly she began to feel better. The two nuns looked at her for a moment in silence, and Sister St. Joseph said something to the Mother Superior which she could not understand. Then the Mother Superior sat on the side of the chair and took her hand.

'Listen, *ma chère enfant* . . . '

133

She asked her one or two questions. Kitty answered them without knowing what they meant. Her lips were trembling so that she could hardly frame the words.

'There is no doubt about it,' said Sister St. Joseph. 'I am not one to be deceived in such a matter.'

She gave a little laugh in which Kitty seemed to discern a certain excitement and not a little affection. The Mother Superior, still holding Kitty's hand, smiled with soft tenderness.

'Sister St. Joseph has more experience of these things than I have, dear child, and she said at once what was the matter with you. She was evidently quite right.'

'What do you mean?' asked Kitty anxiously.

'It is quite evident. Did the possibility of such a thing never occur to you? You are with child, my dear.'

The start that Kitty gave shook her from head to foot, and she put her feet to the ground as though to spring up.

'Lie still, lie still,' said the Mother Superior.

Kitty felt herself blush furiously and she put her hands to her breasts.

'It's impossible. It isn't true.'

'*Qu'est ce qu'elle dit?*' asked Sister St. Joseph.

The Mother Superior translated. Sister St. Joseph's broad simple face, with its red cheeks, was beaming.

'No mistakes is possible. I give you my word of honour.'

'How long have you been married, my child?' asked the Mother Superior. 'Why, when my sister-in-law had been married as long as you she had already two babies.'

Kitty sank back into the chair. There was death in her heart.

'I'm so ashamed,' she whispered.

'Because you are going to have a baby? Why, what can be more natural?'

'*Quelle joie pour le docteur,*' said Sister St. Joseph.

'Yes, think what a happiness for your husband. He will be overwhelmed with joy. You have only to see him with babies, and the look on his face when he plays with them, to see how enchanted he will be to have one of his own.'

For a little while Kitty was silent. The two nuns looked at her with tender interest and the Mother Superior stroked her hand.

'It was silly of me not to have suspected it before,' said Kitty. 'At all events I'm glad it's not cholera. I feel very much better. I will get back to my work.'

'Not to-day, my dear child. You have had a shock, you had much better go home and rest yourself.'

'No, no, I would much rather stay and work.'

'I insist. What would our good doctor say if I let you be imprudent? Come to-morrow, if you like, or the day after, but to-day you must be quiet. I will send for a chair. Would you like me to let one of our young girls go with you?'

'Oh, no, I shall be all right alone.'

56

Kitty was lying on her bed and the shutters were closed. It was after luncheon and the servants slept. What she had learnt that morning (and now she was certain that it was true) filled her with consternation. Ever since she came home she had been trying to think; but her mind was a blank, and she could not collect her thoughts. Suddenly she heard a step, the feet were booted so that it could not be one of the boys; with a gasp of apprehension she realised that it could only be her husband. He was in the sitting-room and she heard herself called. She did not reply. There was a moment's silence and then a knock on her door.

'Yes?'

'May I come in?'

Kitty rose from her bed and slipped into a dressing-gown.

'Yes.'

He entered. She was glad that the closed shutters shadowed her face.

'I hope I didn't wake you. I knocked very, very gently.'

'I haven't been asleep.'

He went to one of the windows and threw open the shutter. A flood of warm light streamed into the room.

'What is it?' she asked. 'Why are you back so early?'

'The Sisters said that you weren't very well. I thought I had better come and see what was the matter.'

A flash of anger passed through her.

'What would you have said if it had been cholera?'

'If it had been you certainly couldn't have made your way home this morning.'

She went to the dressing-table and passed the comb through her shingled hair. She wanted to gain time. Then, sitting down, she lit a cigarette.

'I wasn't very well this morning and the Mother Superior thought I'd better come back here. But I'm perfectly all right again. I shall go to the convent as usual to-morrow.'

'What was the matter with you?'

'Didn't they tell you?'

'No. The Mother Superior said that you must tell me yourself.'

He did now what he did seldom; he looked her full in the face; his professional instincts were stronger than his personal. She hesitated. Then she forced herself to meet his eyes.

'I'm going to have a baby,' she said.

She was accustomed to his habit of meeting with silence a statement which you would naturally expect to evoke an exclamation, but never had it seemed to her more devastating. He said nothing; he made no gesture; no movement on his face nor change of expression in his dark eyes indicated that he had heard. She felt suddenly inclined to cry. If a man loved his wife and his wife loved him, at such a moment they were drawn together by a poignant emotion. The silence was intolerable and she broke it.

'I don't know why it never occurred to me before. It

was stupid of me, but . . . what with one thing and another . . . '

'How long have you . . . when do you expect to be confined?'

The words seemed to issue from his lips with difficulty. She felt that his throat was as dry as hers. It was a nuisance that her lips trembled so when she spoke; if he was not of stone it must excite his pity.

'I suppose I've been like this between two and three months.'

'Am I the father?'

She gave a little gasp. There was just a shadow of a tremor in his voice; it was dreadful that cold self-control of his which made the smallest token of emotion so shattering. She did not know why she thought suddenly of an instrument she had been shown in Hong-Kong upon which a needle oscillated a little and she had been told that this represented an earthquake a thousand miles away in which perhaps a thousand persons had lost their lives. She looked at him. He was ghastly pale. She had seen that pallor on him once, twice before. He was looking down, a little sideways.

'Well?'

She clasped her hands. She knew that if she could say yes it would mean everything in the world to him. He would believe her, of course he would believe her, because he wanted to; and then he would forgive. She knew how deep was his tenderness and how ready he was, for all his shyness, to expend it. She knew that he was not vindictive; he would forgive her if she could but give him an excuse to, an excuse that touched his heart, and he would forgive completely. She could count on him never to throw the past in her teeth. Cruel he might be, cold and morbid, but he was neither mean nor petty. It would alter everything if she said yes.

And she had an urgent need for sympathy. The unexpected knowledge that she was with child had overwhelmed her with strange hopes and unforeseen desires. She felt weak, frightened a little, alone and very far from any friends. That morning, though she cared little for her mother, she had had a sudden craving to be with her. She needed help and consolation. She did not love Walter, she knew that she never could, but at this moment she longed with all her heart for him to take her in his arms so that she could lay her head on his breast; clinging to him she could have cried happily; she wanted him to kiss her and she wanted to twine her arms around his neck.

She began to weep. She had lied so much and she could lie so easily. What could a lie matter when it could only do good? A lie, a lie, what was a lie? It was so easy to say yes. She saw Walter's eyes melt and his arms outstretched towards her. She couldn't say it; she didn't know why, she just couldn't. All she had gone through during these bitter weeks, Charlie and his unkindness, the cholera and all these people dying, the nuns, oddly enough even that funny, drunken little Waddington, it all seemed to have changed her so that she did not know herself; though she was so deeply moved, some bystander in her soul seemed to watch her with terror and surprise. She *had* to tell the truth. It did not seem worth while to lie. Her thoughts wandered strangely: on a sudden she saw that dead beggar at the foot of the compound wall. Why should she think of him? She did not sob; the tears streamed down her face, quite easily, from wide eyes. At last she answered the question. He had asked her if he was the child's father.

'I don't know,' she said.

He gave the ghost of a chuckle. It made Kitty shudder. 'It's a bit awkward, isn't it?'

His answer was characteristic, it was exactly what she would have expected him to say, but it made her heart sink. She wondered if he realised how hard it had been for her to tell the truth (at the same moment she recognised that it had not been in the least hard, but inevitable) and if he gave her credit for it. Her answer, *I don't know, I don't know*, hammered away in her head. It was impossible now to take it back. She got her handkerchief from her bag and dried her eyes. They did not speak. There was a syphon on the table by her bed and he got her a glass of water. He brought it to her and held the glass while she drank. She noticed how thin his hand was, it was a fine hand, slender, with long fingers, but now it was nothing but skin and bone; it trembled a little: he could control his face, but his hand betrayed him.

'Don't mind my crying,' she said. 'It's nothing really; it's only that I can't help the water running out of my eyes.'

She drank the water and he put the glass back. He sat down on a chair and lit a cigarette. He gave a little sigh. Once or twice before she had heard him sigh like that and it always gave her a catch at the heart. Looking at him now, for he was staring with abstracted gaze out of the window, she was surprised that she had not noticed before how terribly thin he had grown during the last weeks. His temples were sunken and the bones of his face showed through the skin. His clothes hung on him loosely as though they had been made for a larger man. Through his sunburn his face had a greenish pallor. He looked exhausted. He was working too hard, sleeping little and eating nothing. In her own grief and perturbation she found room to pity him. It was cruel to think that she could do nothing for him.

He put his hand over his forehead, as though his head were aching, and she had a feeling that in his brain too those words hammered madly: *I don't know, I don't know*. It was strange that this moody, cold and shy man should have such a natural affection for very little babies; most men didn't care much even for their own, but the nuns, touched and a little amused, had more than once spoken of it. If he felt like that about those funny little Chinese babies what would he have felt about his own? Kitty bit her lips in order to prevent herself from crying again.

He looked at his watch.

'I'm afraid I must go back to the city. I have a great deal to do to-day . . . Shall you be all right?'

'Oh, yes. Don't bother about me.'

'I think you'd better not wait for me this evening. I may be very late and I'll get something to eat from Colonel Yü.'

'Very well.'

He rose.

'If I were you, I wouldn't try to do anything to-day. You'd better take it easy. Is there anything you want before I go?'

'No, thanks. I shall be quite all right.'

He paused for an instant, as though he were undecided, and then, abruptly and without looking at her, took his hat and walked out of the room. She heard him go through the compound. She felt terribly alone. There was no need for self-restraint now and gave herself up to a passion of tears.

57

The night was sultry and Kitty sat at the window looking at the fantastic roofs, dark against the starlight, of the Chinese temple, when at last Walter came in. Her eyes were heavy with weeping, but she was composed. Notwithstanding all there was to harass her she felt, perhaps only from exhaustion, strangely at peace.

'I thought you'd be already in bed,' said Walter as he came in.

'I wasn't sleepy. I thought it cooler to sit up. Have you had any dinner?'

'All I want.'

He walked up and down the long room and she saw that he had something to say to her. She knew that he was embarrassed. Without concern she waited for him to summon up his resolution. He began abruptly.

'I've been thinking about what you told me this afternoon. It seems to me that it would be better if you went away. I have spoken to Colonel Yü and he will give you an escort. You could take the amah with you. You will be quite safe.'

'Where is there for me to go?'

'You can go to your mother's.'

'Do you think she would be pleased to see me?'

He paused for a moment, hesitating, as though for reflection.

'Then you can go to Hong-Kong.'

'What should I do there?'

'You will need a good deal of care and attention. I don't think it's fair to ask you to stay here.'

She could not prevent the smile, not only of bitterness but of frank amusement, that crossed her face. She gave him a glance and very nearly laughed.

'I don't know why you should be so anxious about my health.'

He came over to the window and stood looking out at the night. There had never been so many stars in the unclouded sky.

'This isn't the place for a woman in your condition.'

She looked at him, white in his thin clothes against the darkness; there was something sinister in his fine profile, and yet oddly enough at this moment it excited in her no fear.

'When you insisted on my coming here did you want it to kill me?' she asked suddenly.

He was so long answering that she thought he had refused to hear.

'At first.'

She gave a little shudder, for it was the first time he had admitted his intention. But she bore him no ill will for it. Her feeling surprised herself; there was a certain admiration in it and a faint amusement. She did not quite know why, but suddenly thinking of Charlie Townsend he seemed to her an abject fool.

'It was a terrible risk you were taking,' she answered.

'With your sensitive conscience I wonder if you could ever have forgiven yourself if I had died.'

'Well, you haven't. You've thrived on it.'

'I've never felt better in my life.'

She had an instinct to throw herself on the mercy of his humour. After all they had gone through, when they were living amid these scenes of horror and desolation, it seemed inept to attach importance to the ridiculous act of fornication. When death stood round the corner, taking lives like a gardener digging up potatoes, it was foolishness to care what dirty things this person or that did with his body. If she could only make him realise how little Charlie meant to her, so that now already she had difficulty in calling up his features to her imagination, and how entirely the love of him had passed out of her heart! Because she had no feeling for Townsend the various acts she had committed with him had lost their significance. She had regained her heart and what she had given of her body seemed not to matter a rap. She was inclined to say to Walter: 'Look here, don't you think we've been silly long enough? We've sulked with one another like children. Why can't we kiss and be friends. There's no reason why we shouldn't be friends just because we're not lovers.'

He stood very still and the lamplight made the pallor of his impassive face startling. She did not trust him; if she said the wrong thing he would turn upon her with such an icy sternness. She knew by now his extreme sensitiveness, for which his acid irony was a protection, and how quickly he could close his heart if his feelings were hurt. She had a moment's irritation at his stupidity. Surely what troubled him most was the wound to his vanity: she vaguely realised that this is the hardest of all wounds to heal. It was singular that men attached so much importance to their wives' faithfulness; when first she had gone with Charlie she had expected to feel quite different, a changed woman; but she had seemed to herself exactly the same, she had experienced only well-being and a greater vitality. She wished now that she had been able to tell Walter that the child was his; the lie would have meant so little to her, and the assurance would have been so great a comfort to him. And after all it might not be a lie: it was funny, that something in her heart which had prevented her from giving herself the benefit of the doubt. How silly men were! Their part in procreation was so unimportant; it was the woman who carried the child through long months of uneasiness and bore it with pain, and yet a man because of his momentary connection made such preposterous claims. Why should that make any difference to him in his feeling towards the child? Then Kitty's thoughts wandered to the child which she herself would bear; she thought of it not with emotion nor with a passion of maternity, but with an idle curiosity.

'I daresay you'd like to think it over a little,' said Walter, breaking the long silence.

'Think what?'

He turned a little as if he were surprised.

'About when you want to go?'

'But I don't want to go.'

'Why not?'

'I like my work at the convent. I think I'm making myself useful. I should prefer to stay as long as you do.'

'I think I should tell you that in your present condition you are probably more liable to catch any infection that happens to be about.'

'I like the discreet way you put it,' she smiled ironically.

'You're not staying for my sake?'

She hesitated. He little knew that now the strongest emotion he excited in her, and the most unexpected, was pity.

'No. You don't love me. I often think I rather bore you.'

'I shouldn't have thought you were the sort of person to put yourself out for a few stuffy nuns and a parcel of Chinese brats.'

Her lips outlined a smile.

'I think it's rather unfair to despise me so much because you made such a mistake in your judgment of me. It's not my fault that you were such an ass.'

'If you're determined to stay you are of course at liberty to do so.'

'I'm sorry I can't give you the opportunity of being magnanimous.' She found it strangely hard to be quite serious with him. 'As a matter of fact you're quite right, it's not only for the orphans that I'm staying: you see, I'm in the peculiar position that I haven't got a soul in the world that I can go to. I know no one who wouldn't think me a nuisance. I know no one who cares a row of pins if I'm alive or dead.'

He frowned. But he did not frown in anger.

'We have made a dreadful hash of things, haven't we?' he said.

'Do you still want to divorce me? I don't think I care any more.'

'You must know that by bringing you here I've condoned the offence.'

'I didn't know. You see, I haven't made a study of infidelity. What are we going to do then when we leave here? Are we going on living together?'

'Oh, don't you think we can let the future take care of itself?'

There was the weariness of death in his voice.

58

Two or three days later Waddington fetched Kitty from the convent (for her restlessness had induced her immediately to resume her work) and took her to drink the promised cup of tea with his mistress. Kitty had on more than one occasion dined at Waddington's house. It was a square, white and pretentious building, such as the Customs build for their officials all over China; and the dining-room in which they ate, the drawing-room in which they sat, were furnished with prim and solid furniture. They had the appearance of being partly offices and partly hotel; there was nothing homelike in them and you understood that these houses were merely places of haphazard sojourn to their successive occupants. It would never have occurred to you that on an upper floor mystery and perhaps romance dwelt shrouded. They ascended a flight of stairs and Waddington opened a door. Kitty went into a large, bare room with whitewashed walls on which hung scrolls in various calligraphies. At a square table, on a stiff arm-chair, both of blackwood and heavily carved, sat the Manchu. She rose as Kitty and Waddington entered, but made no step forward.

'Here she is,' said Waddington, and added something in Chinese.

Kitty shook hands with her. She was slim in her long embroidered gown and somewhat taller than Kitty, used to the Southern people, had expected. She wore a jacket of pale green silk with tight sleeves that came over her wrists and on her black hair, elaborately dressed, was the head-dress of the Manchu women. Her face was coated with powder and her cheeks from the eyes to the mouth heavily rouged; her plucked eyebrows were a thin dark line and her mouth was scarlet. From this mask her black, slightly slanting, large eyes burned like lakes of liquid jet. She seemed more like an idol than a woman. Her movements were slow and assured. Kitty had the impression that she was slightly shy but very curious. She nodded her head two or three times, looking at Kitty, while Waddington spoke of her. Kitty noticed her hands; they were preternaturally long, very slender, of the colour of ivory; and the exquisite nails were painted. Kitty thought she had never seen anything so lovely as those languid and elegant hands. They suggested the breeding of uncounted centuries.

She spoke a little, in a high voice, like the twittering of birds in an orchard, and Waddington, translating, told

Kitty that she was glad to see her; how old was she and how many children had she got? They sat down on three straight chairs at the square table and a boy brought in bowls of tea, pale and scented with jasmine. The Manchu lady handed Kitty a green tin of Three Castles cigarettes. Beside the table and the chairs the room contained little furniture; there was a wide pallet bed on which was an embroidered head rest and two sandalwood chests.

'What does she do with herself all day long?' asked Kitty.

'She paints a little and sometimes she writes a poem. But she mostly sits. She smokes, but only in moderation, which is fortunate, since one of my duties is to prevent the traffic in opium.'

'Do you smoke?' asked Kitty.

'Seldom. To tell you the truth I much prefer whisky.'

There was in the room a faintly acrid smell; it was not unpleasant, but peculiar and exotic.

'Tell her that I am sorry I cannot talk to her. I am sure we have many things to say to one another.'

When this was translated to the Manchu she gave Kitty a quick glance in which there was the hint of a smile. She was impressive as she sat, without embarrassment, in her beautiful clothes; and from the painted face the eyes looked out wary, self-possessed and unfathomable. She was unreal, like a picture, and yet had an elegance which made Kitty feel all thumbs. Kitty had never paid anything but passing and somewhat contemptuous attention to the China in which fate had thrown her. It was not done in her set. Now she seemed on a sudden to have an inkling of something remote and mysterious. Here was the East, immemorial, dark and inscrutable. The beliefs and the ideals of the West seemed crude beside ideals and beliefs of which in this exquisite creature she seemed to catch a fugitive glimpse. Here was a different life, lived on a different plane. Kitty felt strangely that the sight of this idol, with her painted face and slanting, wary eyes, made the efforts and the pains of the everyday world she knew slightly absurd. That coloured mask seemed to hide the secret of an abundant profound and significant experience: those long, delicate hands with their tapering fingers held the key of riddles undivined.

'What does she think about all day long?' asked Kitty.

'Nothing,' smiled Waddington.

'She's wonderful. Tell her I've never seen such beautiful hands. I wonder what she sees in *you*.'

Waddington, smiling, translated the question.

'She says I'm good.'

'As if a woman ever loved a man for his virtue,' Kitty mocked.

The Manchu laughed but once. This was when Kitty, for something to say, expressed admiration of a jade bracelet she wore. She took it off and Kitty, trying to put it on, found, though her hands were small enough, that it would not pass over her knuckles. Then the Manchu burst into childlike laughter. She said something to Waddington and called for an amah. She gave her an instruction and the amah in a moment brought in a pair of very beautiful Manchu shoes.

'She wants to give you these if you can wear them,' said Waddington. 'You'll find they make quite good bedroom slippers.'

'They fit me perfectly,' said Kitty, not without satisfaction.

But she noticed a roguish smile on Waddington's face.

'Are they too big for her?' she asked quickly.

'Miles.'

Kitty laughed and when Waddington translated, the Manchu and the amah laughed also.

When Kitty and Waddington, a little later, were walking up the hill together, she turned to him with a friendly smile.

'You did not tell me that you had a great affection for her.'

'What makes you think I have?'

'I saw it in your eyes. It's strange, it must be like loving a phantom or a dream. Men are incalculable; I thought you were like everybody else and now I feel that I don't know the first thing about you.'

As they reached the bungalow he asked her abruptly:

'Why did you want to see her?'

Kitty hesitated for a moment before answering.

'I'm looking for something and I don't quite know what it is. But I know that it's very important for me to know it, and if I did it would make all the difference. Perhaps the nuns know it; when I'm with them I feel that they hold a secret which they will not share with me. I don't know why it came into my head that if I saw this Manchu woman I should have an inkling of what I am looking for. Perhaps she would tell me if she could.'

'What makes you think she knows it?'

Kitty gave him a sidelong glance, but did not answer. Instead she asked him a question.

'Do you know it?'

He smiled and shrugged his shoulders.

'Tao. Some of us look for the Way in opium and some in God, some of us in whisky and some in love. It is all the same Way and it leads nowhither.'

59

Kitty fell again into the comfortable routine of her work and though in the early morning feeling far from well she had spirit enough not to let it discompose her. She was astonished at the interest the nuns took in her: sisters who, when she saw them in a corridor, had done no more than bid her good morning now on a flimsy pretext came into the room in which she was occupied and looked at her, chatting a little, with a sweet and childlike excitement. Sister St. Joseph told her with a repetition which was sometimes tedious how she had been saying to herself for days past: 'Now, I wonder,' or: 'I shouldn't be surprised'; and then, when Kitty fainted: 'There can be no doubt, it jumps to the eyes.' She told Kitty long stories of her sister-in-law's confinements, which but for Kitty's quick sense of humour would have been not a little alarming. Sister St. Joseph combined in a pleasant fashion the realistic outlook of her upbringing (a river wound through the meadows of her father's farm and the poplars that stood on its bank trembled in the faintest breeze) with a charming intimacy with religious things. One day, firmly convinced that a heretic could know nothing of such matters, she told Kitty of the Annunciation.

'I can never read those lines in the Holy Writ without weeping,' she said. 'I do not know why, but it gives me such a funny feeling.'

And then in French, in words that to Kitty sounded unfamiliar and in their precision a trifle cold, she quoted:

'And the angel came in unto her, and said, Hail full of grace, the Lord is with thee: blessed art thou among women.'

The mystery of birth blew through the convent like a little fitful wind playing among the white blossoms of an orchard. The thought that Kitty was with child disturbed and excited those sterile women. She frightened them a little now and fascinated them. They looked upon the physical side of her condition with robust common sense, for they were the daughters of peasants and fishermen; but in their childlike hearts was awe. They were troubled by the thought of her burden and yet happy and strangely exalted. Sister St. Joseph told her that they all prayed for her, and Sister St. Martin had said what a pity it was she was not a Catholic; but the Mother Superior had reproved her; she said that it was possible to be a good woman – une brave femme, she put it – even though one was Protestant and le Bon Dieu would in some way or other arrange all that.

Kitty was both touched and diverted by the interest she aroused, but surprised beyond measure when she found that even the Mother Superior, so austere in her saintliness, treated her with a new complaisance. She had always been kind to Kitty, but in a remote fashion; now she used her with a tenderness in which there was something maternal. Her voice had in it a new and gentle note and in her eyes was a sudden playfulness as though Kitty were a child who had done a clever and amusing thing. It was oddly moving. Her soul was like a calm, grey sea rolling majestically, awe-inspiring in its sombre greatness, and then suddenly a ray of sunshine made it alert, friendly and gay. Often now in the evening she would come and sit with Kitty.

'I must take care that you do not tire yourself, *mon enfant*,' she said, making a transparent excuse to herself, 'or Dr. Fane will never forgive me. Oh, this British self-control! There he is delighted beyond measure and when you speak to him of it he becomes quite pale.'

She took Kitty's hand and patted it affectionately.

'Dr. Fane told me that he wished you to go away, but you would not because you could not bear to leave us. That was kind of you, my dear child, and I want you to know that we appreciate the help you have been to us. But I think that you did not want to leave him either, and that is better, for your place is by his side, and he needs you. Ah, I do not know what we should have done without that admirable man.'

'I am glad to think that he has been able to do something for you,' said Kitty.

'You must love him with all your heart, my dear. He is a saint.'

Kitty smiled and in her heart sighed. There was only one thing she could do for Walter now and that she could not think how to. She wanted him to forgive her, not for her sake any more, but for his own; for she felt that this alone could give him peace of mind. It was useless to ask him for his forgiveness, and if he had a suspicion that she desired it for his good rather than hers his stubborn vanity would make him refuse at all costs (it was curious that his vanity now did not irritate her, it seemed natural and only made her sorrier for him); and the only chance was that some unexpected occurrence might throw him off his guard. She had an idea that he would welcome an uprush of emotion which would liberate him from his nightmare of resentment, but that, in his pathetic folly, he would fight when it came with all his might against it.

Was it not pitiful that men, tarrying so short a space in a world where there was so much pain, should thus torture themselves?

60

Though the Mother Superior talked with Kitty not more than three or four times and once or twice for but ten minutes the impression she made upon Kitty was profound. Her character was like a country which on first acquaintance seems grand, but inhospitable; but in which presently you discover smiling little villages among fruit trees in the folds of the majestic mountains, and pleasant ambling rivers that flow kindly through lush meadows. But these comfortable scenes, though they surprise and even reassure you, are not enough to make you feel at home in the land of tawny heights and windswept spaces. It would have been impossible to become intimate with the Mother Superior; she had that something impersonal about her which Kitty had felt with the other nuns, even with the good-humoured, chatty Sister St. Joseph, but with her it was a barrier which was almost palpable. It gave you quite a curious sensation, chilling but awe-inspiring, that she could walk on the same earth as you, attend to mundane affairs, and yet live so obviously upon a plane you could not reach. She once said to Kitty:

'It is not enough that a religious should be continually in prayer with Jesus; she should be herself a prayer.'

Though her conversation was interwoven with her religion, Kitty felt that this was natural to her and that no effort was made to influence the heretic. It seemed strange to her that the Mother Superior, with her deep sense of charity, should be content to leave Kitty in a condition of what must seem to her sinful ignorance.

One evening the two of them were sitting together. The days were shortening now and the mellow light of the evening was agreeable and a little melancholy. The Mother Superior looked very tired. Her tragic face was drawn and white; her fine dark eyes had lost their fire. Her fatigue perhaps urged her to a rare mood of confidence.

'This is a memorable day for me, my child,' she said, breaking from a long reverie, 'for this is the anniversary of the day on which I finally determined to enter religion. For two years I had been thinking of it, but I had suffered as it were a fear of this calling, for I dreaded that I might be recaptured by the spirit of the world. But that morning when I communicated I made the vow that I would before nightfall announce my wish to my dear mother. After I had received the Holy Communion I asked Our Lord to give me peace of mind: Thou shalt have it only, the answer seemed to come to me, when thou hast ceased to desire it.'

The Mother Superior seemed to lose herself in thoughts of the past.

'That day, one of our friends, Madame de Viernot, had left for the Carmel without telling any of her relatives. She knew that they were opposed to her step, but she was a widow and thought that as such she had the right to do as she chose. One of my cousins had gone to bid farewell to the dear fugitive and did not come back till the evening. She was much moved. I had not spoken to my mother, I trembled at the thought of telling her what I had in mind, and yet I wished to keep the resolution I had made at Holy Communion. I asked my cousin all manner of questions. My mother, who appeared to be absorbed in her tapestry, lost no word. While I talked I said to myself: If I want to speak to-day I have not a minute to lose.

'It is strange how vividly I remember the scene. We

were sitting round the table, a round table covered with a red cloth, and we worked by the light of a lamp with a green shade. My two cousins were staying with us and we were all working at tapestries to re-cover the chairs in the drawing-room. Imagine, they had not been recovered since the days of Louis XIV, when they were bought, and they were so shabby and faded, my mother said it was a disgrace.

'I tried to form the words, but my lips would not move; and then, suddenly, after a few minutes of silence my mother said to me: "I really cannot understand the conduct of your friend. I do not like this leaving without a word all those to whom she is so dear. The gesture is theatrical and offends my taste. A well-bred woman does nothing which shall make people talk of her. I hope that if ever you caused us the great sorrow of leaving us you would not take flight as though you were committing a crime."

'It was the moment to speak, but such was my weakness that I could only say: "Ah, set your mind at rest, *maman*, I should not have the strength."

'My mother made no answer and I repented because I had not dared to explain myself. I seemed to hear the word of Our Lord to St. Peter: "Peter, lovest thou me?" Oh, what weakness, what ingratitude was mine! I loved my comfort, the manner of my life, my family and my diversions. I was lost in these bitter thoughts when a little later, as though the conversation had not been interrupted, my mother said to me: "Still, my Odette, I do not think that you will die without having done something that will endure."

'I was still lost in my anxiety and my reflections, while my cousins, never knowing the beating of my heart, worked quietly, when suddenly my mother, letting her tapestry fall and looking at me attentively, said: "Ah, my dear child, I am very sure that you will end by becoming a religious."

' "Are you speaking seriously, my good mother," I

answered. "You are laying bare the innermost thought and desire of my heart."

' "*Mais oui*,' cried my cousins without giving me time to finish, "For two years Odette has thought of nothing else. But you will not give your permission, *ma tante*, you must not give your permission."

' "By what right, my dear children, should we refuse it," said my mother, "if it is the Will of God?"

'My cousins then, wishing to make a jest of the conversation, asked me what I intended to do with the trifles that belonged to me and quarrelled gaily about which should take possession of this and which of that. But these first moments of gaiety lasted a very little while and we began to weep. Then we heard my father come up the stairs.'

The Mother Superior paused for a moment and sighed. 'It was very hard for my father. I was his only daughter and men often have a deeper feeling for their daughters than they ever have for their sons.'

'It is a great misfortune to have a heart,' said Kitty with a smile.

'It is a great good fortune to consecrate that heart to the love of Jesus Christ.'

At that moment a little girl came up to the Mother Superior and confident in her interest showed her a fantastic toy that she had somehow got hold of. The Mother Superior put her beautiful, delicate hand round the child's shoulder and the child nestled up to her. It moved Kitty to observe how sweet her smile was and yet how impersonal.

'It is wonderful to see the adoration that all your orphans have for you, Mother,' she said. 'I think I should be very proud if I could excite so great a devotion.'

The Mother Superior gave once more her aloof and yet beautiful smile.

'There is only one way to win hearts and that is to make oneself like unto those of whom one would be loved.'

61

Walter did not come back to dinner that evening. Kitty waited for him a little, for when he was detained in the city he always managed to send her word, but at last she sat down. She made no more than a pretence of eating the many courses which the Chinese cook, with his regard for propriety notwithstanding pestilence and the difficulty of provisioning, invariably set before her; and then, sinking into the long rattan chair by the open window, surrendered herself to the beauty of the starry night. The silence rested her.

She did not try to read. Her thoughts floated upon the surface of her mind like little white clouds reflected on a still lake. She was too tired to seize upon one, follow it up and absorb herself in its attendant train. She wondered vaguely what there was for her in the various impressions which her conversations with the nuns had left upon her. It was singular that, though their way of life so profoundly moved her, the faith which occasioned it left her untouched. She could not envisage the possibility that she might at any time be captured by the ardour of belief. She gave a little sigh: perhaps it would make everything easier if that great white light should illuminate her soul. Once or twice she had had the desire to tell the Mother Superior of her unhappiness and its cause; but she dared not: she could not bear that this austere woman should think ill of her. To her what she had done would naturally seem a grievous sin. The odd thing was that she herself could not regard it as wicked so much as stupid and ugly.

Perhaps it was due to an obtuseness in herself that she looked upon her connection with Townsend as regrettable and shocking even, but to be forgotten rather than to be repented of. It was like making a blunder at a party;

there was nothing to do about it, it was dreadfully mortifying, but it showed a lack of sense to ascribe too much importance to it. She shuddered as she thought of Charlie with his large frame too well covered, the vagueness of his jaw and the way he had of standing with his chest thrown out so that he might not seem to have a paunch. His sanguine temperament showed itself in the little red veins which soon would form a network on his ruddy cheeks. She had liked his bushy eyebrows: there was to her in them now something animal and repulsive.

And the future? It was curious how indifferent it left her; she could not see into it at all. Perhaps she would die when her baby was born. Her sister Doris had always been much stronger than she, and Doris had nearly died. (She had done her duty and produced an heir to the new baronetcy; Kitty smiled as she thought of her mother's satisfaction.) If the future was so vague it meant perhaps that she was destined never to see it. Walter would probably ask her mother to take care of the child – if the child survived; and she knew him well enough to be sure that, however uncertain of his paternity, he would treat it with kindness. Walter could be trusted under any circumstances to behave admirably. It was a pity that with his great qualities, his unselfishness and honour, his intelligence and sensibility, he should be so unlovable. She was not in the least frightened of him now, but sorry for him, and at the same time she could not help thinking him slightly absurd. The depth of his emotion made him vulnerable and she had a feeling that somehow and at some time she so could work upon it as to induce him to forgive her. The thought haunted her now that in thus giving him peace of mind she would make the only possible amends for the anguish she had caused him. It was a pity he had so little sense of humour: she could see them both, some day, laughing together at the way they had tormented themselves.

She was tired. She took the lamp into her room and undressed. She went to bed and presently fell asleep.

62

But she was awakened by a loud knocking. At first, since
it was interwoven with the dream from which she was
aroused, she could not attach the sound to reality. The
knocking went on and she was conscious that it must be
at the gateway of the compound. It was quite dark. She
had a watch with phosphorised hands and saw that it was
half past two. It must be Walter coming back – how late
he was – and he could not awake the boy. The knocking
went on, louder and louder, and in the silence of the night
it was really not a little alarming. The knocking stopped
and she heard the withdrawing of the heavy bolt. Walter
had never come back so late. Poor thing, he must be tired
out! She hoped he would have the sense to go straight to
bed instead of working as usual in that laboratory of his.

There was a sound of voices, and people came into the
compound. That was strange, for Walter coming home
late, in order not to disturb her, took pains to be quiet.
Two or three persons ran swiftly up the wooden steps
and came into the room next door. Kitty was a little
frightened. At the back of her mind was always the fear
of an anti-foreign riot. Had something happened? Her
heart began to beat quickly. But before she had time to
put her vague apprehension into shape some one walked
across the room and knocked at her door.

'Mrs. Fane.'

She recognised Waddington's voice.

'Yes. What is it?'

'Will you get up at once. I have something to say to
you.'

She rose and put on a dressing-gown. She unlocked the
door and opened it. Her glance took in Waddington in a
pair of Chinese trousers and a pongee coat, the houseboy

holding a hurricane lamp, and a little further back three Chinese soldiers in khaki. She started as she saw the consternation on Waddington's face; his head was tousled as though he had just jumped out of bed.

'What is the matter?' she gasped.

'You must keep calm. There's not a moment to lose. Put on your clothes at once and come with me.'

'But what is it? Has something happened in the city?'

The sight of the soldiers suggested to her at once that there had been an outbreak and they were come to protect her.

'Your husband's been taken ill. We want you to come at once.'

'Walter?' she cried.

'You mustn't be upset. I don't exactly know what's the matter. Colonel Yü sent this officer to me and asked me to bring you to the Yamen at once.'

Kitty stared at him for a moment, she felt a sudden cold in her heart, and then she turned.

'I shall be ready in two minutes.'

'I came just as I was,' he answered. 'I was asleep, I just put on a coat and some shoes.'

She did not hear what he said. She dressed by the light of the stars, taking the first things that came to hand; her fingers on a sudden were so clumsy that it seemed to take her an age to find the little clasps that closed her dress. She put round her shoulders the Cantonese shawl she had worn in the evening.

'I haven't put a hat on. There's no need, is there?'

'No.'

The boy held the lantern in front of them and they hurried down the steps and out of the compound gate.

'Take care you don't fall,' said Waddington. 'You'd better hang on to my arm.'

The soldiers followed immediately behind them.

'Colonel Yü has sent chairs. They're waiting on the other side of the river.'

They walked quickly down the hill. Kitty could not

bring herself to utter the question that trembled so horribly on her lips. She was mortally afraid of the answer. They came to the bank and there, with a thread of light at the bow, a sampan was waiting for them.

'Is it cholera?' she said then.

'I'm afraid so.'

She gave a little cry and stopped short.

'I think you ought to come as quickly as you can.' He gave her his hand to help her into the boat. The passage was short and the river almost stagnant; they stood in a bunch at the bow, while a woman with a child tied on her hip with one oar impelled the sampan across.

'He was taken ill this afternoon, the afternoon of yesterday that is,' said Waddington.

'Why wasn't I sent for at once?'

Although there was no reason for it they spoke in whispers. In the darkness Kitty could only feel how intense was her companion's anxiety.

'Colonel Yü wanted to, but he wouldn't let him. Colonel Yü has been with him all the time.'

'He ought to have sent for me all the same. It's heartless.'

'Your husband knew that you had never seen any one with cholera. It's a terrible and revolting sight. He didn't want you to see it.'

'After all he is my husband,' she said in a choking voice.

Waddington made no reply.

'Why am I allowed to come now?'

Waddington put his hand on her arm.

'My dear, you must be very brave. You must be prepared for the worst.'

She gave a wail of anguish and turned away a little, for she saw that the three Chinese soldiers were looking at her. She had a sudden strange glimpse of the whites of their eyes.

'Is he dying?'

'I only know the message Colonel Yü gave to this

officer who came and fetched me. As far as I can judge collapse has set in.'

'Is there no hope at all?'

'I'm dreadfully sorry, I'm afraid that if we don't get there quickly we shan't find him alive.'

She shuddered. The tears began to stream down her cheeks.

'You see, he's been overworking, he has no powers of resistance.'

She withdrew from the pressure of his arm with a gesture of irritation. It exasperated her that he should talk in that low, anguished voice.

They reached the side and two men, Chinese coolies, standing on the bank helped her to step on shore. The chairs were waiting. As she got into hers Waddington said to her:

'Try and keep a tight hold on your nerves. You'll want all your self-control.'

'Tell the bearers to make haste.'

'They have orders to go as fast as they can.'

The officer, already in his chair, passed by and as he passed called out to Kitty's bearers. They raised the chair smartly, arranged the poles on their shoulders, and at a swift pace set off. Waddington followed close behind. They took the hill at a run, a man with a lantern going before each chair, and at the water-gate the gate-keeper was standing with a torch. The officer shouted to him as they approached and he flung open one side of the gate to let them through. He uttered some sort of interjection as they passed and the bearers called back. In the dead of the night those guttural sounds in a strange language were mysterious and alarming. They slithered up the wet and slippery cobbles of the alley and one of the officer's bearers stumbled. Kitty heard the officer's voice raised in anger, the shrill retort of the bearer, and then the chair in front hurried on again. The streets were narrow and tortuous. Here in the city was deep night. It was a city of the dead. They hastened along a narrow lane, turned a corner, and then at a run took a flight of steps; the bearers were beginning to blow hard; they walked with long, rapid strides, in silence; one took out a ragged handkerchief and as he walked wiped from his forehead the sweat that ran down into his eyes; they wound this way and that so that it might have been a maze through which they sped; in the shadow of the shuttered shops sometimes a form seemed to be lying, but you did not know whether it was a man who slept to awake at dawn or a man who slept to awake never; the narrow streets were ghostly in their silent emptiness and when on a sudden a dog barked loudly it sent a shock of terror through Kitty's tortured nerves. She did not know where they went. The way seemed endless. Could they not go faster? Faster. Faster. The time was going and any moment it might be too late.

63

Suddenly, walking along a blank long wall they came to a gateway flanked by sentry boxes, and the bearers set down the chairs. Waddington hurried up to Kitty. She had already jumped out. The officer knocked loudly on the door and shouted. A postern was opened and they passed into a courtyard. It was large and square. Huddled against the walls, under the eaves of the overhanging roofs, soldiers wrapped in their blankets were lying in huddled groups. They stopped for a moment while the officer spoke to a man who might have been a sergeant on guard. He turned and said something to Waddington.

'He's still alive,' said Waddington in a low voice. 'Take care how you walk.'

Still preceded by the men with lanterns they made their way across the yard, up some steps, through a great doorway and then down into another wide court. On one side of this was a long chamber with lights in it; the lights within shining through the rice paper silhouetted the elaborate pattern of the lattice. The lantern-bearers led them across the yard towards this room and at the door the officer knocked. It was opened immediately and the officer with a glance at Kitty stepped back.

'Will you walk in,' said Waddington.

It was a long, low room and the smoky lamps that lit it made the gloom ominous. Three or four orderlies stood about. On a pallet against the wall opposite the door a man was lying huddled under a blanket. An officer was standing motionless at the foot.

Kitty hurried up and leaned over the pallet. Walter lay with his eyes closed and in that sombre light his face had the greyness of death. He was horribly still.

'Walter, Walter,' she gasped, in a low, terrified tone.

There was a slight movement in the body, or the shadow of a movement,; it was so slight it was like a breath of air which you cannot feel and yet for an instant ruffles the surface of still water.

'Walter, Walter, speak to me.'

The eyes were opened slowly, as though it were an infinite effort to raise those heavy lids, but he did not look, he stared at the wall a few inches from his face. He spoke; his voice, low and weak, had the hint of a smile in it.

'This is a pretty kettle of fish,' he said.

Kitty dared not breathe. He made no further sound, no beginning of a gesture, but his eyes, those dark, cold eyes of his (seeing now what mysteries?) stared at the white-washed wall. Kitty raised herself to her feet. With haggard gaze she faced the man who stood there.

'Surely something can be done. You're not going to stand there and do nothing?'

She clasped her hands. Waddington spoke to the officer who stood at the end of the bed.

'I'm afraid they've done everything that was possible. The regimental surgeon has been treating him. Your husband has trained him and he's done all that your husband could do himself.'

'Is that the surgeon?'

'No, that is Colonel Yü. He's never left your husband's side.'

Distracted, Kitty gave him a glance. He was a tallish man, but stockily built, and he seemed ill at ease in his khaki uniform. He was looking at Walter and she saw that his eyes were wet with tears. It gave her a pang. Why should that man with his yellow, flat face have tears in his eyes? It exasperated her.

'It's awful to be able to do nothing.'

'At least he's not in pain any more,' said Waddington.

She leaned once more over her husband. Those ghastly eyes of his still stared vacantly in front of him. She could not tell if he saw with them. She did not know whether he had heard what was said. She put her lips close to his ears.

'Walter, isn't there something we can do?'

She thought that there must be some drug they could give him which would stay the dreadful ebbing of his life. Now that her eyes were more accustomed to the dimness she saw with horror that his face had fallen. She would hardly have recognised him. It was unthinkable that in a few short hours he should look like another man; he hardly looked like a man at all; he looked like death.

She thought that he was making an effort to speak. She put her ear close.

'Don't fuss. I've had a rough passage, but I'm all right now.'

Kitty waited for a moment, but he was silent. His immobility rent her heart with anguish; it was terrifying that he should lie so still. He seemed prepared already for the stillness of the grave. Some one, the surgeon or a dresser, came forward and with a gesture motioned her aside; he leaned over the dying man and with a dirty rag wet his lips. Kitty stood up once more and turned to Waddington despairingly.

'Is there no hope at all?' she whispered.

He shook his head.

'How much longer can he live?'

'No one can tell. An hour perhaps.'

Kitty looked round the bare chamber and her eyes rested for an instant on the substantial form of Colonel Yü.

'Can I be left alone with him for a little while?' she asked. 'Only for a minute.'

'Certainly, if you wish it.'

Waddington stepped over to the Colonel and spoke to him. The Colonel gave a little bow and then in a low tone an order.

'We shall wait on the steps,' said Waddington as they trooped out. 'You have only to call.'

Now that the incredible had overwhelmed her consciousness, like a drug coursing through her veins, and she realised that Walter was going to die she had but one thought, and that was to make his end easier for him by dragging from his soul the rancour which poisoned it. If he could die at peace with her it seemed to her that he would die at peace with himself. She thought now not of herself at all but only of him.

'Walter, I beseech you to forgive me,' she said, leaning over him. For fear that he could not bear the pressure she took care not to touch him. 'I'm so desperately sorry for the wrong I did you. I so bitterly regret it.'

He said nothing. He did not seem to hear. She was obliged to insist. It seemed to her strangely that his soul was a fluttering moth and its wings were heavy with hatred.

'Darling.'

A shadow passed over his wan and sunken face. It was less than a movement, and yet it gave all the effect of a terrifying convulsion. She had never used that word to him before. Perhaps in his dying brain there passed the thought, confused and difficultly grasped, that he had only heard her use it, a commonplace of her vocabulary, to dogs and babies and motor-cars. Then something horrible occurred. She clenched her hands, trying with all her might to control herself, for she saw two tears run slowly down his wasted cheeks.

'Oh, my precious, my dear, if you ever loved me – I know you loved me and I was hateful – I beg you to forgive me. I've no chance now to show my repentance. Have mercy on me. I beseech you to forgive.'

She stopped. She looked at him, all breathless, waiting passionately for a reply. She saw that he tried to speak. Her heart gave a great bound. It seemed to her that it would be in a manner a reparation for the suffering she had caused him if at this last moment she could effect his deliverance from that load of bitterness. His lips moved. He did not look at her. His eyes stared unseeing at the white-washed wall. She leaned over him so that she might hear. But he spoke quite clearly.

'The dog it was that died.'

She stayed as still as though she were turned to stone. She could not understand and gazed at him in terrified perplexity. It was meaningless. Delirium. He had not understood a word she said.

It was impossible to be so still and yet to live. She stared and stared. His eyes were open. She could not tell if he breathed. She began to grow frightened.

'Walter,' she whispered. 'Walter.'

At last, suddenly, she raised herself. A sudden fear seized her. She turned and went to the door.

'Will you come, please. He doesn't seem to . . .'

They stepped in. The Chinese surgeon went up to the bed. He had an electric torch in his hand and he lit it and looked at Walter's eyes. Then he closed them. He said something in Chinese. Waddington put his arm round Kitty.

'I'm afraid he's dead.'

Kitty gave a deep sigh. A few tears fell from her eyes. She felt dazed rather than overcome. The Chinese stood about, round the bed, helplessly, as though they did not quite know what to do next. Waddington was silent. In a minute the Chinese began to speak in a low tone among themselves.

'You'd better let me take you back to the bungalow,' said Waddington. 'He'll be brought there.'

Kitty passed her hand wearily across her forehead. She went up to the pallet bed and leaned over it. She kissed Walter gently on the lips. She was not crying now.

'I'm sorry to give you so much trouble.'

The officers saluted as she passed and she gravely bowed. They walked back across the courtyard and got into their chairs. She saw Waddington light a cigarette. A little smoke lost in the air, that was the life of man.

64

Dawn was breaking now, and here and there a Chinese was taking down the shutters of his shop. In its dark recesses, by the light of a taper, a woman was washing her hands and face. In a tea-house at a corner a group of men were eating an early meal. The grey, cold light of the rising day sidled along the narrow lanes like a thief. There was a pale mist on the river and the masts of the crowded junks loomed through it like the lances of a phantom army. It was chilly as they crossed and Kitty huddled herself up in her gay and coloured shawl. They walked up the hill and they were above the mist. The sun shone from an unclouded sky. It shone as though this were a day like another and nothing had happened to distinguish it from its fellows.

'Wouldn't you like to lie down?' said Waddington when they entered the bungalow.

'No, I'll sit at the window.'

She had sat at the window so often and so long during the weeks that had passed and her eyes now were so familiar with the fantastic, garish, beautiful and mysterious temple on its great bastion that it rested her spirit. It was so unreal, even in the crude light of midday, that it withdrew her from the reality of life.

'I'll get the boy to make you some tea. I'm afraid it will be necessary to bury him this morning. I'll make all the arrangements.'

'Thank you.'

65

They buried him three hours later. It seemed horrible to Kitty that he must be put into a Chinese coffin, as though in so strange a bed he must rest uneasily, but there was no help for it. The nuns, learning of Walter's death as they learned everything that happened in the city, sent by a messenger a cross of dahlias, stiff and formal, but made as though by the accustomed hands of a florist; and the cross, alone on the Chinese coffin, looked grotesque and out of place. When all was ready they had to wait for Colonel Yü who had sent to Waddington to say that he desired to attend the funeral. He came accompanied by an A.D.C. They walked up the hill, the coffin borne by half a dozen coolies, to a little plot of land where lay buried the missionary whose place Walter had taken. Waddington had found among the missionary's effects an English prayer-book and in a low voice, with an embarrassment that was unusual to him, read the burial service. Perhaps, reciting those solemn but terrible words, the thought hovered in his mind that if he in his turn fell a victim to the pestilence there would be no one now to say them over him. The coffin was lowered into the grave and the grave-diggers began to throw in the earth.

Colonel Yü, who had stood with bared head by the grave-side, put on his hat, saluted Kitty gravely, said a word or two to Waddington and followed by his A.D.C. walked away. The coolies, curious to watch a Christian burial, had lingered and now in a straggling group, their yokes trailing in their hands, sauntered off. Kitty and

Waddington waited till the grave was filled and then placed on the mound, smelling of fresh earth, the nuns' prim dahlias. She had not wept, but when the first shovelful of earth rattled on the coffin she felt a dreadful pang at her heart.

She saw that Waddington was waiting for her to come away.

'Are you in a hurry?' she asked. 'I don't want to go back to the bungalow just yet.'

'I have nothing to do. I am entirely in your hands.'

66

They sauntered along the causeway till they came to the top of the hill on which stood that archway, the memorial to a virtuous widow, which had occupied so large a part of Kitty's impression of the place. It was a symbol, but of what she scarcely knew; she could not tell why it bore a note of so sardonic irony.

'Shall we sit down a little? We haven't sat here for ages.' The plain was spread before her widely; it was tranquil and serene in the morning light. 'It's only a few weeks that I've been here and it seems a lifetime.'

He did not answer and for a while she allowed her thoughts to wander. She gave a sigh.

'Do you think that the soul is immortal?' she asked.

He did not seem surprised at the question.

'How should I know?'

'Just now, when they'd washed Walter, before they put him into the coffin I looked at him. He looked very young. Too young to die. Do you remember that beggar that we saw the first time you took me for a walk? I was frightened not because he was dead, but because he looked as though he'd never been a human being. He was just a dead animal. And now again, with Walter, it looked so like a machine that has run down. That's what is so frightening. And if it is only a machine how futile is all this suffering and the heart pains and the misery.'

He did not answer, but his eyes travelled over the landscape at their feet. The wide expanse on that gay and sunny morning filled the heart with exultation. The trim little rice-fields stretched as far as the eye could see and in many of them the blue-clad peasants with their buffaloes were working industriously. It was a peaceful and a happy scene. Kitty broke the silence.

'I can't tell you how deeply moved I've been by all I've seen at the convent. They're wonderful, those nuns, they make me feel utterly worthless. They give up everything, their home, their country, love, children, freedom; and all the little things which I sometimes think must be harder still to give up, flowers and green fields, going for a walk on an autumn day, books and music, comfort, everything they give up, everything. And they do it so that they may devote themselves to a life of sacrifice and poverty, obedience, killing work and prayer. To all of them this world is really and truly a place of exile. Life is a cross which they willingly bear, but in their hearts all the time is the desire – oh, it's so much stronger than desire, it's a longing, an eager, passionate longing for the death which shall lead them to life everlasting.'

Kitty clasped her hands and looked at him with anguish.

'Well?'

'Supposing there is no life everlasting? Think what it means if death is really the end of all things. They've given up all for nothing. They've been cheated. They're dupes.'

Waddington reflected for a little while.

'I wonder. I wonder if it matters that what they have aimed at is illusion. Their lives are in themselves beautiful. I have an idea that the only thing which makes it possible to regard this world we live in without disgust is the beauty which now and then men create out of the chaos. The pictures they paint, the music they compose, the books they write, and the lives they lead. Of all these the richest in beauty is the beautiful life. That is the perfect work of art.'

Kitty sighed. What he said seemed hard. She wanted more.

'Have you ever been to a symphony concert?' he continued.

'Yes,' she smiled. 'I know nothing of music, but I'm rather fond of it.'

'Each member of the orchestra plays his own little instrument, and what do you think he knows of the complicated harmonies which unroll themselves on the indifferent air? He is concerned only with his own small share. But he knows that the symphony is lovely, and though there's none to hear it, it is lovely still, and he is content to play his part.'

'You spoke of Tao the other day,' said Kitty, after a pause. 'Tell me what it is.'

Waddington gave her a little look, hesitated an instant, and then with a faint smile on his comic face answered:

'It is the Way and the Waygoer. It is the eternal road along which walk all beings, but no being made it, for itself is being. It is everything and nothing. From it all things spring, all things conform to it, and to it at last all things return. It is a square without angles, a sound which ears cannot hear, and an image without form. It is a vast net and though its meshes are as wide as the sea it lets nothing through. It is the sanctuary where all things find refuge. It is nowhere, but without looking out of the window you may see it. Desire not to desire, it teaches, and leave all things to take their course. He that humbles himself shall be preserved entire. He that bends shall be made straight. Failure is the foundation of success and success is the lurking-place of failure; but who can tell when the turning point will come? He who strives after tenderness can become even as a little child. Gentleness brings victory to him who attacks and safety to him who defends. Mighty is he who conquers himself.'

'Does it mean anything?'

'Sometimes, when I've had half a dozen whiskies and look at the stars, I think perhaps it does.'

Silence fell upon them and when it was broken it was again by Kitty.

'Tell me, is: the dog it was that died, a quotation?'

Waddington's lips outlined a smile and he was ready with his answer. But perhaps at that moment his sensibilities were abnormally acute. Kitty was not looking at him, but there was something about her expression which made him change his mind.

'If it is I don't know it,' he answered warily. 'Why?'

'Nothing. It crossed my mind. It had a familiar ring.'

There was another silence.

'When you were alone with your husband,' said Waddington presently, 'I had a talk with the regimental surgeon. I thought we ought to have some details.'

'Well?'

'He was in a very hysterical state. I couldn't really quite understand what he meant. So far as I can make out your husband got infected during the course of experiments he was making.'

'He was always experimenting. He wasn't really a doctor, he was a bacteriologist; that is why he was so anxious to come here.'

'But I can't quite make out from the surgeon's statements whether he was infected accidentally or whether he was actually experimenting on himself.'

Kitty grew very pale. The suggestion made her shudder. Waddington took her hand.

'Forgive me for talking about this again,' he said gently, 'but I thought it might comfort you – I know how frightfully difficult it is on these occasions to say anything that is of the least use – I thought it might mean something to you that Walter died a martyr to science and to his duty.'

Kitty shrugged her shoulders with a suspicion of impatience.

'Walter died of a broken heart,' she said.

Waddington did not answer. She turned and looked at him slowly. Her face was white and set.

'What did he mean by saying: the dog it was that died? What is it?'

'It's the last line of Goldsmith's *Elegy*.'

67

Next morning Kitty went to the convent. The girl who opened the door seemed surprised to see her and when Kitty had been for a few minutes about her work the Mother Superior came in. She went up to Kitty and took her hand.

'I am glad to see you, my dear child. You show a fine courage in coming back here so soon after your great sorrow; and wisdom, for I am sure that a little work will keep you from brooding.'

Kitty cast down her eyes, reddening a little; she did not want the Mother Superior to see into her heart.

'I need not tell you how sincerely all of us here sympathise with you.'

'You are very kind,' whispered Kitty.

'We all pray for you constantly and for the soul of him you have lost.'

Kitty made no reply. The Mother Superior released her hand and in her cool, authoritative tone imposed various tasks upon her. She patted two or three children on the head, gave them her aloof, but winning smile, and went about her more pressing affairs.

68

A week went by. Kitty was sewing. The Mother Superior entered the room and sat down beside her. She gave Kitty's work a shrewd glance.

'You sew very well, my dear. It is a rare accomplishment for young women of your world nowadays.'

'I owe it to my mother.'

'I am sure that your mother will be very glad to see you again.'

Kitty looked up. There was that in the Mother Superior's manner which prevented the remark from being taken as a casual politeness. She went on.

'I allowed you to come here after the death of your dear husband because I thought occupation would distract your mind. I did not think you were fit at that moment to take the long journey to Hong-Kong by yourself, nor did I wish you to sit alone in your house with nothing to do but to remember your loss. But now eight days have passed. It is time for you to go.'

'I don't want to go, Mother. I want to stay here.'

'There is nothing for you to stay for. You came to be with your husband. Your husband is dead. You are in a condition in which you will shortly need a care and attention which it is impossible for you to get here. It is your duty, my dear child, to do everything in your power for the welfare of the being that God has entrusted to your care.'

Kitty was silent for a moment. She looked down.

'I was under the impression that I was of some use here. It has been a great pleasure to me to think that I was. I hoped that you would allow me to go on with my work till the epidemic had come to an end.'

'We are all very grateful for what you have done for us,' answered the Superior, with a slight smile, 'but now that the epidemic is waning the risk of coming here is not so great and I am expecting two sisters from Canton. They should be here very shortly and when they arrive I do not think that I shall be able to make any use of your services.'

Kitty's heart sank. The Mother Superior's tone admitted of no reply; she knew her well enough to know that she would be insensible to entreaty. That she found it necessary to reason with Kitty had brought into her voice a note, if hardly of irritation, at least of the peremptoriness which might lead to it.

'Mr. Waddington was good enough to ask my advice.'

'I wish he could have minded his own business,' interrupted Kitty.

'If he hadn't I should all the same have felt obliged to give it to him,' said the Mother Superior gently. 'At the present moment your place is not here, but with your mother. Mr. Waddington has arranged with Colonel Yü to give you a strong escort so that you will be perfectly safe on the journey, and he has arranged for bearers and coolies. The amah will go with you and arrangements will be made at the cities you pass through. In fact, everything possible for your comfort has been done.'

Kitty's lips tightened. She thought that they might at least have consulted her in a matter which only concerned herself. She had to exercise some self-control in order not to answer sharply.

'And when am I to start?'

The Mother Superior remained quite placid.

'The sooner you can get back to Hong-Kong and then sail to England the better, my dear child. We thought you would like to start at dawn the day after to-morrow.'

'So soon.'

Kitty felt a little inclined to cry. But it was true enough; she had no place there.

'You all seem in a great hurry to be rid of me,' she said ruefully.

Kitty was conscious of a relaxation in the Superior's demeanour. She saw that Kitty was prepared to yield and unconsciously she assumed a more gracious tone. Kitty's sense of humour was acute and her eyes twinkled as she reflected that even the saints liked to have their own way.

'Don't think that I fail to appreciate the goodness of your heart, my dear child, and the admirable charity which makes you unwilling to abandon your self-imposed duties.'

Kitty stared straight in front of her. She faintly shrugged her shoulders. She knew that she could ascribe to herself no such exalted virtues. She wanted to stay because she had nowhere else to go. It was a curious sensation this, that nobody in the world cared two straws whether she was alive or dead.

'I cannot understand that you should be reluctant to go home,' pursued the Superior amiably. 'There are many foreigners in this country who would give a great deal to have your chance!'

'But not you, Mother?'

'Oh, with us it is different, my dear child. When we come here we know that we have left our homes for ever.'

Out of her own wounded feelings emerged the desire in Kitty's mind, malicious perhaps, to seek the joint in the armour of faith which rendered the nuns so aloofly immune to all the natural feelings. She wanted to see whether there was left in the Superior any of the weakness of humanity.

'I should have thought that sometimes it was hard never to see again those that are dear to you and the scenes amid which you were brought up.'

The Mother Superior hesitated for a moment, but Kitty watching her could see no change in the serenity of her beautiful and austere face.

'It is hard for my mother who is old now, for I am her only daughter and she would dearly like to see me once more before she dies. I wish I could give her that joy. But it cannot be and we shall wait till we can meet in paradise.'

'All the same, when one thinks of those to whom one is so dear, it must be difficult not to ask oneself if one was right in cutting oneself off from them.'

'Are you asking me if I have ever regretted the step I took?' On a sudden the Mother Superior's face grew radiant. 'Never, never. I have exchanged a life that was trivial and worthless for one of sacrifice and prayer.'

There was a brief silence and then the Mother Superior, assuming a lighter manner, smiled.

'I am going to ask you to take a little parcel and post it for me when you get to Marseilles. I do not wish to entrust it to the Chinese post-office. I will fetch it at once.'

'You can give it to me to-morrow,' said Kitty.

'You will be too busy to come here to-morrow, my dear. It will be more convenient for you to bid us farewell to-night.'

She rose and with the easy dignity which her voluminous habit could not conceal left the room. In a moment Sister St. Joseph came in. She was come to say good-bye. She hoped that Kitty would have a pleasant journey; she would be quite safe, for Colonel Yü was sending a strong escort with her; and the sisters constantly did the journey alone and no harm came to them. And did she like the sea? *Mon Dieu*, how ill she was when there was a storm in the Indian ocean, *Madame* her mother would be pleased to see her daughter, and she must take care of herself; after all she had another little soul in her care now, and they would all pray for her; she would pray constantly for her and the dear little baby and for the soul of the poor, brave doctor. She was voluble, kindly, and affectionate; and yet Kitty was deeply conscious that for Sister St. Joseph (her gaze intent on eternity) she was but a wraith without body or substance. She had a wild impulse to seize the stout, good-natured nun by the shoulders and shake her, crying: 'Don't you know that I'm a human being, unhappy and alone, and I want comfort and sympathy and encouragement; oh, can't you turn a minute away from God and give me a little compassion; not the Christian compassion that you have for all suffering things, but just human compassion for me?' The thought brought a smile to Kitty's lips: how very surprised Sister St. Joseph would be! She would certainly be convinced of what now she only suspected, that all English people were mad.

'Fortunately I am a very good sailor,' Kitty answered. 'I've never been sea-sick yet.'

The Mother Superior returned with a small, neat parcel.

'They're handkerchiefs that I've had made for the name-day of my mother,' she said. 'The initials have been embroidered by our young girls.'

Sister St. Joseph suggested that Kitty would like to see how beautifully the work was done and the Mother Superior with an indulgent, deprecating smile untied the parcel. The handkerchiefs were of very fine lawn and the initials embroidered in a complicated cypher were surmounted by a crown of strawberry leaves. When Kitty had properly admired the workmanship the handkerchiefs were wrapped up again and the parcel handed to her. Sister St. Joseph, with an *'eh bien, Madame, je vous quitte'* and a repetition of her polite and impersonal salutations, went away. Kitty realised that this was the moment to take her leave of the Superior. She thanked her for her kindness to her. They walked together along the bare, white-washed corridors.

'Would it be asking too much of you to register the parcel when you arrive at Marseilles?' said the Superior.

'Of course I'll do that,' said Kitty.

She glanced at the address. The name seemed very grand, but the place mentioned attracted her attention.

'But that is one of the *châteaux* I've seen. I was motoring with friends in France.'

'It is very possible,' said the Mother Superior. 'Strangers are permitted to view it on two days a week.'

'I think if I had ever lived in such a beautiful place I should never have had the courage to leave it.'

'It is of course a historical monument. It is scarcely intimate. If I regretted anything it would not be that, but the little *château* that we lived in when I was a child. It was in the Pyrenees. I was born within sound of the sea.

I do not deny that sometimes I should like to hear the waves beating against the rocks.'

Kitty had an idea that the Mother Superior, divining her thought and the reason for her remarks, was slyly making fun of her. But they reached the little, unpretentious door of the convent. To Kitty's surprise the Mother Superior took her in her arms and kissed her. The pressure of her pale lips on Kitty's cheeks, she kissed her first on one side and then on the other, was so unexpected that it made her flush and inclined to cry.

'Good-bye, God bless you, my dear child.' She held her for a moment in her arms. 'Remember that it is nothing to do your duty, that is demanded of you and is no more meritorious than to wash your hands when they are dirty; the only thing that counts is the love of duty; when love and duty are one, then grace is in you and you will enjoy a happiness which passes all understanding.'

The convent door closed for the last time behind her.

69

Waddington walked with Kitty up the hill and they turned aside for a moment to look at Walter's grave; at the memorial arch he said good-bye to her, and looking at it for the last time she felt that she could reply to the enigmatic irony of its appearance with an equal irony of her own. She stepped into her chair.

One day passed after the other. The sights of the wayside served as a background to her thoughts. She saw them as it were in duplicate, rounded as though in a stereoscope, with an added significance because to everything she saw was added the recollection of what she had seen when but a few short weeks before she had taken the same journey in the contrary direction. The coolies with their loads straggled disorderly, two or three together, and then a hundred yards behind one by himself, and then two or three more; the soldiers of the escort shuffled along with a clumsy walk that covered five and twenty miles a day; the amah was carried by two bearers and Kitty, not because she was heavier, but for face' sake, by four. Now and then they met a string of coolies lolloping by in line with their heavy burdens, now and then a Chinese official in a sedan who looked at the white woman with inquisitive eyes; now they came across peasants in faded blue and huge hats on their way to market and now a woman, old or young, tottering along on her bound feet. They passed up and down little hills laid out with trim rice-fields and farm-houses nestling cosily in a grove of bamboos; they passed through ragged villages and populous cities walled like the cities in a missal. The sun of the early autumn was pleasant, and if at daybreak, when the shimmering dawn lent the neat fields the enchantment of a fairy tale, it was cold, the warmth later was very grateful. Kitty was filled by it with a sense of beatitude which she made no effort to resist.

The vivid scenes with their elegant colour, their unexpected distinction, and their strangeness, were like an arras before which, like mysterious, shadowy shapes, played the phantoms of Kitty's fancy. They seemed wholly unreal. Mei-tan-fu with its crenellated walls was like the painted canvas placed on the stage in an old play to represent a city. The nuns, Waddington, and the Manchu woman who loved him, were fantastic characters in a masque; and the rest, the people sidling along the tortuous streets and those who died, were nameless supers. Of course it had, they all had, a significance of some sort, but what was it? It was as though they performed a ritual dance, elaborate and ancient, and you knew that those complicated measures had a meaning which it was important for you to know; and yet you could see no clue, no clue.

It seemed incredible to Kitty (an old woman was passing along the causeway, in blue, and the blue in the sunshine was like lapis lazuli; her face with its thousand little wrinkles was like a mask of old ivory; and she leaned, as she walked on her tiny feet, on a long black staff) it seemed incredible to Kitty that she and Walter had taken part in that strange and unreal dance. They had played important parts too. She might easily have lost her life: he had. Was it a joke? Perhaps it was nothing but a dream from which she would suddenly awake with a sigh of relief. It seemed to have taken place a long time ago and in a far-off place. It was singular how shadowy the persons of that play seemed against the sunny background of real life. And now it seemed to Kitty like a story that she was reading; it was a little startling that it seemed to concern her so little. She found already that she could not recall with distinctness Waddington's face which had been so familiar to her.

This evening they should reach the city on the Western River from which she was to take the steamer. Thence it was but a night's run to Hong-Kong.

70

At first because she had not wept when Walter died she was ashamed. It seemed dreadfully callous. Why, the eyes of the Chinese officer, Colonel Yü, had been wet with tears. She was dazed by her husband's death. It was difficult to understand that he would not come into the bungalow again and that when he got up in the morning she would not hear him take his bath in the Suchow tub. He was alive and now he was dead. The sisters wondered at her Christian resignation and admired the courage with which she bore her loss. But Waddington was shrewd; for all his grave sympathy she had a feeling that – how should she put it? – that he had his tongue in his cheek. Of course, Walter's death had been a shock to her. She didn't want him to die. But after all she didn't love him, she had never loved him; it was decent to bear herself with becoming sorrow; it would be ugly and vulgar even to let any one see in her heart; but she had gone through too much to make pretences to herself. It seemed to her that this at least the last few weeks had taught her, that if it is necessary sometimes to lie to others it is always despicable to lie to oneself. She was sorry that Walter had died in that tragic manner, but she was sorry with a purely human sorrow such as she might have felt if it had been an acquaintance. She would acknowledge that Walter had admirable qualities; it just happened that she did not like him; he had always bored her. She would not admit that his death was a relief to her, she could say honestly that if by a word of hers she could bring him back to life she would say it, but she could not resist the feeling that his death made her way to some extent a trifle easier. They would never have been happy together and yet to part would have been terribly difficult. She was startled at herself for feeling as she did; she supposed that people would think her heartless and cruel if they knew. Well, they shouldn't know. She wondered if all her fellows had in their hearts shameful secrets which they spent their time guarding from curious glances.

She looked very little into the future and she made no plans. The only thing she knew was that she wanted to stay in Hong-Kong as short a while as might be. She looked forward to arriving there with horror. It seemed to her that she would like to wander for ever through that smiling and friendly country in her rattan chair, and, an indifferent spectator for ever of the phantasmagoria of life, pass each night under a different roof. But of course the immediate future must be faced: she would go to the hotel when she reached Hong-Kong, she would arrange about getting rid of the house and selling the furniture; there would be no need to see Townsend. He would have the grace to keep out of her way. She would like, all the same, to see him once more in order to tell him what a despicable creature she thought him.

But what did Charles Townsend matter?

Like a rich melody on a harp that rang in exultant arpeggios through the complicated harmonies of a symphony, one thought beat in her heart insistently. It was this thought which gave their exotic beauty to the rice-fields, which made a little smile break on her pale lips as a smooth-faced lad swung past her on his way to the market town with exultation in his carriage and audacity in his eyes, and which gave the magic of a tumultuous life to the cities she passed through. The city of the pestilence was a prison from which she was escaped, and she had never known before how exquisite was the blueness of the sky and what a joy there was in the bamboo copses that leaned with such an adorable grace across the causeway. Freedom! That was the thought that sung in her heart so that even though the future was so dim, it was iridescent like the mist over the river where the morning sun fell upon it. Freedom! Not only freedom from a bond that irked, and a companionship which depressed her; freedom, not only from the death which had threatened, but freedom from the love that had degraded her; freedom from all spiritual ties, the freedom of a disembodied spirit; and with freedom, courage and a valiant unconcern for whatever was to come.

71

When the boat docked at Hong-Kong, Kitty, who had been standing on deck to look at the coloured, gay and vivacious traffic of the river, went into her cabin to see that the amah had left nothing behind. She gave herself a look in the glass. She wore black, the nuns had dyed a dress for her, but not mourning; and the thought crossed her mind that the first thing she must do was to see to this. The habiliments of woe could not but serve as an effective disguise to her unexpected feelings. There was a knock on her cabin door. The amah opened it.

'Mrs. Fane.'

Kitty turned round and saw a face which at the first

moment she did not recognise. Then her heart gave a sudden quick beat and she flushed. It was Dorothy Townsend. Kitty so little expected to see her that she knew neither what to do nor what to say. But Mrs. Townsend came into the cabin and with an impulsive gesture took Kitty in her arms.

'Oh, my dear, my dear, I'm so dreadfully sorry for you.'

Kitty allowed herself to be kissed. She was a little surprised at this effusiveness in a woman whom she had always thought cold and distant.

'It's very kind of you,' murmured Kitty.

'Come on deck. The amah will look after your things and my boys are here.'

She took Kitty's hand and Kitty, allowing herself to be led, noticed that her good-natured, weather-beaten face bore an expression of real concern.

'Your boat's early, I very nearly didn't get down in time,' said Mrs. Townsend. 'I couldn't have borne it if I'd missed you.'

'But you didn't come to meet me?' exclaimed Kitty.

'Of course I did.'

'But how did you know I was coming?'

'Mr. Waddington sent me a telegram.'

Kitty turned away. She had a lump in her throat. It was funny that a little unexpected kindness should so affect her. She did not want to cry; she wished Dorothy Townsend would go away. But Dorothy took the hand that was hanging by Kitty's side and pressed it. It embarrassed Kitty that this shy woman should be so demonstrative.

'I want you to do me a great favour. Charlie and I want you to come and stay with us while you're in Hong-Kong.'

Kitty snatched her hand away.

'It's awfully kind of you. I couldn't possibly.'

'But you must. You can't go and live all by yourself in your own house. It would be dreadful for you. I've prepared everything. You shall have your own sitting-room. You can have your meals there if you don't care to have them with us. We both want you to come.'

'I wasn't thinking of going to the house. I was going to get myself a room at the Hong-Kong Hotel. I couldn't possibly put you to so much trouble.'

The suggestion had taken her by surprise. She was confused and vexed. If Charlie had had any sense of decency he would never have allowed his wife to make the invitation. She did not wish to be under an obligation to either of them.

'Oh, but I couldn't bear the idea of your living at a hotel. And you'd hate the Hong-Kong Hotel just now. With all those people about and the band playing jazz all the time. Please say you'll come to us. I promise you that Charlie and I won't bother you.'

'I don't know why you should be so kind to me.' Kitty was getting a little short of excuses; she could not bring herself to utter a blunt and definite no. 'I'm afraid I'm not very good company among strangers just now.'

'But need we be strangers to you? Oh, I do so want not to be, I so want you to allow me to be your friend.' Dorothy clasped her hands and her voice, her cool, deliberate and distinguished voice, was tremulous with tears. 'I so awfully want you to come. You see, I want to make amends to you.'

Kitty did not understand. She did not know what amends Charlie's wife owed her.

'I'm afraid I didn't very much like you at first. I thought you rather fast. You see, I'm old-fashioned and I suppose I'm intolerant.'

Kitty gave her a passing glance. What she meant was that at first she had thought Kitty vulgar. Though Kitty allowed no shadow of it to show on her face in her heart she laughed. Much she cared for what any one thought of her now!

'And when I heard that you'd gone with your husband into the jaws of death, without a moment's hesitation, I felt such a frightful cad. I felt so humiliated. You've been so wonderful, you've been so brave, you make all the rest of us look so dreadfully cheap and second-rate.' Now the tears were pouring down her kind, homely face. 'I can't tell you how much I admire you and what a respect I have for you. I know I can do nothing to make up for your terrible loss, but I want you to know how deeply, how sincerely I feel for you. And if you'll only allow me to do a little something for you it will be a privilege. Don't bear me a grudge because I misjudged you. You're heroic and I'm just a silly fool of a woman.'

Kitty looked down at the deck. She was very pale. She wished that Dorothy would not show such uncontrollable emotion. She was touched, it was true, but she could not help a slight feeling of impatience that this simple creature should believe such lies.

'If you really mean that you'd like to have me, of course I shall be glad to come,' she sighed.

72

The Townsends lived on the Peak in a house with a wide view over the sea, and Charlie did not as a rule come up to luncheon, but on the day of Kitty's arrival Dorothy (they were Kitty and Dorothy to one another by now) told her that if she felt up to seeing him he would like to come and bid her welcome. Kitty reflected that since she must see him she might just as well see him at once and she looked forward with grim amusement to the embarrassment she must cause him. She saw very well that the invitation to stay had arisen in his wife's fancy and notwithstanding his own feelings he had immediately approved. Kitty knew how great his desire was always to do the right thing and to offer her a gracious hospitality was obviously very much the right thing. But he could hardly remember the last interview of theirs without mortification: to a man so vain as Townsend it must be galling like an ulcer that would not heal. She hoped that she had hurt him as much as he had hurt her. He must hate her now. She was glad to think that she did not hate, but only despised him. It gave her a sardonic satisfaction to reflect that whatever his feelings he would be obliged to make much of her. When she left his office that afternoon he must have hoped with all his heart that he would never set eyes on her again.

And now, sitting with Dorothy, she waited for him to come in. She was conscious of her delight in the sober luxury of the drawing-room. She sat in an armchair, there were lovely flowers here and there, on the walls were pleasing pictures; the room was shaded and cool, it was friendly and homelike. She remembered with a faint shudder the bare and empty parlour of the missionary's bungalow; the rattan chairs and the kitchen table with its cotton cloth, the stained shelves with all those cheap editions of novels, and the little skimpy red curtains that had such a dusty look. Oh, it had been so uncomfortable! She supposed that Dorothy had never thought of that.

They heard a motor drive up, and Charlie strode into the room.

'Am I late? I hope I haven't kept you waiting. I had to see the Governor and I simply couldn't get away.'

He went up to Kitty, and took both her hands.

'I'm so very, very glad you've come here. I know Dorothy has told you that we want you to stay as long as ever you like and that we want you to look upon our house as your home. But I want to tell you so myself as well. If there's anything in the world I can do for you I shall only be too happy.' His eyes wore a charming expression of sincerity; she wondered if he saw the irony in hers. 'I'm awfully stupid at saying some things and I don't want to seem a clumsy fool, but I do want you to know how deeply I sympathise with you in your husband's death. He was a thundering good chap, and he'll be missed here more than I can say.'

'Don't, Charlie,' said his wife. 'I'm sure Kitty understands. . . . Here are the cocktails.'

Following the luxurious custom of the foreigners in

China two boys in uniform came into the room with savouries and cocktails. Kitty refused.

'Oh, you must have one,' insisted Townsend in his breezy, cordial way. 'It'll do you good and I'm sure you haven't had such a thing as a cocktail since you left Hong-Kong. Unless I'm very much mistaken you couldn't get ice at Mei-tan-fu.'

'You're not mistaken,' said Kitty.

For a moment she had a picture before her mind's eye of that beggar with the tousled head in the blue rags through which you saw the emaciated limbs, who had lain dead against the compound wall.

73

They went in to luncheon. Charlie, sitting at the head of his table, easily took charge of the conversation. After those first few words of sympathy he treated Kitty, not as though she had just suffered a devastating experience, but rather as though she had come in from Shanghai for a change after an operation for appendicitis. She needed cheering and he was prepared to cheer her. The best way of making her feel at home was to treat her as one of the family. He was a tactful man. He began talking of the autumn race meeting, and the polo – by Jove, he would have to give up playing polo if he couldn't get his weight down – and a chat he had had that morning with the Governor. He spoke of a party they had been to on the Admiral's flag-ship, the state of affairs in Canton, and of the links at Lushan. In a few minutes Kitty felt that she might have been away for no longer than a weekend. It was incredible that over there, up country, six hundred miles away only (the distance from London to Edinburgh, wasn't it?) men, women and children had been dying like flies. Soon she found herself asking about so and so who had broken a collar bone at polo and if Mrs. This had gone home or Mrs. That was playing in the tennis tournament.

Charlie made his little jokes and she smiled at them. Dorothy with her faint air of superiority (which now included Kitty and so was no longer slightly offensive, but a bond of union rather) was gently ironic about various persons in the colony. Kitty began to feel more alert.

'Why, she's looking better already,' said Charlie to his wife. 'She was so pale before tiffin that I was quite startled; she's really got some colour in her cheeks now.'

But while she took her part in the conversation, if not with gaiety (for she felt that neither Dorothy nor Charlie with his admirable sense of decorum would approve of that) at least with cheerfulness, Kitty observed her host. In all those weeks during which her fancy had been revengefully occupied with him she had built up in her mind a very vivid impression of him. His thick curling hair was a little too long and too carefully brushed, in order to hide the fact that it was greying there was too much oil on it; his face was too red, with its network of mauve veins on the cheeks, and his jowl was too massive: when he did not hold his head up to hide it you saw that he had a double chin; and there was something apelike in those bushy, grizzled eyebrows of his that vaguely disgusted her. He was heavy in his movements, and all the care he took in his diet and all his exercise did not prevent him from being fat; his bones were much too well covered and his joints had a middle-aged stiffness. His smart clothes were a little tight for him and a little too young.

But when he came into the drawing-room before luncheon Kitty received quite a shock (this perhaps was why her pallor had been so marked), for she discovered that her imagination had played an odd trick on her: he did not in the least look as she had pictured him. She could hardly help laughing at herself. His hair was not grey at all, oh, there were a few white hairs on the temple, but they were becoming; and his face was not red, but sunburned; his head was very well placed on his neck; and he wasn't stout and he wasn't old: in fact he was almost slim and his figure was admirable – could you blame him if he was a trifle vain of it? – he might have been a young man. And of course he did know how to wear his clothes; it was absurd to deny that: he looked neat and clean and trim. Whatever could have possessed her to think him this and that? He was a very handsome man. It was lucky that she knew how worthless he was. Of course she had always admitted that his voice had a winning quality, and his voice was exactly as she remembered it: it made the falseness of every word he said more exasperating; its richness of tone and its warmth rang now in her ears with insincerity and she wondered how she could ever have been taken in by it. His eyes were beautiful: that was where his charm lay, they had such a soft, blue brilliance and even when he was talking balderdash an expression which was so delightful; it was almost impossible not to be moved by them.

At last the coffee was brought in and Charlie lit his cheroot. He looked at his watch and rose from the table.

'Well, I must leave you two young women to your own devices. It's time for me to get back to the office.' He paused and then with his friendly, charming eyes on Kitty said to her: 'I'm not going to bother you for a day or two till you're rested, but then I want to have a little business talk with you.'

'With me?'

'We must make arrangements about your house, you know, and then there's the furniture.'

'Oh, but I can go to a lawyer. There's no reason why I should bother you about that.'

'Don't think for a moment I'm going to let you waste your money on legal expenses. I'm going to see to every-thing. You know you're entitled to a pension: I'm going to talk to H.E. about it and see if by making represen-tations in the proper quarter we can't get something extra for you. You put yourself in my hands. But don't bother about anything just yet. All we want you to do now is to get fit and well: isn't that right, Dorothy?'

'Of course.'

He gave Kitty a little nod and then passing by his wife's chair took her hand and kissed it. Most Englishmen look a little foolish when they kiss a woman's hand; he did it with a graceful ease.

74

It was not till Kitty was fairly settled at the Townsends that she discovered that she was weary. The comfort and the unaccustomed amenity of this life broke up the strain under which she had been living. She had forgotten how pleasant it was to take one's ease, how lulling to be surrounded by pretty things, and how agreeable it was to receive attention. She sank back with a sigh of relief into the facile existence of the luxurious East. It was not displeasing to feel that in a discreet and well-bred fashion she was an object of sympathetic interest. Her bereavement was so recent that it was impossible for entertainments to be given for her, but ladies of consequence in the Colony (His Excellency's wife, the wives of the Admiral and of the Chief Justice) came to drink a quiet cup of tea with her. His Excellency's wife said that His Excellency was most anxious to see her and if she would come very quietly to luncheon at Government House ('not a party, of course, only ourselves and the A.D.C.'s!'), it would be very nice. These ladies used Kitty as though she were a piece of porcelain which was as fragile as it was precious. She could not fail to see that they looked upon her as a little heroine, and she had sufficient humour to play the part with modesty and discretion. She wished sometimes that Waddington were there; with his malicious shrewdness he would have seen the fun of the situation; and when alone they might have had a good laugh over it together. Dorothy had had a letter from him, and he had said all manner of things about her devoted work at the convent, about her courage and her self-control. Of course he was skillfully pulling their legs: the dirty dog.

75

Kitty did not know whether it was by chance or by design that she never found herself for a moment alone with Charlie. His tact was exquisite. He remained kindly, sympathetic, pleasant and amiable. No one could have guessed that they had ever been more than acquaintances. But one afternoon when she was lying on a sofa outside her room reading he passed along the verandah and stopped.

'What is that you're reading?' he asked.

'A book.'

She looked at him with irony. He smiled.

'Dorothy's gone to a garden-party at Government House.'

'I know. Why haven't you gone too?'

'I didn't feel I could face it and I thought I'd come back and keep you company. The car's outside, would you like to come for a drive round the island?'

'No, thank you.'

He sat down on the foot of the sofa on which she lay.

'We haven't had the chance of a talk by ourselves since you got here.'

She looked straight into his eyes with cool insolence.

'Do you think we have anything to say to one another?'

'Volumes.'

She shifted her feet a little so that she should not touch him.

'Are you still angry with me?' he asked, the shadow of a smile on his lips and his eyes melting.

'Not a bit,' she laughed.

'I don't think you'd laugh if you weren't.'

'You're mistaken; I despise you much too much to be angry with you.'

He was unruffled.

'I think you're rather hard on me. Looking back calmly, don't you honestly think I was right?'

'From your standpoint.'

'Now that you know Dorothy, you must admit she's rather nice?'

'Of course. I shall always be grateful for her great kindness to me.'

'She's one in a thousand. I should never have had a moment's peace if we'd bolted. It would have been a rotten trick to play on her. And after all I had to think of my children; it would have been an awful handicap for them.'

For a minute she held him in her reflective gaze. She felt completely mistress of the situation.

'I've watched you very carefully during the week I've been here. I've come to the conclusion that you really are fond of Dorothy. I should never have thought you capable of it.'

'I told you I was fond of her. I wouldn't do anything to cause her a moment's uneasiness. She's the best wife a man ever had.'

'Have you never thought that you owed her any loyalty?'

'What the eye doesn't see the heart doesn't grieve for,' he smiled.

She shrugged her shoulders.

'You're despicable.'

'I'm human. I don't know why you should think me such a cad because I fell head over ears in love with you. I didn't particularly want to, you know.'

It gave her a little twist of the heart-strings to hear him say that.

'I was fair game,' she answered bitterly.

'Naturally I couldn't foresee that we were going to get into such a devil of a scrape.'

'And in any case you had a pretty shrewd idea that if any one suffered it wouldn't be you.'

'I think that's a bit thick. After all, now it's all over, you must see I acted for the best for both of us. You lost your head and you ought to be jolly glad that I kept mine. Do you think it would have been a success if I'd done what you wanted me to? We were dashed uncomfortable in the frying-pan, but we should have been a damned sight worse off in the fire. And you haven't come to any harm. Why can't we kiss and make friends?'

She almost laughed.

'You hardly expect me to forget that you sent me to almost certain death without a shadow of compunction?'

'Oh, what nonsense! I told you there was no risk if you took reasonable precautions. Do you think I'd have let you go for a moment if I hadn't been perfectly convinced of that?'

'You were convinced because you wanted to be. You're one of those cowards who only think what it's profitable for them to think.'

'Well, the proof of the pudding is in the eating. You have come back, and if you don't mind my saying anything so objectionable you've come back prettier than ever.'

'And Walter?'

He could not resist the facetious answer which came to his mind. Charlie smiled.

'Nothing suits you so well as black.'

She stared at him for a moment. Tears filled her eyes and she began to cry. Her beautiful face was distorted with grief. She did not seek to hide it, but lay on her back with her hands along her sides.

'For God's sake don't cry like that. I didn't mean to say anything unkind. It was only a joke. You know how sincerely I feel for you in your bereavement.'

'Oh, hold your stupid tongue.'

'I'd give anything to have Walter back again.'

'He died because of you and me.'

He took her hand, but she snatched it away from him.

'Please go away,' she sobbed. 'That's the only thing you can do for me now. I hate and despise you. Walter was worth ten of you and I was too big a fool to see it. Go away. Go away.'

She saw he was going to speak again and she sprang to her feet and went into her room. He followed her, and as he entered, with instinctive prudence, drew the shutter so that they were almost in darkness.

'I can't leave you like this,' he said, putting his arms round her. 'You know I didn't mean to hurt you.'

'Don't touch me. For God's sake go. Go away.'

She tried to tear herself from him, but he would not let her. She was crying hysterically now.

'Darling, don't you know that I've always loved you,' he said in his deep, charming voice. 'I love you more than ever.'

'How can you tell such lies! Let me go. Damn you, let me go.'

'Don't be unkind to me, Kitty. I know I've been a brute to you, but forgive me.'

She was shaking and sobbing, struggling to get away from him, but the pressure of his arms was strangely comforting. She had so longed to feel them round her once more, just once, and all her body trembled. She felt dreadfully weak. It seemed as though her bones were melting, and the sorrow she felt for Walter shifted into pity for herself.

'Oh, how could you be so unkind to me?' she sobbed. 'Don't you know that I loved you with all my heart. No one has ever loved you as I loved you.'

'Darling.'

He began to kiss her.

'No, no,' she cried.

He sought her face, but she turned it away; he sought her lips; she did not know what he was saying, broken, passionate words of love; and his arms held her so firmly that she felt like a child that has been lost and now at last is safe at home. She moaned faintly. Her eyes were closed and her face was wet with tears. And then he found her lips and the pressure of his upon them shot through her body like the flame of God. It was an ecstasy and she was burnt to a cinder and she glowed as though she were transfigured. In her dreams, in her dreams she had known this rapture. What was he doing with her now? She did not know. She was not a woman, her personality was dissolved, she was nothing but desire. He lifted her off her feet, she was very light in his arms, he carried her and she clung to him, desperate and adoring; her head sank on the pillow and his lips clung to hers.

76

She sat on the edge of the bed hiding her face with her hands.

'Would you like a drop of water?'

She shook her head. He went over to the washing-stand, filled the tooth-glass and brought it to her.

'Come along, have a little drink and you'll feel better.'

He put the glass to her lips and she sipped the water. Then, with horrified eyes, she stared at him. He was standing over her, looking down, and in his eyes was a twinkle of self-satisfaction.

'Well, do you think I'm such a dirty dog as you did?' he asked.

She looked down.

'Yes. But I know that I'm not a bit better than you. Oh, I'm so ashamed.'

'Well, I think you're very ungrateful.'

'Will you go now?'

'To tell you the truth I think it's about time. I'll just go and tidy up before Dorothy comes in.'

He went out of the room with a jaunty step.

Kitty sat for a while, still on the edge of the bed, hunched up like an imbecile. Her mind was vacant. A shudder passed through her. She staggered to her feet and, going to the dressing-table, sank into a chair. She stared at herself in the glass. Her eyes were swollen with tears; her face was stained and there was a red mark on one cheek where his had rested. She looked at herself with horror. It was the same face. She had expected in it she knew not what change of degradation.

'Swine,' she flung at her reflection. 'Swine.'

Then, letting her face fall on her arms, she wept bitterly. Shame, shame! She did not know what had come over her. It was horrible. She hated him and she hated herself. It had been ecstasy. Oh, hateful! She could never look him in the face again. He was so justified. He had been right not to marry her, for she was worthless; she was no better than a harlot. Oh, worse, for those poor women gave themselves for bread. And in this house too into which Dorothy had taken her in her sorrow and cruel desolation! Her shoulders shook with her sobs. Everything was gone now. She had thought herself changed, she had thought herself strong, she thought she had returned to Hong-Kong a woman who possessed herself; new ideas flitted about her heart like little yellow butterflies in the sunshine and she had hoped to be so much better in the future; freedom like a spirit of light had beckoned her on, and the world was like a spacious plain through which she could walk light of foot and with head erect. She had thought herself free from lust and vile passions, free to live the clean and healthy life of the spirit; she had likened herself to the white egrets that fly with leisurely flight across the rice-fields at dusk and they are like the soaring thoughts of a mind at rest with itself; and she was a slave. Weak, weak! It was hopeless, it was no good to try, she was a slut.

She would not go in to dinner. She sent the boy to tell Dorothy that she had a headache and preferred to remain in her room. Dorothy came in and, seeing her red, swollen eyes, talked for a little in her gentle, commiserating way of trivial things. Kitty knew that Dorothy thought she had been crying on account of Walter and, sympathising like the good and loving wife she was, respected the natural sorrow.

'I know it's very hard, dear,' she said as she left Kitty. 'But you must try to have courage. I'm sure your dear husband wouldn't wish you to grieve for him.'

77

But next morning Kitty rose early and leaving a note for Dorothy to say that she was gone out on business took a tram down the hill. She made her way through the crowded streets with their motor cars, rickshaws and chairs, and the motley throng of Europeans and Chinese, to the offices of the P. & O. Company. A ship was sailing in two days, the first ship out of the port, and she had made up her mind that at all costs she must go on it. When the clerk told her that every berth was booked she asked to see the chief agent. She sent in her name and the agent, whom she had met before, came out to fetch her into his office. He knew her circumstances and when she told him what she wished he sent for the passenger list. He looked at it with perplexity.

'I beseech you to do what you can for me,' she urged him.

'I don't think there's any one in the Colony who wouldn't do anything in the world for you, Mrs. Fane,' he answered.

He sent for a clerk and made enquiries. Then he nodded.

'I'm going to shift one or two people. I know you want to get home and I think we ought to do our best for you. I can give you a little cabin to yourself. I expect you'd prefer that.'

She thanked him. She left him with an elated heart. Flight: that was her only thought. Flight! She sent a cable to her father to announce her immediate return; she had already cabled to him to say that Walter was dead; and then went back to the Townsends to tell Dorothy what she had done.

'We shall be dreadfully sorry to lose you,' the kind creature said, 'but of course I understand that you want to be with your mother and father.'

Since her return to Hong-Kong Kitty had hestitated from day to day to go to her house. She dreaded entering it again and meeting face to face the recollections with which it was peopled. But now she had no alternative. Townsend had arranged for the sale of the furniture and he had found some one eager to take on the lease, but there were all her clothes and Walter's, for they had taken next to nothing to Mei-tan-fu, and there were books, photographs, and various odds and ends. Kitty, indifferent to everything and anxious to cut herself off completely from the past, realised that it would outrage the susceptibilities of the Colony if she allowed these things to go with the rest to an auction-room. They must be packed and sent to her. So after tiffin she prepared to go to the house. Dorothy, eager to give her help, offered to accompany her, but Kitty begged to be allowed to go alone. She agreed that two of Dorothy's boys should come and assist in the packing.

The house had been left in charge of the head boy and he opened the door for Kitty. It was curious to go into her own house as though she were a stranger. It was neat and clean. Everything was in its place, ready for her use, but although the day was warm and sunny there was about the silent rooms a chill and desolate air. The furniture was stiffly arranged, exactly where it should be, and the vases which should have held flowers were in their places; the book which Kitty had laid face downwards she did not remember when still lay face downwards. It was as though the house had been left empty but a minute before and yet that minute was fraught with eternity so that you could not imagine that ever again that house would echo with talk and resound with laughter. On the piano the open music of a foxtrot seemed to wait to be played, but you had a feeling that if you struck the keys no sound would come. Walter's room was as tidy as when he was there. On the chest of drawers were two large photographs of Kitty, one in her presentation dress and one in her wedding-gown.

But the boys fetched up the trunks from the box-room and she stood over them watching them pack. They packed neatly and quickly. Kitty reflected that in the two days she had it would be easy to get everything done. She must not let herself think; she had no time for that. Suddenly she heard a step behind her and turning round saw Charles Townsend. She felt a sudden chill at her heart.

'What do you want?' she said.

'Will you come into your sitting-room? I have something to say to you.'

'I'm very busy.'

'I shall only keep you five minutes.'

She said no more, but with a word to the boys to go on with what they were doing, preceded Charles into the next room. She did not sit down, in order to show him that she expected him not to detain her. She knew that she was very pale and her heart was beating fast, but she faced him coolly, with hostile eyes.

'What is it you want?'

'I've just heard from Dorothy that you're going the day after to-morrow. She told me that you'd come here to do your packing and she asked me to ring up and find out if there was anything I could do for you.'

'I'm grateful to you, but I can manage quite well by myself.'

'So I imagined. I didn't come here to ask you that. I came to ask if your sudden departure is due to what happened yesterday.'

'You and Dorothy have been very good to me. I didn't wish you to think I was taking advantage of your good nature.'

'That's not a very straight answer.'

'What does it matter to you?'

'It matters a great deal. I shouldn't like to think that anything I'd done had driven you away.'

She was standing at the table. She looked down. Her eyes fell on the *Sketch*. It was months old now. It was that paper which Walter had stared at all through the terrible evening when – and Walter now was ... She raised her eyes.

'I feel absolutely degraded. You can't possibly despise me as much as I despise myself.'

'But I don't despise you. I meant every word that I said yesterday. What's the good of running away like this? I don't know why we can't be good friends. I hate the idea of your thinking I've treated you badly.'

'Why couldn't you leave me alone?'

'Hang it all, I'm not a stick or a stone. It's so unreasonable, the way you look at it; it's so morbid. I thought after yesterday you'd feel a little more kindly to me. After all, we're only human.'

'I don't feel human. I feel like an animal. A pig or a rabbit or a dog. Oh, I don't blame you, I was just as bad. I yielded to you because I wanted you. But it wasn't the real me. I'm not that hateful, beastly, lustful woman. I disown her. It wasn't me that lay on that bed panting for you when my husband was hardly cold in his grave and your wife had been so kind to me, so indescribably kind. It was only the animal in me, dark and fearful like an evil spirit, and I disown, and hate, and despise it. And ever since, when I've thought of it, my gorge rises and I feel that I must vomit.'

He frowned a little and gave a short, uneasy snigger.

'Well, I'm fairly broadminded, but sometimes you say things that positively shock me.'

'I should be sorry to do that. You'd better go now. You're a very unimportant little man and I'm silly to talk to you seriously.'

He did not answer for a while and she saw by the shadow in his blue eyes that he was angry with her. He would heave a sigh of relief when, tactful and courteous as ever, he had finally seen her off. It amused her to think of the politeness with which, while they shook hands and he wished her a pleasant journey, she would thank him for his hospitality. But she saw his expression change.

'Dorothy tells me you're going to have a baby,' he said.

She felt herself colour, but she allowed no gesture to escape her.

'I am.'

'Am I by any chance the father?'

'No, no. It's Walter's child.'

She spoke with an emphasis which she could not prevent, but even as she spoke she knew that it was not the tone with which to carry conviction.

'Are you sure?' He was now roguishly smiling. 'After all, you were married to Walter a couple of years and nothing happened. The dates seem to fit all right. I think it's much more likely to be mine than Walter's.'

'I would rather kill myself than have a child of yours.'

'Oh, come now, that's nonsense. I should be awfully pleased and proud. I'd like it to be a girl, you know. I've only had boys with Dorothy. You won't be able to be in doubt very long, you know: my three kiddies are absolutely the living image of me.'

He had regained his good humour and she knew why. If the child was his, though she might never see him again, she could never entirely escape him. His power over her would reach out and he would still, obscurely but definitely, influence every day of her life.

'You really are the most vain and fatuous ass that it's ever been my bad luck to run across,' she said.

78

As the ship steamed into Marseilles, Kitty, looking at the rugged and beautiful outline of the coast glowing in the sunlight, on a sudden caught sight of the golden statue of the Blessed Virgin which stands upon the church of Sainte Marie de la Grace as a symbol of safety to the mariner at sea. She remembered how the Sisters of the convent at Mei-tan-fu, leaving their own land for ever, had knelt as the figure faded in the distance so that it was no more than a little golden flame in the blue sky and sought in prayer to allay the pang of separation. She clasped her hands in supplication to what power she knew not.

During the long, quiet journey she had thought incessantly of the horrible thing that had happened to her. She could not understand herself. It was so unexpected. What was it that had seized her, so that, despising him, despising him with all her heart, she had yielded passionately to Charlie's foul embrace? Rage filled her and disgust of herself obsessed her. She felt that she could never forget her humiliation. She wept. But as the distance from Hong-Kong increased she found that she was insensibly losing the vividness of her resentment. What had happened seemed to have happened in another world. She was like a person who has been stricken with sudden madness and recovering is distressed and ashamed at the grotesque things he vaguely remembers to have done when he was not himself. But because he knows he was not himself he feels that in his own eyes at least he can claim indulgence. Kitty thought that perhaps a generous heart might pity rather than condemn her. But she sighed as she thought how woefully her self-confidence had been shattered. The way had seemed to stretch before her straight and easy and now she saw that it was a tortuous way and that pitfalls awaited her. The vast spaces and the tragic and beautiful sunsets of the Indian Ocean rested her. She seemed borne then to some country where she might in freedom possess her soul. If she could only regain her self-respect at the cost of a bitter conflict, well, she must find the courage to affront it.

The future was lonely and difficult. At Port Saïd she had received a letter from her mother in answer to her cable. It was a long letter written in the large and fanciful writing which was taught to young ladies in her mother's youth. Its ornateness was so neat that it gave you an impression of insincerity. Mrs. Garstin expressed her regret at Walter's death and sympathised properly with her daughter's grief. She feared that Kitty was left inadequately provided for, but naturally the Colonial Office would give her a pension. She was glad to know that Kitty was coming back to England and of course she must come and stay with her father and mother till her child was born. Then followed certain instructions that Kitty must be sure to follow and various details of her sister Doris's confinement. The little boy weighed so and so much and his paternal grandfather said he had never seen a finer child. Doris was expecting again and they hoped for another boy in order to make the succession to the baronetcy quite sure.

Kitty saw that the point of the letter lay in the definite date set for the invitation. Mrs. Garstin had no intention of being saddled with a widowed daughter in modest circumstances. It was singular, when she reflected how her mother had idolised her, that now, disappointed in her, she found her merely a nuisance. How strange was the relation between parents and children! When they were small the parents doted on them, passed through agonies of apprehension at each childish ailment, and the children clung to their parents with love and adoration; a few years passed, the children grew up, and persons not of their kin were more important to their happiness than father or mother. Indifference displaced the blind and instinctive love of the past. Their meetings were a source of boredom and irritation. Distracted once at the thought of a month's separation they were able now to look forward with equanimity to being parted for years. Her mother need not worry: as soon as she could she would make herself a home of her own. But she must have a little time; at present everything was vague and she could not form any picture of the future: perhaps she would die in childbirth; that would be a solution of many difficulties.

But when they docked two letters were handed to her. She was surprised to recognise her father's writing: she did not remember that he had ever written to her. He was not effusive, and began: dear Kitty. He told her that he was writing instead of her mother who had not been well and was obliged to go into a nursing home to have an operation. Kitty was not to be frightened and was to keep to her intention of going round by sea; it was much more expensive to come across by land and with her mother away it would be inconvenient for Kitty to stay at the house in Harrington Gardens. The other was from Doris and it started: Kitty darling, not because Doris had any particular affection for her, but because it was her way thus to address every one she knew.

Kitty darling

I expect Father has written to you. Mother has got to have an operation. It appears that she has been rotten for the last year, but you know she hates doctors and she's been taking all sorts of patent medicines. I don't quite know what's the matter with her as she insists on making a secret of the whole thing and flies into a passion if you ask her questions. She has been looking simply awful and if I were you I think I'd get off at Marseilles and come back as quick as you can. But don't let on that I told you to come as she pretends there's nothing much the matter with her and she doesn't want you to get here till she's back at home. She's made the doctors promise that she shall be moved in a week. Best love.

Doris.

I'm awfully sorry about Walter. You must have had a hell of a time, poor darling. I'm simply dying to see you. It's rather funny our both having babies together. We shall be able to hold one another's hands.

Kitty, lost in reflection, stood for a little while on the deck. She could not imagine her mother ill. She never remembered to have seen her other than active and resolute; she had always been impatient of other people's ailments. Then a steward came up to her with a telegram.

Deeply regret to inform you that your mother died this morning. Father.

79

Kitty rang the bell at the house in Harrington Gardens. She was told that her father was in his study and going to the door she opened it softly: he was sitting by the fire reading the last edition of the evening paper. He looked up as she entered, put down the paper, and sprang nervously to his feet.

'Oh, Kitty, I didn't expect you till the later train.'

'I thought you wouldn't want the bother of coming to meet me so I didn't wire the time I expected to arrive.'

He gave her his cheek to kiss in the manner she so well remembered.

'I was just having a look at the paper,' he said. 'I haven't read the paper for the last two days.'

She saw that he thought it needed some explanation if he occupied himself with the ordinary affairs of life.

'Of course,' she said. 'You must be tired out. I'm afraid mother's death has been a great shock to you.'

He was older and thinner than when she had last seen him. A little, lined, dried-up man, with a precise manner.

'The surgeon said there had never been any hope. She hadn't been herself for more than a year, but she refused to see a doctor. The surgeon told me that she must have been in constant pain, he said it was a miracle that she had been able to endure it.'

'Did she never complain?'

'She said she wasn't very well. But she never

complained of pain.' He paused and looked at Kitty. 'Are you very tired after your journey?'

'Not very.'

'Would you like to go up and see her?'

'Is she here?'

'Yes, she was brought here from the nursing home.'

'Yes, I'll go now.'

'Would you like me to come with you?

There was something in her father's tone that made her look at him quickly. His face was slightly turned from her; he did not want her to catch his eye. Kitty had acquired of late a singular proficiency at reading the thoughts of others. After all, day after day she had applied all her sensibilities to divine from a casual word or an unguarded gesture the hidden thoughts of her husband. She guessed at once what her father was trying to hide from her. It was relief he felt, an infinite relief, and he was frightened of himself. For hard on thirty years he had been a good and faithful husband, he had never uttered a single word in dispraise of his wife, and now he should grieve for her. He had always done the things that were expected of him. It would have been shocking to him by the flicker of an eyelid or by the smallest hint to betray that he did not feel what under the circumstances a bereaved husband should feel.

'No, I would rather go by myself,' said Kitty.

She went upstairs and into the large, cold and pretentious bedroom in which her mother for so many years had slept. She remembered so well those massive pieces of mahogany and the engravings after Marcus Stone which adorned the walls. The things on the dressing-table were arranged with the stiff precision which Mrs. Garstin had all her life insisted upon. The flowers looked out of place; Mrs. Garstin would have thought it silly, affected and unhealthy to have flowers in her bedroom. Their perfume did not cover that acrid, musty smell, as of freshly washed linen, which Kitty remembered as characteristic of her mother's room.

Mrs. Garstin lay on the bed, her hands folded across her breasts with a meekness which in life she would have had no patience with. With her strong sharp features, the cheeks hollow with suffering and the temples sunken, she looked handsome and even imposing. Death had robbed her face of its meanness and left only an impression of character. She might have been a Roman empress. It was strange to Kitty that of the dead persons she had seen this was the only one who in death seemed to preserve a look as though that clay had been once a habitation of the spirit. Grief she could not feel, for there had been too much bitterness between her mother and herself to leave in her heart any deep feeling of affection; and looking back on the girl she had been she knew that it was her mother who had made her what she was. But when she looked at that hard, domineering and ambitious woman who lay there so still and silent with all her petty aims frustrated by death, she was aware of a vague pathos. She had schemed and intrigued all her life and never had she desired anything but what was base and unworthy. Kitty wondered whether perhaps in some other sphere she looked upon her earthly course with consternation.

Doris came in.

'I thought you'd come by this train. I felt I must look in for a moment. Isn't it dreadful? Poor darling mother.'

Bursting into tears, she flung herself into Kitty's arms. Kitty kissed her. She knew how her mother had neglected Doris in favour of her and how harsh she had been with her because she was plain and dull. She wondered whether Doris really felt the extravagant grief she showed. But Doris had always been emotional. She wished she could cry: Doris would think her dreadfully hard. Kitty felt that she had been through too much to feign a distress she did not feel.

'Would you like to come and see father?' she asked her when the strength of the outburst had somewhat subsided.

Doris wiped her eyes. Kitty noticed that her sister's

pregnancy had blunted her features and in her black dress she looked gross and blousy.

'No, I don't think I will. I shall only cry again. Poor old thing, he's bearing it wonderfully.'

Kitty showed her sister out of the house and then went back to her father. He was standing in front of the fire and the newspaper was neatly folded. He wanted her to see that he had not been reading it again.

'I haven't dressed for dinner,' he said. 'I didn't think it was necessary.'

80

They dined. Mr. Garstin gave Kitty the details of his wife's illness and death, and he told her of the kindness of the friends who had written (there were piles of sympathetic letters on his table and he sighed when he considered the burden of answering them) and of the arrangements he had made for the funeral. Then they went back into his study. This was the only room in the house which had a fire. He mechanically took from the chimney-piece his pipe and began to fill it, but he gave his daughter a doubtful look and put it down.

'Aren't you going to smoke?' she asked.

'Your mother didn't very much like the smell of a pipe after dinner and since the war I've given up cigars.'

His answer gave Kitty a little pang. It seemed dreadful that a man of sixty should hesitate to smoke what he wanted in his own study.

'I like the smell of a pipe,' she smiled.

A faint look of relief crossed his face and taking his pipe once more he lit it. They sat opposite one another on each side of the fire. He felt that he must talk to Kitty of her own troubles.

'You received the letter your mother wrote to you to Port Saïd, I suppose. The news of poor Walter's death was a great shock to both of us. I thought him a very nice fellow.'

Kitty did not know what to say.

'Your mother told me that you were going to have a baby.'

'Yes.'

'When do you expect it?'

'In about four months.'

'It will be a great consolation to you. You must go and see Doris's boy. He's a fine little fellow.'

They were talking more distantly than if they were strangers who had just met, for if they had been he would have been interested in her just because of that, and curious, but their common past was a wall of indifference between them. Kitty knew too well that she had done nothing to beget her father's affection, he had never counted in the house and had been taken for granted, the bread-winner who was a little despised because he could provide no more luxuriously for his family; but she had taken for granted that he loved her just because he was her father, and it was a shock to discover that his heart was empty of feeling for her. She had known that they were all bored by him, but it had never occurred to her that he was equally bored by them. He was as ever kind and subdued, but the sad perspicacity which she had learnt in suffering suggested to her that, though he had probably never acknowledged it to himself and never would, in his heart he disliked her.

His pipe was not drawing and he rose to find something to poke it with. Perhaps it was an excuse to hide his nervousness.

'Your mother wished you to stay here till your baby was born and she was going to have your old room got ready for you.'

'I know. I promise you I won't be a bother.'

'Oh, it's not that. Under the circumstances it was evident that the only place for you to come to was your father's house. But the fact is that I've just been offered the post of Chief Justice of the Bahamas and I have accepted it.'

'Oh, father, I'm so glad. I congratulate you with all my heart.'

'The offer arrived too late for me to tell your poor mother. It would have given her a great satisfaction.'

The bitter irony of fate! After all her efforts, intrigues and humiliations, Mrs. Garstin had died without knowing that her ambition, however modified by past disappointments, was at last achieved.

'I am sailing early next month. Of course this house will be put in the agent's hands and my intention was to sell the furniture. I'm sorry that I shan't be able to have you to stay here, but if you'd like any of the furniture to furnish a flat I shall be extremely pleased to give it you.'

Kitty looked into the fire. Her heart beat quickly; it was curious that on a sudden she should be so nervous. But at last she forced herself to speak. In her voice was a little tremor.

'Couldn't I come with you, father?'

'You? Oh, my dear Kitty.' His face fell. She had often heard the expression, but thought it only a phrase, and now for the first time in her life she saw the movement that it described. It was so marked that it startled her. 'But all your friends are here and Doris is here. I should have thought you'd be much happier if you took a flat in London. I don't exactly know what your circumstances are, but I shall be very glad to pay the rent of it.'

'I have enough money to live on.'

'I'm going to a strange place. I know nothing of the conditions.'

'I'm used to strange places. London means nothing to me any more. I couldn't breathe here.'

He closed his eyes for a moment and she thought he was going to cry. His face bore an expression of utter misery. It wrung her heart. She had been right; the death of his wife had filled him with relief and now this chance to break entirely with the past had offered him freedom.

He had seen a new life spread before him and at last after all these years rest and the mirage of happiness. She saw dimly all the suffering that had preyed on his heart for thirty years. At last he opened his eyes. He could not prevent the sigh that escaped him.

'Of course if you wish to come I shall be very pleased.'

It was pitiful. The struggle had been short and he had surrendered to his sense of duty. With those few words he abandoned all his hopes. She rose from her chair and going over to him knelt down and seized his hands.

'No, father, I won't come unless you want me. You've sacrificed yourself enough. If you want to go alone, go. Don't think of me for a minute.'

He released one of her hands and stroked her pretty hair.

'Of course I want you, my dear. After all I'm your father and you're a widow and alone. If you want to be with me it would be very unkind of me not to want you.'

'But that's just it, I make no claims on you because I'm your daughter, you owe me nothing.'

'Oh, my dear child.'

'Nothing,' she repeated vehemently. 'My heart sinks when I think how we've battened on you all our lives and have given you nothing in return. Not even a little affection. I'm afraid you've not had a very happy life. Won't you let me try to make up a little for all I've failed to do in the past?'

He frowned a little. Her emotion embarrassed him.

'I don't know what you mean. I've never had any complaint to make of you.'

'Oh, father, I've been through so much, I've been so unhappy. I'm not the Kitty I was when I went away. I'm terribly weak, but I don't think I'm the filthy cad I was then. Won't you give me a chance? I have nobody but you in the world now. Won't you let me try to make you love me? Oh, father, I'm so lonely and so miserable; I want your love so badly.'

She buried her face in his lap and cried as though her heart were breaking.

'Oh, my Kitty, my little Kitty,' he murmured.

She looked up and put her arms round his neck.

'Oh, father, be kind to me. Let us be kind to one another.'

He kissed her, on the lips as a lover might, and his cheeks were wet with tears.

'Of course you shall come with me.'

'Do you want me to? Do you really want me to?'

'Yes.'

'I'm so grateful to you.'

'Oh, my dear, don't say things like that to me. It makes me feel quite awkward.'

He took out his handkerchief and dried her eyes. He smiled in a way that she had never seen him smile before. Once more she threw her arms round his neck.

'We'll have such a lark, father dear. You don't know what fun we're going to have together.'

'You haven't forgotten that you're going to have a baby.'

'I'm glad she'll be born out there within sound of the sea and under a wide blue sky.'

'Have you already made up your mind about the sex?' he murmured, with his thin, dry smile.

'I want a girl because I want to bring her up so that she shan't make the mistakes I've made. When I look back upon the girl I was I hate myself. But I never had a chance. I'm going to bring up my daughter so that she's free and can stand on her own feet. I'm not going to bring a child into the world, and love her, and bring her up, just so that some man may want to sleep with her so much that he's willing to provide her with board and lodging for the rest of her life.'

She felt her father stiffen. He had never spoken of such things and it shocked him to hear these words in his daughter's mouth.

'Let me be frank just this once, father. I've been foolish and wicked and hateful. I've been terribly punished. I'm determined to save my daughter from all that. I want her to be fearless and frank. I want her to be a person, independent of others because she is possessed of herself, and I want her to take life like a free man and make a better job of it than I have.'

'Why, my love, you talk as though you were fifty. You've got all your life before you. You mustn't be down-hearted.'

Kitty shook her head and slowly smiled.

'I'm not. I have hope and courage.'

The past was finished; let the dead bury their dead. Was that dreadfully callous? She hoped with all her heart that she had learnt compassion and charity. She could not know what the future had in store for her, but she felt in herself the strength to accept whatever was to come with a light and buoyant spirit. Then, on a sudden, for no reason that she knew of, from the depths of her unconscious arose a reminiscence of the journey they had taken, she and poor Walter, to the plague-ridden city where he had met his death: one morning they set out in their chairs while it was still dark, and as the day broke she divined rather than saw a scene of such breath-taking loveliness that for a brief period the anguish of her heart was assuaged. It reduced to insignificance all human tribu-lation. The sun rose, dispelling the mist, and she saw winding onwards as far as the eye could reach, among the rice-fields, across a little river and through undulating country the path they were to follow: perhaps her faults and follies, the unhappiness she had suffered, were not entirely vain if she could follow the path that now she dimly discerned before her, not the path that kind funny old Waddington had spoken of that led nowhither, but the path those dear nuns at the convent followed so humbly, the path that led to peace.